HER HOPEFUL HEART

Vicki Rowell

CONTENTS

Title Page

Copyright

Introduction

Prologue

Chapter 1   1

Chapter 2   5

Chapter 3   9

Chapter 4   13

Chapter 5   20

Chapter 6   27

Chapter 7   31

Chapter 8   39

Chapter 9   46

Chapter 10   50

Chapter 11   55

Chapter 12   61

Chapter 13   65

Chapter 14   69

Chapter 15   74

Chapter 16   79

Chapter 17   85

Chapter 18   92

Chapter 19   98

Chapter 20   106

Chapter 21   114

Chapter 22   121

Chapter 23   128

Chapter 24   134

Chapter 25   140

Chapter 26   150

Chapter 27   155

Chapter 28   163

Chapter 29   170

Chapter 30   178

Chapter 31   186

Chapter 32   191

Chapter 33   195

Chapter 34   200

Chapter 35   205

Chapter 36   212

Chapter 37   215

Chapter 38   220

Chapter 39   223

Chapter 40   230

Chapter 41   237

Chapter 42   244

Chapter 43   251

Epilogue   258

Vicki's Books   263

INTRODUCTION

This book contains sexually explicit themes as well as mature language and therefore is only suitable for adults.

Mention of parental death off page.

Mention of miscarriage.

Mention of domestic violence off page.

PROLOGUE

It's funny how you think you know yourself, know how you'll react to certain situations. This isn't my first rodeo getting my life screwed over. I'm not being dramatic, my life to this point has been nothing short of a shit show. And every time the universe decides to send me another test, I either fight or I run. Admittedly, I don't always choose the right one, but it's always one or the other. The night the social workers turned up to finally take me away, even though my 6-year-old brain knew I was in all kinds of danger where I was, I ran and hid in a cupboard. When a girl at school made fun of me for wearing clothes two sizes too big for me, I punched her straight in the nose and laughed while she cried. I either fought in, or ran from, every foster home I was placed in. If I'd ever bothered to turn up to the therapy sessions that I was encouraged to attend, maybe I'd have changed my course. Or at least that's what my best friend Olivia thinks. Only friend if we're being technical. Not even sure I can still call her any type of friend to be honest, given we haven't spoken in months. I should probably call her now that I can. But I'm getting off track. Which brings me back to my original point; I know myself, I know how I react. Until now. Because now I'm not fighting, I'm not running, I'm not actually doing anything. I know there are Doctors and police still in the room. I can hear the false sympathy in the voices of the hospital staff as they float textbook platitudes in my direction. "Sorry for your loss", "Let me call someone for you, you shouldn't be alone right now". I should have laughed at that one. I've always been alone and maybe if I'd stayed that way I wouldn't be in this current situation. But I can't laugh, I can't fight, I can't run. All I can do is sit on this hospital bed, completely numb, staring out of the window into the dark night, wondering what on earth I do next. Because this time I don't have a plan. Stuart is dead. The pregnancy I only found out about last week is over. My chance to finally have a family of my own is gone. So, I'm going to continue to sit here, silently contemplating the enormity of the latest card to be dealt to me and try not to fight or run. Maybe a different reaction will help, maybe the hits will stop coming, maybe I won't completely drown in the grief I can feel seeping into my mind. Maybe it's time I rethink that therapy suggestion.

CHAPTER 1
Jake

Fuck my life. As if the business meeting I dragged my ass to Glasgow for wasn't a complete waste of my time, now I was rushing through a packed train station with no hope of getting home any time soon. I should have been landing about now, back in time for Belle's bath time, a relaxing night of beers with the boys and football on TV. Instead, after an afternoon spent hoping my plane would get off the ground, I'm now rushing to catch a train. A fucking train. I don't do public transport at the best of times, and to make matters worse my assistant couldn't even get me a ticket in first class.

I run along the platform, cursing as I go, and finally make it to my carriage. The train is just as bad as the station. Clearly, I'm not the only one who needed to find an alternative way back to London when all the flights were grounded due to 'technical issues'. I move along the carriage and finally find a seat. There's already someone in the window seat, although they're facing away and buried so far inside a hoodie, I'm not even sure if it's a man, woman or child. Still, they look like they won't bother me much, so I slump down and finally take a breath. I pull out my phone and shoot a quick text to my sister.

Me: Finally on a train, so sorry to land you with this, are you staying over or taking her back to your place.

I barely get my phone in my pocket when it buzzes with a reply.

Jen: Like it's a hindrance to have extra snuggle time with my favourite human. We're heading back to mine and I'll take her straight to school in the morning.

Jake: Have I told you lately how amazing you are? Thanks Jen, give her snuggles from me and tell her I love her.

I smile as I put my phone away again. My sister has been my absolute rock since Belle came along and their bond fills me with love, not to mention easing the guilt that never leaves me when it comes to my daughter. Still, I'll never not be grateful that she at least has my sister as a positive female influence in her life. The train eases away from the station and I settle in. I need a drink. Although I'm not holding out much hope for a decent whiskey, but maybe I'll at least find a beer when the trolley comes through.

I'd planned to do some work while I was travelling, however I barely fit my six foot four bulky frame in the seat as it is, so I'm not even going to attempt to set my laptop up on the tiny fold down table. Sighing, I resign myself to being happy with using my phone to clear some emails and check in with my assistant. It's not long before my phone starts lighting up with messages from the group chat.

Matt: We still on for tonight?

Damien: Yup, heading out in the next hour

Sean: You'd better have good snacks this time

Me: Sorry boys, not happening tonight, fucking planes are grounded so I'm currently on a train back to London but we only just left

Matt: Erm did you say train?

Damien: Are there private trains we don't know about?

Me: Fuck off, no it's a normal train, cramped seats, no privacy, barely any signal. I am in hell.

Sean: Oh fuck, this is hilarious, we need a selfie to confirm, this

may be the first time you've travelled like a regular person in the last decade

Sean: I should send this to print...breaking news, the mighty Jake Holmes spotted on a train, he'll be the one rocking in his seat crying as he tries and fails to find a drinks waitress

Me: Fuck off arsehole, I'm not that out of touch

Matt: You really are

Sean: Too funny

Damien: They're not wrong bro

Me: Whatever, none of you are any better, catch up later in the week

They actually weren't wrong. I have a driver at home and whenever I travel. I always fly first class. But in my defence, I'm often working at the same time and let's be honest, I can afford it so why wouldn't I. I'm pulled from my thoughts of the night I'm missing out on by movement from the window seat, making a move to get up. Before they can speak, I'm out of my seat to let them pass. Then I hear it, it's only one word, "thanks", but the voice that sounds it is the softest, most melodic I've ever heard. So much so that I want to hear more of it. Jesus, this train is making me crazy, since when did I get so excited by someone's voice, at least I know I'm sitting next to a woman now.

Sitting back down, I drift off into my own world until I feel a presence beside me. Looking up my breath catches, standing in the aisle is one of the most beautiful women I've ever seen. Blonde hair is piled on top of her head in a messy bun, with strands falling down to frame her face. And what a face it is. Big blue eyes, framed with long lashes, a delicate nose, leading down to large plump lips that have my cock twitching in my pants. She's wearing a white vest that hugs her perfect handful tits to perfection. A hoodie is tied around her waist making it difficult to appreciate the curves I'm imagining it covering, but her skintight jeans show off long legs. Legs that would look perfect wrapped around my body. I realise I've been staring but I own it, smirking slightly before finding my voice.

"Can I help you?" I ask with a raise of my brow.

I see a look of confusion on her face but don't miss the slight blush creeping over her cheeks, apparently my cock also approves.

"Erm, I just wanted to get back to my seat."

It's my turn to look confused for a second, then my brain recognises the voice that had me excited a few minutes ago. Holy shit! The wrapped up unknown that left her seat has returned as a fucking knock out. Realising I'm still just sitting here staring like a chump, I stand to let her pass, her scent hitting me as she does, she smells like lemon and vanilla and again my cock is very much here for that. Adjusting myself as I slide back into my seat, I groan internally; well this journey just got a lot more interesting.

CHAPTER 2
Rori

Taking my seat, I purposely root around in my bag to give myself a minute to breathe. I was one of the first people on the train, wanting to make sure I could get my suitcases stacked away on the luggage racks before finding a seat. I'd rushed around so much this morning, getting the last of my things together and handing back the keys to my flat, that I was exhausted once I finally sat down. The emotions of my big move had also started to get to me and not wanting a trip down memory lane, I'd put my headphones in, pulled my hood up and snuggled into the window as best as my five foot seven height would allow me.

I'd felt someone taking the seat next to me, but I didn't bother looking to see who it was. Well, I'd certainly seen now. He was out of his seat before I could ask him to move when I'd gotten up to use the toilet, so I hadn't even glanced at him. Despite the cold weather when I set off today, I was over heating from the stuffy train, so I'd taken off my hoodie and pulled my hair up to try and cool down. But as I made my way back to my seat, I finally got a good look at the man I was sitting next to, and my my, a man he certainly was. He was stunning. Brown hair, not too long but enough to grab hold of, a strong jaw with just the right amount of stubble to feel good in all the right places. Although he was sitting, he was clearly tall and well built, although his suit was doing well to hide whatever was underneath. But it was his eyes that took my breath away, especially as I got to the seats, and he looked up. I watched him take me in, but I couldn't look away from the piercing green eyes that swept over me. They were intense, dangerous, yet comforting at the same time. When he finally spoke, his deep voice rolled over me, turning me on in a way I'd never experienced before, and I knew I was blushing. After the confusion of him not realising I was sitting next to him, he'd finally stood and I could see I'd been right about his height, he must be over six foot.

I realise I've been buried in my bag for too long so I pull out my water and finally try to relax into my seat, avoiding looking to my right at all costs, even though I can feel his gaze on me. He clears his throat then speaks,

"I'm sorry about that, I clearly wasn't paying attention when you got up or I would have known the vision that I looked up to was my seating partner when you returned, although even then I would still have been silenced by your beauty."

His grin lights up his face and instantly puts me at ease, grinning back I reply,

"smooth, I'm sure lines like that get you out of all kinds of trouble."

His gaze hardens and I try to look away, but I'm caught in those piercing eyes.

"I don't use lines, when I say you're beautiful I mean it."

He moves to stand and for a second I think I might have offended him, but then he grins again as he says,

"I'm going to find some drinks, back soon."

And with that, he's marching down the aisle leaving me wondering what the hell is going on. Don't get me wrong, I'm a relatively confident woman. Surprising given my past. But over the last 4 years, with a lot of help, I've laid a lot of demons to rest and grew into the woman I always wanted to be. So while I might look in a mirror and be proud of who looks back at me, while I might flirt with men who hit on me and have no issues spending the night with some of them, I don't think I've ever had someone pay me a compliment in such a way that makes me weak at the knees, especially when he looks like he should be the model on a magazine cover.

I'm still contemplating Mr Model when he returns with four very full paper bags. Without asking, he reaches over and pulls my tray down from the seat in front before unfastening his own.

"I wasn't sure what you'd like so I got a choice."

I watch as he pulls out small bottles of wine, two red and two white, a few miniatures of vodka, coke, beer and lastly some bags of crisps, spreading them across the two tables.

"So," he grins again, "what would you like?"

Managing to pull my gaze from his big hands as they arrange his haul, I find my voice, "I usually find out someone's name before I join them for a picnic, but I'll take a beer for now."

He looks at me and laughs, "You're sassy, I like that, and I'm Jake by the way."

"Rori," I reply, as I take the hand he offers.

And if I thought his stare had me clenching my thighs, his touch is a whole new level of heat and spark that has me wishing I didn't blush so easily. Letting go of my hand, he opens a beer and pours it into a plastic cup before handing it to me.

"So Rori, now that we're having a picnic together, tell me about you. How did I end up with the pleasure of such beautiful company for my journey?"

Taking a drink, I also try to swallow my nerves, he might look intimidating, but his eyes are filled with warmth, and it settles me.

"I'm moving back to London actually, how about you?"

"Oh yeah? I'm just travelling for work, I was supposed to

fly but the issues at the airport changed my plans, although now I'm not so pissed off about that."

He winks and takes a drink of his own beer.

"So Rori, we have a few hours to kill on this train, a wide range of alcohol, how about we play a game and get to know each other?"

His eyes are boring into mine again, he might be smiling innocently but I see the look he's giving me. And while I don't want to share my story with a stranger, I do want to have some fun.

"What kind of game?"

"Well…. How about 20 questions to ease us in a bit, and then a few rounds of never have I ever to really get to the good stuff?"

He winks again. I raise my eyebrow and take a minute before answering,

"I have one rule, in keeping with the fun element, let's not make it too serious, no boring stuff like families and work, just fun stuff like favourite film, favourite book etc, and if either of us don't want to answer the question we can opt to take a drink instead?"

I can see him giving it thought, maybe wondering why I don't want to share life stories with him, but something about the look on his face makes we wonder if he isn't a bit relieved by that, maybe he doesn't want to share too much of himself either. That works for me.

"Okay that's fair, and since I'm such a gentleman I'll even let you go first"

His cocky grin is back, and I find myself wondering what I'm getting myself into, oh well, time to have fun.

CHAPTER 3
Jake

I have no idea who I am right now. Since my daughter was born, I haven't dated, not once. I have occasional one-night stands where we both know what we want and why we're there. I barely learn more than their first name and I never stay the night. I never bring them home, in fact I also avoid going to their place, preferring to book into a hotel. And I don't feel guilty. Belle is my priority, nothing is more important than her, and given she's already been let down by the one person who should have loved her unconditionally, I don't intend to put her through any more pain when it comes to relationships. So, I avoid them. Yet here I am, several drinks in and laughing ridiculously at the story Rori is currently telling me about a disastrous first date.

We've been playing this game for a couple of hours and the time has flown over, mainly because she's so much fun. Okay and hot, very hot. The urge to touch her is intense, I want to pull the hairband out and run my fingers through her blonde hair, I want to bite on her plump bottom lip, I want… well let's face it, I want to be balls deep in her. But aside from that, she's funny, she's not over the top flirting or trying to find out how much I earn, I feel like I'm chatting with an old friend not a relative stranger.

"So yeah, the moral of that story is, ask more questions before agreeing to go on a date that's an hours drive from home with no transport links."

She finishes her drink and glances out of the window at the passing scenery. I don't speak, taking advantage of her facing away to stare at her more. When she turns back, I smile at her.

"So that was your worst date. What's been your best date, or what would your ideal date be?"

I don't know why I asked that. *Because you want to ask her out.* No, I want to fuck her. *And date her.* No fuck her. I ignore the internal argument I'm currently waging and wait for her answer.

"Erm, I'm not sure I have an ideal first date as such. I think it's more important that whatever it is, I feel like they've taken the time to plan something I'd really enjoy. I'm not high maintenance, don't get me wrong I enjoy getting dressed up for a night of dancing or a nice meal. But I don't expect that, and I'd much prefer to stay casual and get to know someone."

Damn, I like her. It's like she can read my mind. So far, we've had heated debates about movies and books, even sports. We enjoy the same things just not always from the same opinion and its exciting. But hearing she'd rather chill out and get to know someone than be taken to a fancy dinner at an expensive restaurant has me wanting to ask her out on that date. Fuck, I need to pull myself together. I can't date. Time to lower the tone and have some fun.

"Okay, we're only half an hour from Kings Cross, let's have that game of never have I ever."

I smirk as I see her cheeks go pink again and fuck if I don't want to see how far that blush would travel if I touched her. We're both down to our last drinks so I flip the tables back up and turn in my seat as best I can, making it harder for her to look away from me but also blocking anyone's view who might walk past, as best as possible. Here goes nothing.

"So, I ask a question and if you've done it you drink, ready?"

She nods her head looking a little nervous, she should be, I'm about to ambush her and see where the cards land.

"Okay, never have I ever met a woman so beautiful I enjoy my first ever train picnic"

I smile as I take a drink myself.

"You're such a charmer, I thought the point was to ask things you'd never done to try and catch me out, so I drink?"

My smile gets wider as I respond, "That's the traditional game yes, but I'm changing things up, and I'm asking all the questions"

She looks like she's about to argue then thinks better of it and just raises her brow. I lower my voice, so the conversation stays as private as possible, but stay in the same position, not getting any closer to her, yet.

"Never have I have spent two hours wondering how soft someone's lips are."

I glance down at her lips before meeting her gaze and taking a sip of my drink. There's that pink again, but she doesn't look away.

"Never have I ever sat on a train and wanted to run my hands through someone's hair until it's wrapped around my fist."

This time I see her quickly nip at her bottom lip and I have to stop myself from groaning out loud. I lean in a little and lower my voice more.

"Never have I ever been so turned on I had to go to the toilet to give my cock a talking to."

Her eyes widen with shock, but she doesn't call me out, she doesn't push me away and demand I leave my seat. This time I lean in so close I'm whispering in her ear as I say,

"Never have I ever met a stranger on a train and kissed her before reaching the station."

She's so still I'm not sure she's breathing.

"I finished my drink on the last question, but even if I hadn't, I wouldn't be taking a drink for that question right now."

I use my finger to guide her chin around so I can look her in the eye. Bright blue eyes that I could get lost in look up at me with a mixture of innocence and hunger and that's all I need to carry on.

"Rori," I'm practically touching her lips when I whisper, "If I ask the same question in five minutes will I need a new drink?"

Time stands still as I wait for her to respond, really hoping I haven't misread this and totally screwed up, in fact I'm so caught up in wondering if this was the worst idea ever that I nearly miss it, nearly miss her mouth opening and the barely audible, "Yes", leave those cock hardening lips. But I do hear it, and I don't wait to question further, I close the gap and softly bring my lips to hers. One hand finds the back of her head and I pull her against my mouth to deepen the kiss. My tongue is about to seek access to her when we're interrupted by the speakers announcing we'll shortly be arriving at Kings Cross. I pull away but keep my grip on the back of her head.

"Looks like I need another drink Rori, wanna join me?"

I grin at her this time, praying she enjoyed that as much as I did. The moment she smiles back I know I got it right, and she confirms that when she utters, "I do".

Best train ride ever.

CHAPTER 4
Rori

It's official, hottest kiss of my life. It wasn't even that long or dirty, no tongues even, but the heat from his gaze and the way he held my head, especially after the build-up of questions and whispering in my ear. Just wow. It's fair to say I've also never been so turned on while still fully clothed. But now I'm freaking out. I said yes to joining him, but what did he mean? I know he mentioned needing a drink but the way he looked at me didn't suggest he wanted to hit up the nearest bar. God, I wish I could ring Liv for advice. I might have been in a long-term relationship, although some wouldn't refer to it quite like that, and I've had a few dates and one-night stands since, but I'm not exactly experienced. Maybe I just need to take the lead. This is a new start, new me, I can do this. Can I? I can feel his gaze on me while I'm having this internal freak out, once again rummaging in my bag to avoid him.

"Rori, I can feel you freaking out from here, if you've changed your mind you don't have to worry, it's always your choice," he murmurs.

And that right there, that is the moment I drop all of my for and against debate in my head and take the reins. Looking into his eyes, full of sincerity, I take a leap of faith that I'm right to trust he isn't an axe murderer.

"I have two large suitcases as well as my rucksack and handbag, do you want to come back to my hotel?"

I rush the ending, I know I'm bright red this time never mind a gentle blush. I'm barely finished speaking though when he replies with a confident,

"Yes, I very much want to do that."

I take a deep breath and relax into my seat, Jake takes my hand and rests it on his thigh as the train arrives at the station.

We don't speak as we wait for the carriage to clear, before getting our luggage. He only has an overnight bag, so he positions it on top of one of my cases, then pulls them both along the platform. It occurs to me that I don't know if he even lives in London. I know he's travelling for work, but he could have meant that work was in Glasgow. I don't suppose it matters, this is likely to be a one time thing and I'm going to enjoy it as that. We find a cab easily and I give the driver my hotel details. Jake takes my hand again as we head away from the station, and again, we fall into a relaxed silence.

The drive doesn't take too long, but I can still see how expensive it's going to be, and when we arrive, I'm too busy checking everything is out of the taxi to realise Jake has paid the driver.

"Hey, you didn't need to do that, I needed a cab regardless, let me give you the money."

His face flickers for a second and I can't tell what it means, before he recovers and shakes his head,

"Don't worry about it, I can claim it on expenses."

He heads to the hotel shop for some water while I check in, then we head up to my room, nerves kicking in again. We've barely spoken since we kissed, and while it's not been uncomfortable silence, I'm not sure what's going to happen when we get to the room. What if he's changed his mind? I needn't have worried. As soon as he's dumped my cases in a corner he turns and fixes me with his stare as he walks towards me and pulls me into his arms, before his lips crash down on mine. While our first kiss was gentle, this is the opposite, he cups my face as his tongue pushes along my bottom lip then drives into my mouth. He reaches up with one hand to ease the hairband out of my messy bun, then pulls back as it cascades over my shoulders and down my back.

"So fucking gorgeous," he growls, before descending on my lips again.

Without breaking the kiss, I feel him walk me backwards to where I know the bed is. When my legs hit the bed, he stops and takes a step back, looking at me with such heat and lust I can feel my wetness soaking into my knickers. We both take a breath then he speaks.

"You're stunning Rori, I want you so much in so many ways, but you haven't said much since the train, so I just want to check this is still what you want before we go any further."

His sincerity turns me on even more, surely my face is all the answer he needs, but I find my words anyway.

"I want this Jake, I want you, touch me."

And then I'm falling as he pushes me down onto the bed. I'd put my hoodie back on as we left the train and now his hands find their way under the hem and move up my body, stopping to cup my breasts and I groan in approval. He tries to kiss down to my neck, but he's stopped by the thick material, and he pulls away.

"Too many clothes Rori, I need your skin."

He sits me up and pulls my hoodie over my head, throwing it to the floor before running his hands back down my body to remove my vest. Laying me back down, he kisses his way from my lips, down my neck, until his lips skim over the lace of my bra, hardening my nipples. His hands reach for the buttons on my jeans, and I gasp as his fingers trail inside. Standing up, he pulls them gently down my legs, stopping to remove my shoes before he goes back to my jeans and drags them off my legs. He stands fully and looks down at me, slowly running his eyes over my body. I flinch slightly, not wanting to remember previous comments about my body. Apparently, I don't hide it well enough because he stops and brings his gaze back to my eyes. His gaze makes me feel more naked than my current state of undress.

"Don't do that, whatever just came into your head has no place in this room. There's only room for you and me in this bed, not whoever made you think your body is anything other than exquisite, am I understood?".

Where the fuck did this man come from? I didn't think I could get more wet without him touching me, but his words shoot straight to my pussy.

"I said, am I understood?"

I swallow before looking up at him again, "Yes."

Stepping back, he shrugs off his suit jacket and drops it onto a chair. He lost his tie at some point on the train, so he moves to unbutton his shirt, still holding me in place with his darkened green eyes. As he pulls his shirt away, my gaze drops to his chest and I'm immediately in awe. His body is amazing, I don't know what he does but he clearly works out somewhere because his arms and chest are all toned muscles and mouth-watering definition. I'm still staring when he drops his trousers and briefs at the same time and now my mouth literally hangs open. He lets out a dark laugh, but I still can't look away from his thick thighs and imposing dick, standing to attention and already oozing pre-cum.

"See something you like baby?" he says, amusement in his tone.

I tear my gaze away and meet his eyes again, "I do".

He drops to his knees and pulls my underwear down my legs, spreading them open so I'm bare in front of him. Keeping his hands on the inside of my thighs, he doesn't miss a beat as he lowers his head, flattens his tongue against my lips and drags it through my wetness to my throbbing clit.

"Rori, you're so fucking wet for me", he groans, before diving back in.

He laps, sucks and nips at my clit as I groan and wriggle on the bed, feeling the heat building inside me. I feel his hand move over my stomach, pinning me in place before he slides two fingers from his other hand inside me and I cry out.

"Fuck, Jake, don't stop."

I look down to see his fingers still stroking inside me as he grins up at me,

"I don't plan to baby, not until you're cumming all over my face."

Then he turns his attention back to my clit as his fingers work deeper and faster, bringing me closer and closer to what I need. I grip onto the sheets as I feel myself getting closer, the pressure building and building with every stroke of his fingers and lick of his tongue. Just when I think I can't take anymore he curls his fingers inside me and at the same time sucks hard on my clit and I go crashing over the cliff, freefalling into one of the most intense orgasms I've ever had. I hear him moan as he removes his fingers but continues to lap me with his tongue, my body still rippling with aftershocks. As I come down from the high, he stands, pinning me with his stare again as he slowly sucks his fingers into his mouth,

"You taste amazing baby, if I wasn't so desperate to get inside you, I could eat you all night."

And just like that I'm wet for him again. I've never had someone talk to me like this during sex and let me tell you, it is absolutely working for me right now.

He pulls a new box of condoms from his discarded trousers and must see the look on my face as he gently cups my face, looking sheepish as he tells me,

"Before your head runs away with you, I don't generally carry condoms wherever I go, I didn't really need a bottle of water when I ducked in the shop while you were checking in but I didn't want to come right out and tell you I was going to buy condoms."

Relaxing into his touch I smile up at him, "I'm glad you did, that was amazing and I'm not ready for it to be over."

Swiping his thumb over my cheek, he straightens up and slides the condom over his straining cock.

"Oh baby, I am nowhere near done with you yet"

And then he pushes me up the bed and his lips crash down on mine again, igniting my body with every swipe of his tongue. Kneeling between my legs, he gently lines his cock up to my entrance and pushes inside. We both moan loudly as he sinks inside me until he's all the way in, filling me up like I've never felt before. He stays still inside me, propped up on one elbow as his other hand roams over my body. When I can't take it anymore, I speak up.

"Jake, I need you to move, fuck me."

He grins slowly before running his tongue up my neck to my ear.

"You don't need to ask me twice," and then he pulls back out of me slowly before slamming his cock back inside me.

He continues thrusting deep inside me, filling me with every stroke. My hands finally have access to his body, and I make the most of it, gliding them up his chest and over his shoulders, feeling his muscles flex as I do. He really is a beautiful man. He picks up his pace and I grip onto his shoulders as my orgasm builds again.

"Fuck, baby, your pussy feels so good gripping my cock."

His words stoke the fire already building inside me and I moan loudly as he leans down and sucks my nipple into his mouth.

"Jake I'm so close."

"Rori let go, cum for me."

Then he twists my nipple again and that's all it takes to send my orgasm crashing through me. His cock driving into me until he follows seconds later, letting out a deep groan as he gives in to his release. Still panting, I watch as he gets up and bins the condom then comes back to lie on the bed. I don't think I can speak, I've never had sex like it, I can barely remember my own name. He reaches out and runs his fingers over my stomach and I can't stop the moan that slips out from his touch. He laughs again before propping himself on his elbow to look down at me.

"Right, it's time for food, you're gonna need sustenance cos that was only round one."

CHAPTER 5

Jake

I t's still dark when I wake up. My morning brain fog is just clearing when I feel movement next to me. Which is when reality hits me, shit, I fell asleep. I slide out of bed carefully, not wanting to disturb Rori, then head to the bathroom to relieve my bladder.

Coming back into the room, I find my phone in my jacket and see it's 5am. The room is basic, so I sit in one of the two chairs in the corner and rub my hand over my face. What was I thinking? I never stay the night, I don't fall asleep with anyone, I don't cuddle. Then again, I don't usually wear myself out so much. After ordering burgers from room service, I suggested a shower, which Rori was totally on board with, especially when that shower gave her two more orgasms. But it didn't stop there, we carried on fucking until the early hours, every time I thought I was done I got another look at her amazing body and got hard all over again. I didn't consciously make a decision to stay, I'd cuddled her into me after our last round, intending to get dressed and leave, and that was the last thing I remember until I woke up. Even more confusing to me is why I don't seem to know what to do now. I should be getting dressed and running before she wakes up, especially considering how much work I need to do after being out of the office all day yesterday. Instead, I'm still sitting in this chair, watching her sleep like a weird stalker. I need to pull myself together, this is ridiculous. Yet I'm still not moving, because try as I might, I can't stop running the images through my head of the best night of sex I've ever had. The memory of her tits bouncing in my face as she rode me, has my dick twitching to life again. Seriously, I'm surprised its not chafed, how am I still getting hard for her?

I need to leave. I get up and dress as silently as possible, so I don't disturb her. Finding my bag, I head to the door, but I stop. I can't just leave. I want more of her, sex that good shouldn't end after one night. I might not do relationships, I might have only had a handful of one and done experiences over the last few years, but even I'm not stupid enough to walk away from sex this good. As long as she's up for more fun what's the harm in another meet up.

I still don't want to wake her up, despite the noises she made last night, she might not want a replay, so I should give her an out. I get a notepad and pen from my bag and sit back down. I'll write a note, explain my position, leave my number and then wait for her to decide. Once I was happy with my wording, I ripped the page out and left it on the bedside table, then taking one last look, I stop myself from waking her for another session and slip out of her room. I don't want to hang around waiting for my driver to get here so I grab a cab outside the hotel and head home.

The benefit of Belle staying at Jen's is I can go into the office as early as I like. Before Belle, I worked long hours, especially when I first set up my company. I thought nothing of getting to my desk at six a.m and not leaving until gone nine p.m. But Belle changed all of that. I was a single Dad from the beginning, and I didn't want my daughter raised by nannies. My own mother passed away when I was fifteen, but she'd been poorly for a while and my dad was never particularly present, I didn't want that for Belle.

When I found out I was going to be a father I didn't know what to do. My company was already very successful by that point, I'd already made my first million and more, but I didn't want to walk away from it. That's when my sister literally became my rock. She was only ten when mum died, and she felt just as strongly as me about how Belle should be raised. She was due to finish her degree and wanted to take some time out before deciding on a career path. When I told her about Belle and my fears, she didn't hesitate to offer help. She moved in with me to look after Belle when I couldn't. After taking some time off when Belle was first born, I eventually returned to work leaving Auntie Jen to dote on her. But even though she was with family, I still wanted to spend as much time with her as possible. So, I made sure I never worked more than a nine to five with no weekends. My management team are excellent and thankfully they took this change in their stride, making the change seamless with no adverse effects on our clients or profit.

Belle is five now and at school, Jen moved out a few months ago to get back to her own life. I now have a nanny, but only for a couple of hours after school. But their bond is still as strong as ever and Jen insists on Belle having a weekly sleepover so I can have time to myself. Which is mostly spent with my boys. I've been friends with Sean, Matthew and Damien since school. They were there for me when my mum died, and we've been like brothers ever since. We're now all back in London and see each other several times a week. They all adore Belle and spoil her, not just with presents but their time. My weekly night to myself is usually spent in the pub with the boys, but they all drop in whenever they want to see Belle.

I hit the gym when I get home, I'm exhausted but I know it will make me feel better if I stick to my routine. After I'm done, I send a message to my driver to let him know I'm going in early then hit the shower.

I can't remember the last time I was at work this early and I enjoy the silence while I work. Until the group chat starts up that is. I'd ignored it on the train and only caught up on the messages on the way home this morning and then not bothered replying to them.

Sean: You alive Jake or did the train see you off

Me: Ha ha, alive and kicking dickhead

Sean: you know how upset I get when you ignore us, my delicate ego can't handle the rejection

Me: poor baby, did you cry yourself to sleep

Damien: No joke mate, he was a knob all night wondering why you weren't replying to anything

Matthew: Makes me wonder if there's something he needs to tell us

Sean: You know you want me Matthew

Sean: but seriously bro where were you

Me: busy

Sean: how busy can you possibly be when you're stuck on a train for nearly 5 hours

Me: you'd be surprised

Damien: consider me intrigued, spill

Matthew: yeah he's hiding something

Me: don't know what you mean, now leave me alone I'm working

Damien: why are you already in the office, where's Belle

Me: she stayed at Jen's last night, so I didn't have the school run this morning

Sean: hang on that means when your train got in at what, 9pm, you were completely child free, yet we still didn't hear from you

Damien: oh he is absolutely hiding something

I exit the group chat and put my phone away, this could go on all day, and I'd never hear the end of it if I told them now.

Why I thought ignoring them would help I don't know.

An hour later I hear them before I see them, which gave me approximately thirty seconds to put on my game face before they barge into my office. Throwing down my pen, I look up at them and raise my eyebrows,

"Seriously, do you not all have jobs to get to, I told you I was working."

Sean outright laughs at me before taking a seat on the couches, Matthew shrugs and follows, Damien is the only one to actually respond.

"Mate we own those companies, you ignore us, blatantly withhold from us then try to go back to ignoring, what did you expect?"

Then he also throws himself down in a seat and they all start unloading breakfast onto the table. Right then, looks like we're doing this now. Taking a seat, I take the coffee Matthew holds out for me.

"You're all drama queens, I would have replied eventually I was just playing catch up this morning from being out of the office, I'm not hiding anything, I couldn't reply last night, like I said, I was busy......getting laid."

Everyone stops and looks at me, Damien is the first to respond with a fist pump, followed by Matthew's,

"About fucking time,"

and then Sean's horrified,

"On a train!!"

"No not on a train dickhead, I met her on the train then went to her hotel."

"Oh, fair enough."

He pauses, I can see the cogs turning in his brain and I know I'm not going to get away with ending it at that.

"Hang on", here it is, "That still doesn't explain why you

didn't reply when you got home last night, even just to tell us you finally broke your drought."

While Sean had been contemplating this, Damien had dished out breakfast sandwiches, so I pick mine up and take a huge bite, avoiding Sean's last comment. But he doesn't let it go.

"So why the silence?"

Swallowing my food, I avoid looking up as I mumble,

"I didn't get home last night, I got home at 6 this morning, hit the gym them came straight here to work."

It's the silence that makes me look up, all three of them in various states of shock. Sean's eyes are practically the size of his head, Damien is paused with his coffee halfway to his mouth and Matthew literally has his mouth dropped open. Then they all start talking at once....

"The fuck!"

"Were you drugged?"

"You actually spent the night, like the whole night, damn that must have been good pussy."

And that's when I snap.

"Enough, don't talk about her like that, Christ you really are drama queens, yes I spent the night, we had fun, I was worn out and fell asleep, it's not a big deal, I woke up at five and headed home soon after, which is when I caught up with all the messages, are we all happy now?"

I look around and they're silent again, sometimes I wish they didn't know me so well, actually that's a lie, I'd be lost without them, doesn't mean I don't want to throw them out on the street though. This time its Damien who speaks first.

"You just defended her honour bro," he says with a smirk.

"What! That's what you took from that, it's not cool to talk about women like that and you know it, I'd say the same if you were talking about someone you slept with."

I'm trying to cover my arse and they all know it, but they let it go for now.

"So, you snuck out of her room this morning before she could get all clingy on you?"

That's from Matthew.

"Erm, well…" now I'm in trouble, "I didn't want to wake her so early, so I left a note and erm… my number."

Sean is practically jumping up and down in his seat like an excitable puppy at this revelation.

"Who the fuck are you?"

Damien is looking at me like I've grown a second head.

"Look, she was fun, we had a good time, would I go there again, absolutely, I'm not suggesting I date her, but extending the fun if we're both up for it, then that's good with me. It's not like I'm gonna be cut up if she doesn't get in touch, can we drop it now, because I know you do all have companies you need to turn up to today."

With that I go back to my breakfast and they seem to let it go, although none of them look like they believe me, I'm not sure I believe myself.

CHAPTER 6
Rori

I woke from one of the best sleeps I've had in months, probably a direct result of the hours long workout I got last night. The curtains are open and it's bright outside so I know it's late and I immediately realise I'm alone in bed. I shouldn't be disappointed. I knew what it was when I invited him here, and if I didn't, I only wanted fun myself. Still, it would have been nice to say goodbye. I shift up to sitting and reach for the bottle of water on the bedside table. That's when I notice the sheet of paper next to it. Picking it up I'm soon grinning as I read.

'*Morning sexy, hope you slept well and enjoyed a lie in, I had to get to work, and I didn't want to disturb you. Look I want to be honest with you, my life is complicated, and I don't have time for relationships. So, if that's what you're looking for then I'll say thank you for an amazing night and wish you well. However, if you want another night of fun, and I really hope you do, then get in touch, I'm leaving the decision in your hands while I hang on to my memories of your tits in mine*'

Oh my god, he'd ended the note with his number. It really had been an amazing night. I'd lost count of the orgasms he'd given me, and I was more than a little sore this morning from the number of times he thrust into me without mercy.

I get up and find my phone, then save the number, tucking the note away in my handbag. I won't contact him yet; I need to decompress and think things through before I make a decision. I might have made a rash decision yesterday, but years of therapy has taught me to not let that spiral into more, and instead, step back and process my feelings. So instead, I take a shower and get dressed.

I'm moving in with my best friend, Liv, and her housemate Jen, on Saturday. Liv thinks that's when I'm getting the train, but I wanted a couple of days alone when I first got here, unsure how my emotions would handle being back in London. I'd grown up here and met Liv when I spent a brief period in the same foster home as her. She was the only link to my old life. I'd also met Stuart here, but we'd left London eight years ago and I hadn't been back since. A lot had happened since then, but I wasn't the person I was when I was last here, I wasn't even the person I was four years ago when my life hit rock bottom. I'm strong now, it was time to move on fully with my life, which meant leaving Glasgow.

I'd reconnected with Liv after everything happened and soon realised, the bond we had forged in childhood held strong. She'd been to visit me regularly, and now I had a job that I was starting on Monday, and we'd finally be sharing a house again. So, I'd booked a hotel for three nights so I could wander around alone, re-acquainting myself with the city, knowing I could process my emotions alone when I needed to.

Once I was dressed, I headed out. It was after eleven and I was starving, so I decided to find a coffee shop and contemplate my next move. Once I was settled with a very large cappuccino, cheese and ham toastie and a large slice of chocolate cake, I turned my thoughts to the events of last night, and Jake's subsequent note. He was hands down the most impressive man I'd ever been with, his body was what dreams are made of and the way he looked at me, I don't think I've ever felt that desired. But did I want more? Well, yes, yes I did. Was it a good idea though, that was a more complicated question.

Despite the years of hell I went through with Stuart, I'd

worked hard to not assume every man was the same. I'd finally conceded to trying therapy and it had changed me for the better. It was hard, so hard, but I no longer constantly blame myself for getting into that situation, although I do sometimes slip back to those thoughts. However, while I'm open to starting a relationship in the future, right now all I want to do is enjoy my life, have fun, get settled in my job and hopefully find a way to get my book published. Love can wait. But Jake doesn't want love either. He said so in his note. I'm sure some women would be offended by his note, but I appreciate his honesty. I didn't need to know why his life was complicated, I didn't need to know why he didn't want a relationship. None of that impeded his ability to give me multiple orgasms. And I was absolutely here for those. Okay, decision made, I'd text him, open the line of communication and see where it went, hopefully back to my bed. I order another coffee then take my phone out.

Me: Hi, I did sleep well, in fact I'm only just venturing out now. Your note was a nice surprise, I honestly didn't expect you to stay, but I agree, it would be a shame not to have more fun. I'm at the hotel until Saturday morning then I'll be busy moving into my new place and starting my job, let me know if you wanna meet up before then

I re-read the text I'd composed several times before I hit send, then I got started on my cake and coffee. My phone buzzed just as I was finishing.

Jake: Hey gorgeous, I envy your lie in, I was at was at work by 7.30, I'm glad you text and that you understand what I can offer you, I could come by the hotel tomorrow afternoon, maybe around 1 if that works for you

Me: Sounds good, I'll be waiting

Jake: Oh baby, you'll sound more than good when you're screaming my name again

I nearly drop my phone, that dirty mouth turning me on even by text. Deciding to leave it there, given I was very much in public, I put my phone away. Now that I'd eaten, I wanted to get out, deciding a long walk was the best way to remind myself of the city I'd left behind.

I wander the streets and parks, memories hitting me from every angle. But I don't run from them, I let myself feel them, the good and the bad, and then I tuck them away, because I could let myself remember without spiralling back to that time. I walk for hours, feeling proud of myself for how I was dealing with everything. When I eventually get back to the hotel, I'm exhausted, so I decide a bath and TV will be my plan for the night.

CHAPTER 7
Jake

When I walk through the door to my apartment, I'm instantly hit with the sound of my daughter's giggles, lifting me in a way nothing else could. As I walk into the kitchen, I'm surprised to find Sean stood at the island, Belle dangling over his shoulder, shrieking in delight as he tickles her.

"Hey, twice in one day, what are you doing here?"

"Daddy!!"

Realising I'd walked in, Belle squirms in his arms until he lowers her to the ground so she can launch herself at me. Gathering her up in my arms, I hold her tight.

"Well hello there Angel, I missed you so much, did you enjoy your night with Aunt Jen?"

"Of course Daddy, we watched my movie."

My daughter is obsessed with all things princess, and since she'd discovered Beauty and the Beast, and realised she shared a name with her newest heroine, it was all she wanted to watch. I'd watched it so many times I could probably re-enact it word for word if the TV broke. My nanny, Diana, walks in soon after, and I turn my attention to her.

"Hi Diana, anything I need to know?"

"No everything's been fine Mr Holmes, she's had some

play time at the park and a small snack while we walked home."

"Thanks Diana, you can get yourself away, I'll see you tomorrow."

Sean interrupts before she can walk away,

"Actually that's why I'm here, it's been ages since I had a date with Princess Belle, I was hoping she'd agree to let me escort her from school tomorrow and keep me entertained for the afternoon."

Belle is shrieking again,

"Daddy Daddy yes, please let me go with Uncle Sean."

I smile at my daughter then look towards Diana, "Looks like you've got a day off, we'll see you Monday."

Thanking me she heads off for the night. I knew she wouldn't mind, I pay her well for the few hours a week she cares for Belle and I never reduce her pay for days I don't end up needing her. Sean gets up to leave soon after, and by his face I know he has a date. Sean loves dating. Like really loves it. He puts effort in, plans things, how he's never found the one to settle down with baffles us all. As I walk him to the door, he turns to grin at me.

"So, did she get in touch".

My mind goes back to the messages I exchanged with Rori earlier today, I really shouldn't be so excited that she's contacted me, but the thought of tasting her again has me wishing away the hours until tomorrow.

"Actually, yeah she did, I'm meeting her at her hotel tomorrow afternoon."

He beams back at me.

"Oh are you now, well isn't that convenient seen as you now don't need to be home as early as usual, I'm happy for you man, glad you're finally getting out there."

I roll my eyes at him.

"Don't get any ideas Mr Romantic, I'm not you, it's just sex, a repeat performance with someone I enjoyed spending the night with."

Still grinning like a dick, he wanders out to the lift, calling over his shoulder as he goes,

"Yeah yeah mate, whatever you say, I'll have her back for bedtime but don't rush home, I can handle it."

My friends really are the best.

The rest of my night is spent with Belle. We eat and play until it's time for her bath, then I snuggle up on her bed to read to her. We were working our way through her favourite princess books, currently reading Sleeping Beauty, again. Tiredness took over once she was asleep, probably last night catching up with me, so I decide to get an early night and head to bed myself.

The next morning, I drop Belle at school then head to the office. Friday is always a slow day for me, which is why I feel no guilt for leaving early to meet Rori. I decide to send her a quick text to make sure she's still happy to meet.

Me: Morning beautiful, just checking you still want to see me later

Rori: Absolutely, see you when you get here

I'm not going to lie; I'm relieved she's replied. After not hearing back from her yesterday, I thought I'd pushed too far with my last text about making her scream.

My morning flew over and I left on time, heading down to my driver. I wondered if I should take her anything, but then I stopped myself, this was just sex, mutual fun, not the start of something else.

I head up to her room and knock, I am not prepared for what stands on the other side when she opens the door. Her hair is already down, blonde waves flowing over her shoulders. Her blue eyes shine bright, her face fresh with barely any make-up. Sweeping my eyes down I take in her black robe, not fully closed, showing off her incredible tits covered by a black lace bra. The robe lands mid-thigh and her bare legs go on for days until I land at her feet. Moving back up her body, I pause for a second on her plump pink lips, before meeting her eyes again. She shudders under my gaze and takes a step back as I enter the room and kick the door shut.

"Fuck Rori, I hope you're not expecting me to last long opening the door looking like that."

She giggles as I pick her up and walk to the bed, laying her down when I get there. Once again, the scent of lemons and vanilla make me want to lick every inch of her.

"You approve then," she smiles up at me.

I look down at her as I start to undress in record time.

"Oh yeah, I'm going to show you just how much I approve, several times, and I promise to make you cum again and again as I worship your body, but right now, I need to be inside you."

Running my hand up and down my hard length I rip open a condom packet.

"Now roll over and get on your hands and knees baby."

She doesn't need telling twice. Kneeling behind her I run my hands up the back of her smooth thighs, gripping her arse cheek with one hand, I run the other down, slipping under her lace thong until I find her already dripping pussy and slide a finger inside.

"Mmm, already so wet for me, good girl."

She lets out a moan, I already know how much she likes the dirty talk from last time. I continue to rub her pussy as I grip the elastic of her pants and pull, tearing them off her body.

"Fuck Jake, that's so hot."

I can't hold back any longer, gripping her thighs in my

hands I sink my cock inside her until I'm fully seated, then start to pound into her. Jesus, she feels so good.

"So tight baby, your pussy fits me like a glove."

Her moans and whimpers spur me on, harder and harder I drive inside her, the force pushing her down onto her elbows. I lean over her, holding her around the waist to keep her in place and I plant my other hand on the bed for support. I can feel myself getting closer, each thrust into her warmth taking me closer to the edge.

"Rori, I need to cum baby, touch yourself."

I hear her gasp and briefly wonder if she'll refuse, before I feel her hand move down to find her clit. Her moans get louder as I continue to slam my cock into her, faster and faster, until I feel her body go rigid, before she shatters in my arms, screaming my name. That's all it takes for me to let go, two more thrusts inside her quivering pussy and one of the most powerful orgasms tears through me as I grip onto her to stop myself falling. I fall to her side so I don't hurt her, both of us panting hard.

"Jake, that was…"

"That was incredible Rori."

We both fall back into silence, waiting for our breathing to return to normal.

I slide out of bed to bin the condom then crawl back over her, leaning down to take her lips with mine I slowly caress her mouth, dipping my tongue gently inside, sliding over hers before sucking it gently. Pulling back I look down at her flushed face and glazed eyes.

"That's how I should have said hello, but then you opened the door looking like a goddess and I couldn't hold back, you really are stunning Rori."

I can see the emotion in her eyes.

"Thank you, I…erm."

I put my fingers over her lips.

"Stop, you don't have to thank me for telling the truth, and the fact you look so shocked by my words makes me want to find and punch anyone that's ever let you feel less than the beautiful woman you are. Now, I seem to remember promising to worship this body once I'd filled you with my cock, it's time to make good on that."

I start with her mouth again, slow strokes with my tongue while my fingers trace lines up and down her arm, goosebump spring up where I touch. Moving my lips across her jaw I lick around her ear before sucking gently underneath as she arches under me.

"Mmm you like that."

She doesn't answer, just grips my hair, keeping my head in place as I repeat the movement. I move my other hand down from her arm to her thigh. Tracing circles, I coast upwards, getting close but not landing on her pussy. My mouth moves lower, kissing along her collar bone as my hand dusts over her stomach. Her breath is shortening, her hands gripping the sheets to give her leverage to twist under me to try and guide me where she wants me. That isn't going to work for me. I stop my movements to take both her hands in mine and hold them above her head.

"I'm in charge right now baby, hold still."

Her eyes are pooled with lust and frustration and fuck if it doesn't turn me on even more, my dick hardening against her leg. Resuming my position my free hand finds it's way to one of her perfect tits, while my mouth found the other. My tongue circles one nipple while my fingers find the other, feeling them both harden under my touch. I suck it into my mouth and bite down gently as I roll the other between my finger and thumb.

"Mmm, Jake that feels so good, so so good."

She was already so responsive to me but as I glanced up to her face, watching her bite down on her lower lip, her head thrown back, it was clear she was enjoying this more and more. I'd planned to carry on down her body, but I was so transfixed by her moans and the joy on her face, that I stayed fixed in place. Working her nipples simultaneously, sucking, licking, biting, I switch my mouth and hands so I can taste her other glorious peak. I'm learning her body after making her cum so many times, and the way she's moaning and breathing suggests she's close, but I'm still only playing with her tits. I want to stop and ask if she can cum like this, but I don't want to ruin the moment, so I stay quiet and carry on.

A moment later I have my answer as she starts shaking.

"Ahhhh Jake."

Well fuck me, I'd never made a woman cum like this. I'm so shocked I can't speak, and in the haze of my surprise it takes me a minute to realise I haven't stopped sucking on her nipple, and that's when I realise her orgasm isn't stopping. It's as if she's just rolling from one to the next, never completely coming down before her body spasms and she cries out. So I don't stop, I want to see how long I can draw this out, how much pleasure I can wring out of her. I've counted six when she finally tries to push my away.

"Jake, please, stop, I can't take any more."

Laughing, I release my grip on her and move to the side.

"What the hell was that?" she looks just as shocked as I feel.

"Baby that was one of the best things I've ever seen, I never expected you to orgasm like that."

"Neither did I! That's never happened to me before, it was so intense yet mind-blowingly relaxing all at the same time, until I couldn't take any more, there was just no reprieve before the next one rippled through me, shit I'm babbling now aren't I"

Chuckling again I pull her against my chest, not ignoring the pride bursting out of me that I did this to her.

"Enjoy the high baby, I think you need a break."

I'm not sure she even hears the end of that sentence, when she doesn't reply I look down to see her eyes are closed and she's asleep. She's breathtaking. But it's still just sex, still just fun, still nothing more. Apart from I don't see any time soon that I'll get bored by this, that I won't want to find new ways to pleasure her. I can already hear the boys laughing at me, I'm screwed, absolutely screwed.

CHAPTER 8

Rori

When I wake up Jake is getting dressed.

"Hey, what happened, did I fall asleep on you?"

He must see how horrified I am as he stops with his shoes and comes over to sit on the edge of the bed, cupping my face.

"You did gorgeous, it's hardly surprising after what we did, don't stress about it, you're cute when you sleep. But I'm afraid I have to go, today was amazing, I know you've got a lot on the next few days, maybe we can meet up next week sometime if you're free?"

That's when the niggle starts. Why does he have to leave? What is it making his life complicated? It's not that I want to know his life story, or even what the complications are, but there are some lines I won't cross, and my conscience gets the better of me. I pull myself up to sitting and cross my legs, creating a barrier in case this ends in disaster.

"Look Jake, we've had fun, a lot of fun, and I would absolutely want to keep on having fun, I won't ask you for anything more when you've already said you can't give it and if I'm honest I don't want it either, but there is something I do need from you, I need you to tell me that whatever is complicating your life isn't a wife or girlfriend, cos I won't be that girl"

I inhale a deep breath, not wanting to look at him but

knowing I have to. When I meet his gaze, I see the sincerity that's always been there.

"Rori, I can assure you, I am not that man either, no wife, no girlfriend, in fact no other anything, I'm not leaving to meet another woman, and even though this is just fun, you will be the only person I have that fun with while its happening, I promise. I'm just not in a position to offer you a relationship or share the details of my life. It's always your choice though, I don't want you to feel any pressure to carry on with something if it makes you uncomfortable."

I smile and lean forward to kiss him, "Oh you make me uncomfortable, in all the best kinds of ways, I had to ask, thanks for being honest, next week sounds good."

And with that said, I sweep my tongue over his lips one more time then head to the bathroom.

He's gone when I come back out, I knew he would be, I could see him getting turned on again and he clearly had somewhere to be. When I check the time it's just after seven, so I order some room service then started packing up all of my stuff ready to take to Liv's in the morning. She thinks I'm arriving in the afternoon, so my plan is to surprise her in the morning before she leaves to meet me.

The cab pulls up at my new building at eleven the next morning. I've never seen the outside before, but I've seen the apartment plenty of times when we've facetimed. Liv wouldn't generally have been able to afford this place. It's a three-bedroom apartment in a nice area and Jen owns it. From what Liv has told me, Jen lived with her extremely wealthy brother until a few months ago, helping him with childcare. When she decided it was time to focus back on her own life, he bought this apartment for her as a thank you for everything she'd done for him and because he wanted to know his daughter was safe when she stayed over, which she does. I know, we all want a brother like that. Liv and Jen went to Uni together, although they didn't study the same subject their paths crossed so often with mutual friends, they eventually became close. When Liv's lease was due to run out on the shitty flat she was renting, Jen offered her a room at a really good rate. When I mentioned to Liv that I wanted to come home she immediately spoke to Jen. I'm almost certain Liv's told her some of my history, but I like Jen, so I don't mind, plus it means I also have a really nice place to live for a fraction of the cost.

What didn't occur to me before I formed this plan, was that I wouldn't actually be able to get up to the apartment without a lift fob, so I have to wait in the foyer while the doorman phones up to them. Five minutes later the lift doors open, and Liv is rushing towards me screaming,

"Oh my god, Aurora you're here, how? Why? What happened?"

She's hugging me by this point and bouncing up and down until I can't help but join in her excitement.

"Surprise!"

We start to pull my things over to the lift and I decide to get the explanation out of the way early.

"I know I said I was arriving today but I actually got here on Wednesday, please don't be mad at me, I just felt like I needed to have a couple of days on my own so I could get used to being back in London and deal with any emotions that unearthed. So, I came early and stayed in a hotel for a couple of days first."

"Ah Aurora, of course I'm not mad, this is a massive step for you, I'm glad you did it your way. I'd like to think if I'd known I would have left you to it for two days, but let's face it, as soon as I knew you were here, I'd have been camped outside your hotel room."

We're both laughing as we reach the apartment door because that is absolutely what she would have done.

I'd first met Liv when she was twelve. She'd come to the

foster home I was in at the time for a two-week respite stay while her foster family were dealing with an emergency. I'd like to say we clicked straight away, but we didn't. I was angry at the world back then and I didn't let anyone in. But Liv wasn't put off. By the time she'd gone home, I'd begrudgingly agreed to hang out with her, and our friendship built from there. Whenever I tried to push her away, she kept coming back, and over time, I learned to trust her. Unlike me, she was happy with her foster parents and lived with them until she went to Uni, she still sees them regularly.

I know how much I hurt her when I cut contact with her. Well, I say I cut contact with her, it wasn't exactly my choice, just another way for Stuart to control me. I'd reached out after everything happened, expecting her to ignore me, but she didn't, she was the same Liv, welcoming me with open arms and helping me through my trauma. Liv is also the only person who has ever called me by my full name; Aurora. I hated it growing up, my mother was probably high when she named me, so as soon as I could, I asked to be called Rori. Liv wouldn't have it though. She told me my name was beautiful and regardless of where it came from, it was who I was, so that was what she'd call me. Yeah, Liv isn't someone many people argue with.

"Okay let me take you through to dump your stuff then I'll get the kettle on, and we can catch up properly."

We pull my bags down the corridor and in through a door on the left. My room is amazing, facetime didn't do it justice. It's painted all white, giving it such a bright and airy feel. Even the curtains are white. The hardwood flooring is a dark brown and a fluffy white rug covers the floor at the foot of a double bed. There's a set of drawers and a wardrobe along one wall and a vanity table on the other.

"Wow! Liv this is amazing, it's the nicest bedroom I've ever had."

"Isn't it! Mine is about the same size, Jen's is bigger and she has an ensuite, I'll show you where the other bathroom is when we head through."

"Cool, where is Jen?", I ask as we leave my room.

"She's gone to pick up Belle, her niece. She stays over every Saturday night and sometimes during the week, she's really sweet, you'll like her."

I love kids, love spending time with them, so I'm happy I get to meet Jen's niece today.

The hallway of bedrooms leads into an open plan living area, just as light and airy as my bedroom. The main living area has three big chunky sofas that look like they'd be amazing to curl up on with a book and a glass of wine. A dining table separates the area from the kitchen, which again has white units and looks well stocked with gadgets. I'm not much of a cook, but I have found a passion for baking over the last couple of years so I'm going to enjoy using this space.

We're just settling down at the table with a cuppa when the front door opens and a bundle of energy comes tearing through the room, Jen following closely behind. I stand to greet her and much like Liv, she squeals and throws her arms around me.

"Oh wow you're here, it's so good to finally meet you in person!"

"Hi Jen, you too, it's weird to have talked to someone so often and never been in the same room, thank you again for letting me move in, this place is amazing."

"Oh you're more than welcome, I spend so much time alone with work, so I like to have people around me in my free time."

While we've been talking, the little girl, now stood at Jen's side, has been quietly gazing up at me. Her brown hair is pulled into bunches at each side, green eyes looking up at me probably wondering who I am, with a shy smile on her face.

She's adorable. She tugs on Jen's leg, prompting her to make introductions.

"So, this gorgeous girl is my niece Belle, Belle this is my friend Aurora, she's going to be living here as well from now on."

Belle gasps and her mouth drops open. Unsure why, I drop down to my knees and offer her a gentle smile, maybe she's just shy.

"Hi Belle, it's so nice to meet you, I hope we can be friends as well."

Without warning she darts forward and hugs me tight, taking me by surprise for a minute before I return the hug.

"I knew my wish would come true."

Confused I look up to Jen, but she doesn't seem to know what's going on either.

"What wish sweetie?", she asks as she also drops to her knees trying to find an explanation.

"On my birthday I blew out all of my candles and I wished that another princess would come and find me so we could be friends and have princess tea parties together."

That's when the penny drops, my name, because Liv has always called me by my full name, Jen does as well, and that's how she introduced me to Belle. Recovering quickly, I put on my best smile.

"Well of course I would love to come to tea parties with you, Princess Belle."

Belle giggles, seemingly happy with my answer, and sits down at the table. As we both stand, Jen explains,

"She's obsessed with princesses, it's only gotten worse since she made the connection between her name and Beauty and the Beast. In fact, I'm pretty sure my brother said they were currently reading Sleeping Beauty at bedtime."

"Well that makes sense, she's so cute, I love kids, especially when they're little."

"I'm not little I'm five", pipes up a voice from the table.

"I'm so sorry princess Belle, I just meant you're little compared to me, but wow, five, you're definitely a big girl."

Face beaming with my response, she digs into the juice and biscuits that Liv has put on the table for her.

"So," Liv starts, "tell me everything you've been doing since you got here."

Jen looks confused so I explain my two-day early arrival before responding to Liv's question.

"Erm I will, but it's actually quite the story and definitely not suitable for delicate ears."

I indicate towards Belle, now colouring in.

"Well, that sounds like a wine and pizzas story for later."

"Absolutely", Jen giggles.

I giggle along with them, and even though I've only been here an hour, for the first time in so long I feel like I'm right where I'm supposed to be. Living my life for me, with friends who I can drink and gossip with, not worrying about the repercussions. I'm so happy I'm here.

CHAPTER 9
Jake

The boys are already here when I get to the pub. Saturday nights are our weekly get together, even though I see all of them during most weeks, we still all meet up in the same pub every Saturday night, just to shoot the shit and relax. Jen had insisted on it soon after Belle was born, wanting me to still have time with my friends to unwind. Since she's moved out, it has become her girl's night with Belle, something they both love.

"Evening lover boy," Sean smirks out, pushing a glass towards me.

Flipping him off, I pick it up and take a drink of the golden whiskey held inside.

"Don't try to deny it, I saw the hearts dancing in your eyes when you got back last night."

Before I get the chance to respond Damien cuts in,

"What the fuck! are you seriously falling for her?"

He looks horrified, which might have made me laugh, if it wasn't me he was talking about. Out of all of us, Damien is the biggest man whore, never seeing the same girl twice and adamant he would never commit. Understandable given his past. Sighing I look at all of them,

"Of course I'm not falling for her, you know what Mr Romantic is like. It's just sex, just fun, neither of us want more."

Matthew is the first to respond.

"You sure about that? Because aside from the occasional hook up, it's been years since you've seen anyone twice, never mind spending the night."

I take another drink, not liking where this conversation is heading. Matthew is the quietest of us all, a deep thinker, he knows us all better than ourselves at times, and I didn't like the look he was giving me.

"Yes, I'm sure, look she's a nice girl, absolutely stunning and the sex is amazing. But you know I only have one priority and that's Belle. I'm not looking for a relationship, I won't put Belle through the pain of someone else leaving. Now can we please just drop it?"

Draining my drink, I get up and head to the bar for another round. I watch them as I wait for the drinks, they're clearly talking about me, but as I head back to the table, they all put their game face on and change the subject. Setting down the drinks, it's as if the previous conversation hasn't happened, and I'm grateful they're letting it go so we can enjoy the rest of the night.

I'm just finishing lunch when I hear Jen and Belle coming through the apartment. I go to greet them, and my daughter launches herself into my arms.

"Hey Angel, I missed you, did you have fun with Aunt Jen?"

Kissing her head, I sit down, keeping her on my knee.

"Oh Daddy it was so good, I have a new best friend and she's a princess and we're going to have tea parties and so much fun!"

Wow, my baby is hyper today.

"You did? That's so cool, did you make friends at the park?"

I assume Jen took her on the way home this morning.

"Don't be silly Daddy, Aurora is a big girl like Aunt Jen, and she lives at her house."

Confused I look up at Jen for clarity.

"Liv's friend moved in, I've known her a while as well, she's nice and she was really good with Belle."

I take a minute to stop myself overreacting. Jen hadn't told me someone else was moving in. I knew Liv a little, she was a good friend to Jen, and I was comfortable with Belle spending time with her. But a stranger is different. I open my mouth to say something when Jen cuts me off.

"I'm sorry JayJay, I should have told you. She really is lovely, Liv has known her since they were kids, she's her closest friend. And, well, she hasn't had a great life for reasons I won't share, so when I found out I could help, I did, I really am sorry."

My annoyance leaves me immediately, I never could stay angry at my sister, especially when she uses her childhood nickname for me.

"It's ok, I was a little taken aback, and I do wish you'd told me first, but you've always put Belle first, and I trust Liv, so it's all good."

She looks relieved as she stands.

"I'm going to head straight off, we're going to help Aurora get settled then have a girl's night."

Belle jumps up to say goodbye. Many kisses and cuddles later and it's just the two of us. My favourite time.

After lunch, we spend the afternoon doing her favourite things, playing princesses and watching movies. It was clear Jen's new housemate had certainly made an impression when Belle asked to watched Sleeping Beauty instead of Beauty and the Beast, and I was glad for the change.

When Belle is in bed, I settle down on the sofa with a

beer, thinking about my week ahead. Rori flitted through my thoughts, and I wanted to wish her luck with her new job tomorrow, but I stop myself, that's not what we were. As hot as she is, and fuck she's hot, I'd meant what I said to the boys. I couldn't put Belle in the position to lose someone else. Not just that, I might not date, but I knew women, I see how they look at me when they know who I am, wondering what I can do for them, what they can get from me. I like the anonymity I have with Rori. We know nothing about each other, she isn't looking at me thinking about my bank balance or wishing I didn't have the responsibilities that I do. And that was how it needed to stay, for as long as she was happy with it. Because I was more than happy with it.

Even thinking about her body and the ways I'd made her cum had my cock hardening in my pants. Checking on Belle one last time I head for my room, needing to relieve the pressure. Stripping out of my clothes I head for the shower and as soon as it's hot enough, I step inside. The water pours over me as I reach for my cock, stroking up and down my shaft. I imagine her mouth around me; something we haven't done yet, but I hope to change. Her on her knees looking up at me. Those perfect lips sucking me down her throat as I twist her hair in my grip. It doesn't take long for the familiar feeling to take over my body, my grip tightening around my dick as I brace myself against the shower wall with my other hand. With one last tug I shoot my load against the wall, my body sagging as I watch it wash away. Cleaning the wall and then myself I head to bed, still thinking about those lips wrapped around me.

CHAPTER 10
Rori

I wake to the sun filtering through my curtains and sigh happily. Finally, the weekend. What a week it had been. I'd started my job in the admin department of tech firm on Monday. It wasn't my ideal job, but it paid well enough to make this move possible and I enjoyed the work. I'd spent my first week getting to know the systems and my new colleagues, fun but tiring days. Spending so much time with Liv had been amazing, making me realise how much I'd missed out on over the last few years. Jen was a real bonus as well. I'd liked her from the chats we'd shared before I moved back, but she was fast becoming a good friend now that I was here. We'd had so much fun gossiping on Saturday night. Jake had been the main topic of conversation, although they'd referred to him as 'hot train dude' from the start, so I don't think I actually mentioned his name. I didn't tell them everything either, too embarrassed to go into detail about the intimate things we'd done. But they knew how amazing he'd made me feel and encouraged me to make the most of this no strings fun. Liv in particular had gotten a little emotional, so happy that I seemed to be moving on and enjoying life again.

On Tuesday, Jen had brought Belle over for tea and I'd really enjoyed seeing her again, she was such a cute kid. She'd gotten dressed up in her princess costume and we'd played with her tea set. I'd also seen Jake on Thursday night. He'd text me on Wednesday to see if I was free to meet up and suggested 'our hotel' for the night. I wasn't sure at first; meeting up at a hotel felt a little bit icky. But then I reminded myself this was just some much needed fun. An opportunity to escape with a gorgeous man and earth-shattering sex. So, I'd met him at the hotel after work and he had not disappointed. He'd spent two hours taking me to ecstasy, time and time again, both of us a sweaty mess by the time we'd stopped. He couldn't stay, I didn't ask why, and even though he'd paid for the room for the night I still came home.

Now it's the weekend and I need to get up and go shopping. Belle is staying tonight and, after checking with Jen, I planned to bake with her this afternoon. I take a quick shower and dress, then go in search of coffee. Liv is in the kitchen, and she pours me one when she sees my approach.

"Morning, how glad are you that it's the weekend!"

I take the mug and smile.

"I am glad, but you look especially happy this morning, what's going on?"

She'd been out on a date with her boyfriend last night and I'd already been asleep when she got home.

"I'm going away for the night! Jason surprised me with it last night and he's picking me up in ten minutes"

Liv has been with Jason for a couple of months, but it seems like things are getting more serious.

"That's great Liv, have a great time," I say, hugging her.

Liv works hard and deserves the chance to get away, even if it is only for the night. Her childhood had motivated her to want to help kids like we'd been, and she'd become a social worker. It amazed me that she could take all of that on and I was always telling her how in awe of her I was.

"What about you?", she asks as I let her go, "got plans with 'hot train dude' this weekend?".

She winks at me as she sips her own coffee.

"Nah not this weekend, we didn't make plans the other night, and anyway, I have plans to bake up a storm with Belle this afternoon."

Her face grows more serious, and she grips onto my hand.

"Aurora, are you sure you're ok spending time with her? It must be so hard for you."

"It's really not", I smile at her, "she's a great kid and I've always loved kids. It wasn't meant to be for me but there's no point dwelling on it."

Sensing I don't want to carry on the conversation, she gives me another quick hug then sets her mug down.

"Right I'm off, have a great weekend babe."

Once she was gone, I sat down to make a list of ingredients I need then head out to the shop. It's a lovely day, so I wander through the park on my way home, laughter and squeals filling the air where several kids are enjoying the swings and slides in a gated off part of the park. By the time I get back, Jen is home with Belle, and she comes running to greet me.

"Princess Aurora you're here!"

She hugs my legs tight. I'm impressed with her speech, even the first time we were introduced she said my name perfectly.

"Well hello there Princess Belle, I heard you'd be in residence today and I thought we could have some fun in the kitchen."

Her face lights up as she pulls away from me.

"Really!?"

"Really," I smile back at her, "I've been shopping for supplies and we're going to bake some cakes together."

Belle starts jumping up and down with the biggest smile

on her face and I laugh as we head to the kitchen together. Putting everything on the counter I turn to Belle.

"Ok then, let's get our hands clean and get baking."

The afternoon flies over. We make cookies, cupcakes and brownies. Belle helps me measure and mix everything and then decorate them when they're cool. By the time we're finished we're both covered in flour and sprinkles and the kitchen is a mess, but I don't care. I grab my phone and turn to Belle.

"How about a princess selfie?", I ask, crouching down next to her to take the picture.

We're both smiling into the camera as Jen comes over.

"Wow guys you're covered! But everything smells so good. Come on munchkin, you're having a bath to get cleaned up then we can taste your cakes."

I clean the kitchen then head for the shower myself. It's been such a good afternoon. I know I told Liv I was fine, and I am, mostly. But a family is all I've ever wanted, the chance to give a child what I never got.

After Belle goes to bed Jen opens a bottle of wine and we settle on the sofa.

"You really are so good with her Aurora."

She looks like she wants to say more and by her face I know she knows.

"Thank you, she's a great kid. I don't know how much Liv told you about my past, but from your face I can see she told you about my miscarriage. I'm not upset with her so don't worry, it's not something I talk about a lot, but I don't mind you knowing."

Jen looks relieved as she replies, "she told me a little, I didn't know if you wanted me to know so I haven't said anything but I wanted to tell you how sorry I am for what you've been through and if you ever want to talk I'm here."

I spend a couple of minutes lost in my own world before

making the decision to share some of my story with her.

"Thank you. It's not that I don't trust you, it's just not a pleasant story and I don't like to get swallowed up in the memories. That's probably why I've enjoyed writing my books so much, it's a good escape from reality."

She gives me an understanding smile.

"That's totally understandable, but the offer is always there. Also, you've piqued my editor interest, I'd love to read what you've written."

"You would?" I ask.

"Yeah, I mean I can't guarantee I can help, but if nothing else, I will be honest with you and help you fine tune the editing if you need it."

"Thank you, I'd love that, I'll email them over to you."

We move on to lighter topics as we finish our wine. When I eventually head to bed, I feel content with how things are for the first time in a long time. I might not have told Jen my story, but it feels good to know she cares, and I'm genuinely happy with the direction my life has taken.

CHAPTER 11
Jake

I 'm having a bad day. I've been dealing with pain in the arse clients all morning, I have a monster headache and all I want to do is go back to bed then start this day again. I'm about to make my next call when the boys walk in.

"Does it ever occur to any of you to call my assistant before you turn up, or even just knock?" I ask, frustrated.

"Someone got out of the wrong side of bed this morning," comments Damien.

"Maybe the issue is it was his bed he was getting out of…. alone", chimes in Sean.

They all snigger.

"Fuck off, arseholes, I've got a shit ton of work to get done and my head is pounding, what do you want?"

They don't get the chance to respond before my sister comes waltzing in behind them.

"Hey boys, it's been a while, still breaking hearts all over London are we?"

She grins as she hugs them one by one. My sister has known the boys as long as I have. She might have started out as my annoying little sister, but when our lives fell apart, they stepped up, not just for me. They included her when they came over, suggested days out she would enjoy and generally just showed up for her. She's now like a sister to all of them and they'd drop anything to help her out if she needed it. She also knows what our track record with women is like and doesn't miss an opportunity to wind any of us up.

"It not us you should be looking at this time little Jen," Damien pipes up and I swear I could knock him out right now.

Gritting my teeth, I pause as she swings round and sets the look on me.

"Jayjay, are you seeing someone! What have you been keeping from me?"

It's the look she gives Belle when she's checking if she really brushed her teeth.

"No", I reply as the others chime yes and laugh like schoolkids.

"For fuck sake, no I am not seeing anyone, I'm just having some fun, can we move on?"

"Bullshit," coughs Matthew as Sean shakes his head.

She focuses on Damien.

"Give me the gossip Damien, you know you want to."

I'm about to shout at all of them to leave when Damien starts.

"He's been with the same woman three times, claims it's just fun, but spent the night at least once and gets a soppy look on his face that he thinks we haven't noticed whenever we bring her up."

"Are you fucking kidding me?" I bark as I toss a pen at him.

Catching it easily, he looks over.

"What, you know what that look does to me, I haven't been able to say no to her since she was ten, she's fucking scarier than some of the executives I deal with."

I sit down in defeat and rest my head back against my chair.

"Why are you all here?" I ask.

"We thought you might want to get lunch," Matthew starts, "but it's clear your day is busier than ours, so we'll get out of your hair and leave you to Jen's interrogation."

More sniggers.

As they head for the door Jen stop him.

"Matthew, while you're here, can I ask a favour?"

It comes out sounding a lot softer than she did a minute ago. She's never been as confident when it comes to Matthew, probably because they work in a similar industry. Matthew runs a hugely successful publishing company. Jen is a freelance editor. When she first showed an interest in the world of books, I offered to ask Matthew to help her out, but she refused. She wanted to do it herself. So I'm surprised to hear her asking him for something.

"Sure Jen, if I can, what's up?"

"My new housemate is an author. What I mean is, she's never had anything published, but I offered to read what she has and it's good. Believe me, this girl was born to do this, and I could go through my normal routes to help her, but she's had a rough time and she deserves a break. If I email something over to you, will you read it?"

"Of course, my week is pretty quiet, send it over and I'll let you know what I think asap."

When he leaves, Jen flops into the chair on the other side of my desk and fixes me with the look again.

"Spill it big bro."

Groaning I drop my head in my hand.

"There's nothing to spill Jen, I hooked up with her, had

fun, decided to have more fun, nothing else to say."

I look away, hoping she shuts up, no such luck.

"You do realise this is me you're talking to don't you, as in the sister who's been around for the last twenty six years, the same sister who knows you've barely looked at a woman since Belle came along, never mind going back for more, she's different."

I close my eyes; I really don't want to continue this conversation.

"Look, Jake, I know you don't want to hear this, but I've kept my mouth shut long enough. Not every woman is Melinda."

"Jen", I warn, my tone telling her how close I am to losing my shit.

"No Jake, let me finish."

She leans forward now, and I know I won't like what comes next.

"I was there, both times, I know why you tried again, I know how much Mum dying changed you. But you can't let it stop you moving on and finding love, you deserve it. She was never right for you and what she did was beyond redemption. But what if this girl is who you're meant to be with, and you lose her because you can't let go of the past?"

I'm silent for what feels like hours, my eyes staying closed. I can't look at her because I don't want to see the pity on her face, and I can't speak because I honestly don't know what will come out of my mouth.

"I'm going to head off as well, I only came up to say hi while I was passing. I love you Jayjay." I still don't look at her, but I do find my voice.

"I love you too Jen."

Then she's gone, leaving me with an even worse headache and no idea what I'm feeling.

I let my assistant know I'm done for the day and ask her to rearrange my scheduled appointments. Instead of texting my driver I decide to take a walk to clear my head. When I get to the park I sit at a bench, sun shining on me and a gentle breeze washing over my face. My mind replays everything Jen said, all of the comments the boys have made over the last couple of weeks and then finally her face fills my head. I'm not an idiot, it's not like I'm lying to them and I'm really in love with her. I don't know her. We connect intensely on a physical level, but we've never talked beyond that. Apart from on the train, where admittedly, we did seem to have similar interests, we've kept it just about sex. So, there's a chance we wouldn't be good together anyway. The problem, and yes, it is absolutely a problem, is that I've started to want to know her. To want to find out if we could be more. And that fucking terrifies me.

I'll never forgive my child's mother for walking away, never understand how she could do that. My own mother fought as hard as she could not to leave us, that's what a mother does. Belle is the best thing that's ever happened to me. I would give up everything in exchange for her. She doesn't ask about her Mum, she's always accepted how our life is. But now she's at school, making friends with kids who have both parents, or even just a mum at home, I know the questions will come. I don't want to add to the pain I know she'll suffer when we have those conversations. What if I start dating Rori, introduce her to Belle, and then it doesn't work out. Belle will be crushed. She's so loving and gets attached so easily. Jesus, she's only known Jen's housemate a week and she's smitten with her. She came home on Sunday raving about her afternoon of baking. She was so proud of herself for what she'd created and couldn't wait to tell me all about how she'd helped weigh out the ingredients and decorate the cakes. She'd even brought some home for me to try, which I did immediately and then heaped more praise on her. I didn't even have to fake it, they were fucking good. But it's easy to let her get attached in this way, Aurora lives with Jen so is likely to be in her life for a while, and Belle only expects to see her if she's visiting Jen. Having a girlfriend would be different, they'd spend more time together, maybe she'd stay the night. And if that all came crashing down; how would my wonderful, funny, sensitive little girl cope with that loss.

Sending a text to my driver to come get me, I also send another to the nanny to say she's not needed today. I'm not wasting this early finish, I'll pick Belle up myself, knowing how excited she'll be to see me at school, then take her to the park closer to home and for ice cream. An afternoon with my angel is just what I need today.

CHAPTER 12
Rori

I've just gotten home on Thursday when my phone buzzes a text.

Jake: Hey beautiful, are you free tomorrow night? Your pussy is like a drug and I need my next hit

My days, his mouth, I'm turned on just reading it. It's been nearly a week since I've seen him, with no texts either, so I'd wondered if he'd gotten bored and moved on. It seems that isn't the case.

Rori: How can I say no when you ask like that, where and when

Jake: Our hotel? 7? I don't have to rush off this time, I can feast on you all night long

Jake: and I intend to

Jake: ALL NIGHT LONG

And now I'm completely wet for him.

Rori: can't wait, see you then

Jake: indeed you will gorgeous

I put my phone down and change out of my work clothes then go to find the girls in the living room. Before I can speak Jen jumps up from the couch.

"Oh my god Aurora I have the best news. And an apology, but I'm really hoping you'll forgive me for that bit when you hear the good news part.”

I can see the excitement on her face, and she must see the confusion on mine, so she carries on.

“So obviously you know I’m an editor, but what I didn’t mention is that one of my brother’s best friends owns a publishing company. I don’t work with him, I didn’t want any favours when I was starting out, but I read your work Aurora and it’s so good, I lost myself in it, you have a real talent.”

She finally takes a breath, so I jump in,

“thanks Jen, that means a lot but why are you sorry?”

Now she looks sheepish and I glance at Liv to see if she knows what this is about, but she just shrugs.

“Well like I said, my brother’s best friend is a publisher, so I spoke to him and he agreed to read it, that was Tuesday, he called me today, he loved it as well, he loved it so much he wants you to come in for a meeting to talk about next steps!”

I’m speechless, I don’t even think I blink, I just stare at her silent and unmoving. It’s Liv that pulls me out of it, jumping up and grabbing me into a hug.

“Oh Aurora this is amazing news, I’m so happy for you!”

I look at Jen.

“Is this for real, he actually likes my stuff?”

Her gaze softens as she grips my arm.

“Yeah, he really does, and he’s not just doing it to shut me up, he has a good reputation and wouldn’t take a risk just to keep his best friends baby sister happy.”

A look passes over her face when she says the last bit and I wonder if there’s a story hidden in that comment. But I’m too excited to question her.

“Thank you so much Jen, you’ve been amazing since I got here, I don’t know what I’d do without you both.”

The tears fall freely now, and the girls pull me in for another hug. I can't believe this is happening, that I might actually get to see my words in print.

Liv moves to the kitchen and opens the fridge.

"We need to celebrate," she says, producing a bottle of fizz.

Soon, we're a little bit tipsy and talk moves on to men.

"So, Aurora", Liv starts, "how's things with hot train dude."

I giggle at his nickname.

"He actually text just before I came out here, asking to meet up tomorrow night."

"Ooo you are getting laid tomorrow!" Jen says, topping up our drinks.

"Is it still just a fun hook up orrr? Are you happy with that?".

I think about the question. The sex is amazing, there's no question I'm having a lot of fun. But when I thought he might have moved on, it's also true that it bothered me a bit. I still know nothing about him, or why his life is complicated. I also know that I'm not sure I could offer him a relationship even if he wanted one. I might have worked hard to move on from my past, but the scars are still there. The self-doubt, the feeling of never being worthy, it never really goes away. I'm so much more confident than I was, I'm proud of the progress I've made, but I've still got work to do. Looking back at the girls I answer honestly.

"It's still just a hook up and I'm happy with where things are, I'm not ready for a full on relationship, but I do think I want to learn more about him, I can't deny how much I enjoy spending time with him. I'm just mindful that I bring a lot of baggage with me, and I don't want burden him with that."

Liv looks at me, I can see her getting a little emotional as she speaks.

"Aurora, for the right person, it won't be baggage, it will be another reason to love you. I understand why you're not ready to fully commit to the idea of really dating again, I really do. But I still remember the bright, sassy bitch that didn't take shit from anyone. Stuart destroyed a lot of things, but that girl is still in there, and she's amazing. So, try to be open to possibilities, but in the meantime…keep riding that hot train dick, I mean dude."

And with that we all burst out laughing. I heard all of her words, I know she's right, but I'll analyse that later, right now I'm just enjoying the high of finally having someone read my stories and the anticipation of another night with Jake.

CHAPTER 13

Jake

I get to the hotel early. This time, Matthew had been the one to offer his doting Uncle services and Belle had been more than happy to spend time with him, mainly because he always brought more books to read to her. Opening the door, I drop my briefcase and continue inside. I'd thought a lot over the last few days. Ran through every scenario I could, weighing up the possible outcomes. But no matter how much I focused on the negatives, I still came back to the same image of Rori curled up in bed the morning after we first met. I didn't want this to stop, not only that but I wanted to know more about her. So, I was going to talk to her tonight, tell her a little bit of my life, then see if she was open to maybe dating, slowly, very slowly. I realised I was taking a risk, not just the risk of what happened if she said yes but also if she said no. If she didn't want more, she was unlikely to want to continue as we were, it would be too awkward. So, my plan was to fuck her first, just in case I never got to have her again. Selfish I know, but what could I do, I needed her body wrapped around mine again.

Thinking of the time she'd answered the door in the robe, I decide I'll return the visual and strip out of my suit, getting a robe from the bathroom. As I come back to the bed my phone rings, seeing it's Matthew I take the call.

"Hey bro, is everything ok?" I ask.

"Yeah, we're all good, but my little sidekick got a little

upset because she forgot to say goodnight to you so I hoped we could catch you before you were, erm, occupied?"

I laugh at him trying to choose his words for my daughter's ears.

"Put her on."

"Daddy Daddy it's me," her voice calls out.

He's put me on speaker.

"Hi baby girl, I love you so much, I can't wait to see you in the morning."

I hear the gasp and before I even turn, I know it has come from Rori and not my daughter. I freeze, my eyes widening, seeing the look of betrayal on her face, while still listening to Belle chatter in my ear. She's still holding on to the door she's just come through and, reacting quicker than me, she turns and flees.

"Rori wait!" I yell after her, but she's already gone.

I run for the door to see her disappearing behind the closing lift doors. My phone still in my hand, I hear Matthew telling Belle I have something to deal with and we can talk later, then the line disconnects. I dial Rori's number, but she doesn't pick up. Rushing around the room, I pull my clothes back on then rush back to the hallway, hoping she hasn't gotten far. It's then I see my briefcase in the doorway, it must have stopped the door closing fully when I came in, so she'd been able to open it without me hearing.

When I reach the lobby, she's nowhere to be seen and I run to the street, looking left and right, but nothing. She's gone. I make my way back inside and up to the room, trying her number over and over again. She doesn't answer. Fuck. She clearly hadn't heard the start of my conversation and must have come in to the sound of me calling someone baby and telling them I loved them. Fucking fuck. I'd hoped she might have changed her mind and come to the room to shout at me, but the corridor is empty when I return. Going back into the room I sit on the bed and try her phone again, nothing. I need to talk to her.

Jake: Rori, it's not what you think, please either call me or come back so we can talk

I'd only gotten half-dressed to chase after her, so I go back to the rest of my things and finish getting dressed. I had no new messages so I go back down to the bar, choosing a seat where I can see the main entrance of the hotel in case she comes back. Ordering a whiskey, I pull out my phone again, still nothing, so I try to ring her again. This time it doesn't even ring. Pulling up our text thread I see my message hasn't even been delivered. She's either turned her phone off or blocked me. Out of ideas I drain my drink and head home.

When I get back, I found all three of my boys sat around the kitchen island with a bottle between them. Matthew speaks first.

"She's in bed, already sound asleep."

I nod as I reach for the bottle and pour a good measure.

"What happened?"

That's from Sean.

Letting out a sigh I explain what went down in the hotel room, they're all silent once I've finished. Damien breaks the silence.

"Well it's shit that it's ended like this, but it was just sex, right? You were just having fun yeah? So onwards and upwards to the next one."

I slam my glass on the counter and move for the bottle to top it up.

"That's what I thought," he adds.

"What does that mean?" I growl at him.

"It means I was right when I called bullshit, this wasn't

just sex was it?" he accuses.

I take a steadying breath, they all know the truth, it's pointless trying to lie to them now.

"No, it wasn't, don't get me wrong I wasn't about to propose but I was going to talk to her tonight about maybe trying to actually date."

I finally look up at them, waiting for their views, but they're all silent again.

"Yeah, I know, how fucked up is this, I finally decide to entertain the idea of dating and I fuck it all up before I can even ask her out. In five years, she's the only woman I've felt any kind of connection to."

My words sit between us before Matthew speaks.

"Jake, I know this is shit, but it's a massive step you were prepared to take, a step we've all been hoping you would take for a long time. You never know, she might reach out, but even if she doesn't, don't let this send you backwards again."

I don't answer, I can't, I don't want to think or analyse my choices. What I want is to drink my weight in whiskey until I forget my own name….and hers. I don't remember much else, or how I got to bed, but I do remember the look on her face when I turned around. The hurt, the anger, the betrayal, and it haunts my fucking dreams.

CHAPTER 14
Rori

"I love you so much, I can't wait to see you in the morning"

I heard the words over and over in my head as I run from the hotel. I can't think straight and jump in the first cab I see, giving him my address. My phone is buzzing constantly in my pocket, but I ignore it, I know it's him. How could he do this? It was the only question I'd asked him, the only stipulation I had before we continued to hook up; I wouldn't be that girl. Yet that's exactly what he's turned me into. By the time I get home I'm sick of the constant buzzing in my pocket, so I take out my phone and turn it off without checking the notifications. I'm grateful I'm alone in the apartment. I'm not sure where Liv and Jen are, or what time they'll be back, but I need time to gather my thoughts before I unload on them.

Deciding a bath will help, I go straight to the bathroom and set the water away, adding a relaxing bubble mix as I undress. Soaking into the water, I lay my head back and close my eyes. What an absolute clusterfuck. There was nothing complicated about his life at all, he was just a total prick, wanting his fun while his partner was oblivious. Oh god, what if they're married? What if he has kids? I feel sick. Why does this happen in my life? I think about all the work I've done to work on my reactions to bad situations, to not either run or fight but to stop and think. Well, I'm sure my therapist would agree that running tonight was a way better idea than staying and kicking him in the balls. I stay in the bath until the water starts to get cold, letting the bubbles soothe my body.

When I finally get out and dressed into comfortable lounge clothes, I drag myself to the living room and find a bottle. I was just pouring my first shot of vodka when both Jen and Liv arrive home together. They take one look at me and dive for the sofa, sitting either side of me as Liv asks,

"What happened? What did he do?"

I down my shot without answering, reaching for two more glasses before pouring another round.

"He's not single," I mumble as I take my next shot.

I hear their intake of breath before they also down the shots I'd poured.

"That bastard."

"Fucking prick."

They both speak at the same time.

"Tell us what happened," Liv adds.

This time she pours the drinks, and after finishing mine I sit back and tell them what I'd walked in on.

"None of this is your fault Aurora, he's a tool of the highest order, but you asked him, he's the one who lied, don't be too hard on yourself."

Jen's words help. I'd already started feeling guilt for whoever was on the other end of that phone call.

"This calls for more vodka and pizza," Liv states, with her glass raised, "we've got you, don't worry, by tomorrow morning you'll be over that giant cockwomble."

I laugh out loud at that and slip more and more into a happier place, as the alcohol works through my system, grateful once again for my girls.

I'm not so grateful, for the alcohol at least, when I wake up the next morning. My head is pounding, and my tongue is stuck to the roof of my mouth. Turning my head, I groan but I'm thankful to see I'd brought a bottle of water to bed with me. Rolling slightly to get a better angle, I gulp down as much as I can. It isn't cold but at least I can swallow properly now. I still haven't turned my phone back on, so I drag myself out of bed, not knowing what time it was. When I get to the living area, I find both Liv and Jen sitting at the table nursing mugs of coffee. Liv silently stands and goes to pour me one as I join them at the table.

"What time is?" I croak out.

"Eleven," Jen answers, sounding rough but not nearly as bad as I do.

"God, I feel like shit, I think I need to sleep the day away."

I put my head on my arm, raising it when I feel Liv slide the mug towards me.

"I have a better idea," announces Jen.

"It's Saturday don't forget, which means it's Belle day, and Belle makes everyone feel better. But you need to clear your head first, or it'll explode before the first tea party ends."

I smile at that, Belle certainly is a whirlwind.

"What do you suggest?" I ask.

"I suggest we get dressed, head out for some brunch and then we take a walk. I'm picking her up from the park so we can get her while we're out."

I don't like the sound of any of that, apart from the ending when I get to see Belle, so I begrudgingly agree to the rest of the plan. Half an hour later I'm showered and dressed, still rough as fuck, wearing dark sunglasses with my leggings and hoodie.

"Cute," Liv laughs as we meet in the hallway.

We stop at a nearby café for food, all ordering coffee and

orange juice to go with bacon sandwiches. By the time we've finished I feel marginally better and more willing to walk to the park.

We take a slow walk, although they are both pretty much fully recovered, they take pity on my blatant hangover. It's a nice enough day, dry and warmish but the sky isn't bright, so I probably look ridiculous in my sunglasses. As we approach the play area the sounds of kids screeching gets a lot louder and I hope Belle won't want to hang around after we collect her from Jen's brother. Just as I'm about to look around, I hear the now familiar voice of my favourite little person.

"Aunt Jen, Princess Aurora, Liv, I'm here I'm here!".

And then she comes cannoning towards us. She launches herself at Jen first and I watch as they hug like they've been apart for weeks. Then she dives out of Jen's arms into mine. Still not feeling great I lower her to the ground and crouch in front of her for a hug.

"Well hello there Princess Belle, it's so good to see you."

I hear several sets of footsteps approaching from behind, and Belle shouts over my shoulder,

"Daddy come and meet my princess."

Standing up slowly, I raise my glasses to the top of my head as I turn to meet her dad.

I freeze, stunned, not believing what I'm seeing. In front of me, Belle is in her dad's arms, arms I know well, arms that have held me, arms that belong to 'hot train dude'.

"Rori," he barks out, clearly as shocked as I am.

"Jake," I whisper.

I suddenly become aware of our surroundings. Belle looks confused, she'd never heard anyone call me Rori, and gives Jake a stern look.

"No Daddy, this is Aurora, my new friend."

The three men that are with him seem to cotton on quicker than any of us and are looking at me with giant smiles on their faces. Liv and Jen are standing with their mouths literally hanging open. Jake and I just stand, staring at each other, neither of us speaking. Belle breaks our gaze when she wriggles in his arms to get down.

"I want to go back and play, Aurora will you push me on the swings?"

Before I can respond one of the other men speaks up.

"Hey Belle, I haven't had a turn to push you yet and you promised, let's go."

She hurries after him, happy that someone is going to push her. Jake looks back at me.

"Rori, I don't understand, what are you doing here?"

I don't get the chance to respond, Liv finds her voice first.

"Holy shit! Are you hot train dude?" she says, looking at Jake.

This pulls Jen from her frozen state as she looks between the two of us. She turns to Jake first.

"Is this the girl the boys have been teasing you about?" she smiles, then she stops, the smile dropping from her face and she looks a little sick, turning to me her eyes are wide.

"Eww Aurora, are you telling me the best sex of your life was with my brother!"

The man who'd left to push Belle chose this moment to return to the group and all of them burst into laughter. Jake at least shoots them a scalding look and I cringe and drop my head, staring intently at the ground, wishing it to open up and swallow me.

This is not how I saw my day going.

CHAPTER 15
Jake

W hat the fuck is going on right now? If my hangover isn't bad enough, my head is now completely fucked by the events of the last ten minutes. When Belle woke me up this morning, I felt like I'd been hit by a truck. When we got to the kitchen, I realised the boys had stayed over last night and like the legend that he is, Damien was already cooking breakfast. A full English no less. The food helped clear the fog and we all gave in to Belle's demand to take her to the park. The fresh air worked wonders, but I was still feeling a little green when Belle suddenly called out to Jen and took off. By the time I turned in the direction she'd ran, she was already in Jen's arms. I could see Liv standing near them and another woman with her back to me. Registering that Belle had called out other names, I assumed she was Jen's new housemate.

The four of us started to make our way over, just as Belle launched herself into the other woman's arms and they crouched to the floor for a hug. The action made me stall. I'd never seen Belle do that with any woman other than Jen and it flooded me with emotions. Pain, regret, guilt. But I couldn't ignore the tug of longing as well, wishing things could have been different. Especially if I hadn't royally fucked up last night.

Then Belle was on me, and the woman was standing and turning slowly towards me, as she pushed away her sunglasses. It was like all of the air was sucked out of me. It was Rori, my

Rori. I could hear Belle correcting me and telling me she was Aurora, but I couldn't speak, couldn't move, could only stare at her. She had her hair piled on top of her head in a bun, a big baggy hoodie covering her perfect curves. Her eyes suggested she'd also hit the drink last night but fuck me, she was perfect. Absolutely stunning. I was vaguely aware of Damien taking Belle back to the swings, but I couldn't stop staring into her big blue eyes, trying to read what she was thinking. They were filled with confusion mostly. I didn't blame her, I was confused as fuck right now.

It was Jen that pulled me out of my mute state.

"The best sex of your life was with my brother!"

Then the laughter of the boys behind me. Her eyes hit the ground, clearly mortified. Turning to look at the idiots beside me I fix them with a glare to shut the fuck up. They at least tried to quieten down. I glance at Jen, her eyes are wide as saucers, and she's mimicking throwing up. So fucking mature, my friends and family are really not helping right now.

"Rori," I take a step forward, she didn't move, didn't take her eyes from the floor. "Rori look at me."

I reach out and put my finger under her chin, tipping her face up to meet my eyes. There are so many things I want to say, so many questions about how she was standing in front of me right now, but I knew where I needed to start.

"Rori, I was talking to Belle on the phone last night, she was with Matthew and he called me because she was upset that she'd forgotten to say goodnight."

I see the relief in her eyes, but she still doesn't speak. Then Belle is back, jumping all around us, asking if it's time to leave.

"Princess Aurora, are we going to bake again today?"

Thankfully Jen jumps in.

"Hey precious girl, so Aurora has somewhere to be this

afternoon, that's why she came to the park so she could see you first."

Belle's face falls, and it's like a shot to the heart. Rori must notice as well because she finally finds her voice and crouches down again.

"Princess Belle don't be sad, I brought this with me so you could have fun with Aunt Jen on the way home, and I promise the next time I see you we'll bake again."

She produces a giant bubble wand from her sleeve and hands it to my daughter, who throws herself in for another hug. My brain can't cope with these images, it's too much. I turn away and look at the boys for help. Help none of them seem to want to give. Arseholes know how to stay silent now don't they? The three of them start to edge away and Sean says with a grin,

"Well it's time we made a move, things to do, people to see."

They all give Belle hugs before waving their goodbyes and walking away. Still grinning like fools. Arseholes. As I turn back to Rori, Liv is giving her a hug and saying something in her ear, then Jen does the same, this time a blush creeping over her skin. Fuck knows what my sister is saying to her. Then she approaches me, and I reach out to hug her automatically. As I pull her close, she whispers in my ear.

"Don't make me want to throat punch you, I like her."

And before I can reply she'd moved away, Belle now replacing her in my arms.

"Be good for Aunt Jen sweetie, I'll see you tomorrow, I love you."

"Love you Daddy"

Then they're gone, making their way across the park, bubbles flying everywhere.

I look at Rori, back to staring at the ground, gently biting her bottom lip. God she was gorgeous, my cock agreed, and I silently begged it to stand down. For now. She clearly isn't going to speak anytime soon so I need to take the lead.

"Well, this is a massive head fuck I wasn't expecting this morning," I laugh out.

She looks up, smiling slightly.

"Yeah, me neither," she breathes out.

"Look Rori…. actually, is it Rori, I'm beyond confused right now, I know you've got plans but could we talk."

I hold my breath as she considers what I've said.

"Actually I don't have plans, well I had plans to walk off this hangover then distract myself entertaining.." she paused, seeming to be searching for the right words, "erm, entertaining your daughter, but your sister seems to have changed those plans for me," she finishes with a wry smile.

My sister is a meddler, a wonderful meddler right at this moment, although I will never admit that.

"Ok, so maybe we could take a walk, get a coffee?" I ask hopefully.

She still doesn't look completely sure but nods her head in agreement and we start to walk.

"So, maybe we could start with your name," I prompt.

She laughs now, it's not loud but it's like music to my ears and I want to keep hearing it.

"Ah yeah, my name. So… my name is Aurora, but I've never liked it, from a young age I shortened it to Rori. Liv, however, wouldn't have it. She said it was my name and it was beautiful, so she's always called me Aurora. Which is what she introduced me as to Jen and therefore what Jen called me when I first met Belle", she says with a shrug.

The mention of my daughter pulls my mind back to the

images of them together. Although brief, it was clear they'd developed a bond and right now that was fucking with my head.

"Erm yeah…so…I have a daughter," I sigh out.

"You do," she replies, "you have a beautiful, funny, clever, loving daughter Jake. You should be proud."

The warmth I feel at her comments is intense, my heart beating faster. I need to have a word with myself, I barely know her, and this is not how I expected things to turn out.

"Thank you, and I am, every single day, she's my world, everything I do is for her. She's also one of the reasons my life is complicated. I wasn't lying when I said that, it wasn't just a brush off to hide another woman. I hope you believed what I said about it being Belle on the phone last night."

There were some tables ahead of us near a coffee stand, so I guide us towards them as I wait for her to answer.

"I do believe you, I'm sorry I didn't stick around for an explanation last night, but at the time I didn't think there was any other explanation."

We're still walking side by side, but I need more eye contact with her, need to see her beautiful face fully while we talk.

"Good, let's get a coffee and sit for a bit."

I don't pose it as a question, I don't want to give her the chance to say no, so I make my way to a table and pull out a seat for her. Thankfully she follows.

"Right then, what can I get you?"

CHAPTER 16
Rori

While Jake stands in the queue for coffee, I take a minute to catch my breath. He looks amazing. Every other time I've seen him he's been in a suit, which he looks hot in of course. But casual Jake is something else. He's wearing jeans that sit low on his hips and from this angle I can see exactly how well they mould over his arse and thighs. The white t-shirt he has on is skin-tight, showing off the rippling muscles I know are hidden underneath it. He finished it all off with a leather jacket, so hot. Looking up to his face, I can see he hasn't shaved today, his stubble is dark and enticing, the thought of it rubbing over my body makes me squirm in my seat. I need to stop this fantasy. My two worlds have crashed together, and I don't know how I feel about it, now is not the time for drooling.

I'm still staring when he turns his head towards me, those piercing green eyes locking on mine, a cocky smile tugging at his lips. Yeah, he knows I'm checking him out. He's next to be served and soon he's on his way back to our table and setting down the paper cups.

"So, what did my sister say to you before she left?" he asks, and I know I'm blushing.

Looking anywhere but at him I answer truthfully.

"She told me you were a good man and to listen to what you had to say, but also that we're never discussing my sex life ever again."

I see him grinning from the corner of my eye and I know what he's thinking about before he says,

"So what you're saying is, you can't discuss the best sex you've ever had with her anymore."

The grin doesn't stop. I'm mortified. Looking for any kind of distraction I throw the question back at him, knowing she also spoke to him before she left. He takes a minute before answering.

"She told me she likes you and then told me if I hurt you she'd come for me, and let me tell you, I've seen my sister mad more than once, I don't take her threats lightly."

I smile at this, relaxing more, talking about Jen feels like common ground.

"Jen's been really good to me, I'm lucky to have her and Liv as friends."

"She's the best sister I could've hoped for, she's done more for me the last few years than I can ever pay her back for."

I know he's talking about how much she's cared for Belle, but I don't want to admit that, given it now feels a little weird to know more about him than he's told me. He must read the look on my face as he continues,

"I'm sure she's told you she moved in with me when Belle was born and only moved out a few months ago."

"She did, but if you're worried about what else she might have told me then the answer is nothing, she mentioned that because I commented on the amazing bond they share, she hasn't spoken about you in any other way."

He looks relieved, I don't blame him, his casual fun just rocked up in his world, already knowing his daughter and sister, he's probably wondering how to let me down gently without it getting awkward.

"Look, Rori, I'm just going to be honest with you."

Here it comes.

"If things had gone differently last night, I'd planned to talk to you then. My life is complicated, I'm a single dad for a start. I also run my own company, I'm wealthy, which can bring its own problems. I haven't dated since before Belle was born, in fact I've barely been with anyone since then, certainly not more than once. She's my number one priority, not just of my time but for emotional stability, I don't want to do anything that could open her up to pain and loss."

This man is perfect, he might be about to tell me he never wants to see me again, but his motives are making me want him even more.

"And then you came along. And that first night, rocked my world in ways I wasn't expecting. I knew I wanted more than one night. Your body is insane Rori, I needed to touch you again. You're not the only one who thinks it's the best sex they've ever had."

Wow, just wow. I am blown away right now. And yeah, completely turned on. I don't have to speak though as he takes a breath and continues.

"I've realised this week though that I wasn't just thinking about the sex, I was thinking about you, wondering how your new job was going, or if you'd gotten everything organised at your new apartment. So many times, I wanted to text and ask but that wasn't what we agreed to, so I didn't. The boys knew, that's why they were laughing so much. They know my reservations, but they also saw how much you were affecting me. So last night I was going to talk you and tell you about my situation, I wanted to know if you'd still want to spend time with me once you knew I wasn't as single as you thought I was. And by spend time with me, I don't mean more random hours in a shitty hotel room. I mean, I want to take you on a date, get to know you. Don't get me wrong, I want my hands and mouth all over you as well."

He winks at me and I melt, again.

"But I want more than just sex. I know this is a lot to take in, and I know you were just as keen as me to just have fun, so I understand if this is all too much for you."

He's right, this is a lot to take in. It's not as simple as just seeing how things go with him. I live with his sister, I've bonded with his daughter. If things go wrong, then I'll lose all of that. I'll be on my own, again. I've lost enough. Suddenly I'm restless and my knee is bouncing. Standing abruptly, I see his face fall, I'm not sure what I want but I don't want him to think his situation is deal breaker in the way he thinks.

"Let's walk again," I suggest.

Looking relived again he nods, and we move off, taking the winding paths through the park again.

He doesn't speak, we both know it's my turn to talk, I just don't know what to say yet. We continue in silence for a few minutes while I work out where to start.

"I was thinking the same, in the run up to last night I mean, I was thinking, that I was wondering things about you and your life that felt more than just our having fun arrangement. If last night had gone off the way you'd planned, my answer would have been easier, I would have wanted to take it very slow, but I would have said yes."

He stops walking for a second, looking confused, I don't blame him.

"I'm sure you're wondering why I'm not immediately saying yes now if I would have before I knew who your family were. That's kind of the issue...I know who they are. Look, you have your own reasons for protecting yours and Belle's heart, I understand that completely, probably more than you realise. But I also have my own reasons for protecting mine. I've just moved back here, I'm starting my life again, I really like living with your sister and I love hanging out with Belle, what happens if we start something, and it goes wrong. I'll be the one that loses my home and friends, and honestly, I'm not strong enough to deal with that."

I'm not sure I'd wanted to blurt all of that out but it's the truth, so he might as well hear it. He's looking at me again and I can't read his face, he doesn't look angry or even hurt by what I've said, in fact if anything he looks kind of happy.

"You might actually be perfect Rori," he says, as he takes my hand and laces out fingers together.

Well now I'm confused. However, as confused as I am, I can't help but look at our hands joined together and think how good it looks. I also can't ignore the energy that shoots through me when he touches me.

He starts walking again, not letting go of my hand, so I have no choice but to follow. He laughs before pulling me over to a bench and sitting us down again.

"Ok, my turn again and I don't want to walk and talk. I understand everything you said, I'm not brushing off your concerns. Believe me, my concerns are huge. But the fact that you have them is what gives me hope. You know I have a daughter, but you also know I'm a wealthy man, yet you're not just jumping at the chance to see how much you can get out of me."

I start to pull my hand away, frankly I'm offended, but he holds on tighter.

"I didn't say I've ever thought you were like that," he says softly, "but that is what I've experienced a lot, fake people who only see my bank balance. So, this is what I'm suggesting. I want us to get to know each other without any expectations. I want to keep things as separate as possible while we do. By that I mean I don't want Belle to know anything. I want to take things really slow, see each other once or twice a week maybe. Belle already has a bond with you, and I don't want that to change so I'm not going to ask you to stay away from her when she's at Jen's, just not tell her about us. If we decide not to take things any further, then we stop, and nobody has to lose anything. I would never ask Jen to kick you out or stop Belle visiting Jen's apartment. Like I said, my daughter always comes first, and I can already see how much she enjoys seeing you."

I look into his eyes and all I see is sincerity, he believes what he's telling me, and I really want to, I do. But I've been hurt so much I don't know if I can cope with this. But then if I never take another chance, all of this working on myself will be for nothing. I can't treat every man I meet like they're another Stuart. I felt a connection to him from the first conversation we had on the train, and the sex really is mind-blowingly good. I let out a shaky breath and give him an answer.

"Slow Jake, really really slow, but yes, I'll go on a date with you."

CHAPTER 17
Jake

I let out the breath I'd been holding as I heard her agree to a date. Relief mixes with the desire I feel for her, and I tug her towards me needing to taste her. Cupping the back of her neck I close the gap between us fully and press my lips to her. Running my tongue along the seam, I groan as she opens for me and I push inside her mouth, seeking out hers. I kiss her like I'm starved, not caring who sees. My other hand caresses her thigh, and I groan again as I continue to explore the warmth of her mouth. When I eventually pull away, we're both panting, and my need to be inside her is consuming. Taking her hand again I stand, tugging her up as I tell her,

"Good, then let's go."

Still dazed from the kiss she looks at me confused.

"Go where?" she asks, staying still when I try to move us.

"On a date, obviously," I state.

Now she looks shocked as she stutters,

"What now!? Are you serious? Where are we going, I'm not dressed for a date, we can plan something for later Jake."

What she doesn't realise, is I'd chosen the paths we walked on purpose, the ones leading to the exit closest to my apartment. Nor does she know that when I'd been stood in line for coffee, I'd been texting my assistant and driver to help me with my plan. My employees are paid well for good reason, they always come through no matter what I need or how quickly. Cupping her face, I look into her nervous eyes.

"Firstly, I didn't think I'd ever see you again after last night, so I'm not wasting the opportunity of a first date right now. Secondly, you look stunning no matter what you wear gorgeous, and what you're wearing right now is perfect for this date."

She tries to cut me off with no doubt an objection to her leggings and oversized hoodie being perfect for anything, but I carry on.

"And thirdly, like we said, we're taking things slow and not mixing our worlds right now, which means we need to make the most of Belle being with Jen today."

She swallows down her objections and smiles,

"Where exactly are we going for this date then?"

Finally getting her to walk with me, I grin as I answer, "My place, of course."

If I couldn't see the look of hunger in her eyes, the blush sliding over her cheeks would have confirmed exactly what she's thinking, and fuck if that doesn't turn me on even more. Grinning again, I stroke her hand in mine.

"Rori, Rori, such a dirty mind. Don't get me wrong, I've wanted to get you naked since I first saw you today, and I fully intend to do so, eventually. But I'm not just taking you back to my place for sex, I told you I wanted a date, and that's what you're going to get."

Before she can answer we're coming out of the park and my car is waiting for us. Guiding her over, my driver gets out and opens the door for us.

"Mr Holmes, we're all set," he tells me as I motion for Rori to get in first.

Sliding in after her, I thank Clive, and he closes the door

behind us. Rori's eyes are wide. I'd debated over whether it was too soon to show her this side of me, but I'm about to take her to my apartment so there's no hiding how wealthy I am.

"Something wrong beautiful?" I question.

"No, yes, no," laughing at her own indecision she starts to relax. "I just wasn't expecting the driver. I mean I know you're wealthy, you said, and obviously Jen told me her brother bought her apartment for her, but it's still taking my brain time to see you as the same person," she shrugs.

Before I can reply she speaks again.

"It doesn't make a difference to me though. I want you to know that. I've never been motivated by money, there are so many more important things in life. I just wanted to say that, so you don't think I'm interested in you for that."

Fuck, I want this woman. Pulling her into my side I stroke her shoulder as I say,

"I've already told you, I don't think you're anything like that."

Satisfied with my answer we settle into silence until we pull up at my building and Clive opens the door for us to exit the car. I take her hand again and we cross the entrance and ride the lift to the top floor. Leading Rori into my apartment I see the look of awe on her face as she takes it in. My apartment is bigger than Jen's, it's the entire top floor of the building, and one entire side is filled with floor to ceiling windows showing off the views of the city. We're standing in my living room, well, one end looks like a living room, with large comfy sofas, a flat screen tv mounted on the wall opposite the windows and other furniture placed around the space. The other end looks like an explosion in a toy shop.

"Wow, Jake these views are amazing," she comments.

Snaking my arm around her waist from behind and bending to dip my head into her neck I mumble, "They just got a hell of a lot better."

Laughing she turns in my arms, "I seem to recall you brought me here for a date not a quickie."

Shaking my head at her I grab her hips and pull her closer again. Bending down I tuck the loose hair behind her ear then slowly run my tongue over her lobe before whispering,

"Rori, if you haven't learned in the time we have already spent together, that when it comes to your body and making you scream, there will never be any such thing as a quickie, it's clear I need to remind you. Slowly, very very slowly."

She shivers listening to my words, and I want more than anything to take her straight to my bedroom, or just the nearest flat surface, but I stop myself and stand tall again.

"But you're right, we are here for a date, follow me."

I grin as I lead her down the hallway, there's a lot more to see but that can wait. I take her to the door I want, taking a key out of my pocket to unlock it I explain,

"This door stays locked at all times so Belle can't get up here without me knowing."

Then I lead her up the staircase to where I hope she will be blown away by the date I have planned for us. She gasps as she sees the space in front of her.

My apartment came with a private roof space, secured with glass panelling, tall enough, and set from the edge, so it was safe for Belle. I'd had it decked over and the space included comfy seating and a firepit.

That firepit was lit now, along with the heaters dotted around the space. Rather than taking her to the seating area I head to another area next to the firepit, where, thanks to my staff, a large rug has been laid out, covered in a range of food with pop up coverings to keep it fresh, and large bean bags at the edge for us to sit on.

"What do you think," I ask, "will this work for our date?"

Taking it all in she looks at me astonished.

"Jake this is perfect, how did you do all of this?"

I pull us down on the bean bags and start to pour champagne into the glasses next to it.

"Well, you said on the train that your ideal date wouldn't be about going somewhere fancy, but that you'd rather spend time getting to know someone. And given that I learned that while we were having a train picnic, I thought it would be fitting to have another one so we could find out more about each other. And in answer to your question, I may have sent a couple of texts while I was getting us coffee, in the hopes you would say yes," I admit.

She looks like she might cry and for a second I'm thinking of all the ways I can make up for this clear error of judgement, but then she smiles as she takes the glass from me.

"This is perfect Jake, it might be one of the nicest things anyone has ever done for me," she whispers as she leans over and kisses me gently on the cheek.

I want to pull her onto my lap right then and feel those soft lips everywhere, as well as ask her how it was possible that a picnic on a roof was the nicest thing anyone had ever done for her. I might be freaked out by this idea of finally having a relationship again, but regardless of that, I know this girl deserves everything and more from the people in her life.

"I'm glad you like it, now eat, you need the fuel, if this date goes well, I'm hoping you'll be expending a lot of energy later," I smirk.

Laughing at me she reaches towards the food and soon we've both filled our plates.

Before I can speak again my phone starts blowing up in my pocket and I know exactly who it will be.

"You're popular, do you need to get that?" Rori asks, taking another sip of champagne.

Grimacing I take my phone out of my pocket and without reading any of the shit they've put in the group chat I send a message telling them to get fucked and put my phone away.

"Just the group chat with the boys, nothing important, I've just told them I won't be seeing them tonight," I answer as I start to eat.

"Did you already have plans? Jake we can do this another time, I don't want to stop your time with your friends."

She bites her lip as she speaks, and my control goes straight out the window. Leaning forward I suck her lip into my mouth before plunging my tongue inside hers. She responds instantly, her hands sliding up my arms as she returns my kiss. Pulling away I settle back into my seat and look at her.

"Trust me, there's nowhere else I want to be right now, I see enough of those fuckers, they can last a night without me."

She smiles back at me, happy with my answer.

"Tell me about them, is that who you were with today?"

"Yeah, it was. We've been friends since we were kids."

I wonder how much to tell her but then decide the entire point is to get to know each other, so I don't hold back.

"We were your average group of kids, went to school together and hung out in our spare time. But then my mum died when I was fifteen and they were my rocks, they got me through it."

She looks at me and I se sympathy and maybe understanding in her eyes.

"I'm so sorry Jake, I had no idea, Jen didn't mention it."

She rests her hand on my thigh and squeezes gently.

"She doesn't talk about it a lot, neither of us do really, she was ten when it happened. Cancer. Anyway, the boys stepped up for both of us, they were always around, planning fun things to cheer us up or just sitting around when I couldn't do anything, they always included Jen. We've been more like brothers ever since. Belle calls all of them Uncle and they dote on her. Have done since she was born. So yeah, we usually spend Saturday nights together with that being the only night I don't have Belle, but I see them multiple times a week, so they'll cope without me tonight."

I grin, wanting to steer the conversation away from the sadness.

"They sound great Jake, it's good you have people around you that you can count on."

Wanting to find out more about her I steer the conversation away from the boys.

"So what about you and Liv, how long have you known each other."

"Since we were kids as well, she's my best friend, probably my only friend to be honest."

She looks sad but I don't want to push her.

"Well that's not true or my sister wouldn't have threatened me before she left this morning."

She laughs and the brief moment of sadness passes from her face. We carry on eating and chatting, her telling me about her new job and me sharing the history of my business. She congratulates me on my success but doesn't ask much about the ins and outs or how wealthy it has made me, which only makes me like her more. Wanting to know more about her I move the conversation back to family.

"So, you know about Jen, she's my only actual sibling, what about you, do you have a big family?"

CHAPTER 18

Rori

The afternoon is going so well. Jake is so easy to spend time with and every time he touches me, I want more from him. I knew he would ask about my past and family eventually, I just don't know how to handle it. We're so new, it's too soon to tell him everything. In fact, it may never be time to tell him everything. But I have to say something.

"Actually, I don't have any family. I grew up in care, well from when I was six anyway, so it's just me."

I look away once I've said it, I don't want to see the sympathy or judgement on his face, but he won't let me. He holds my chin and turns my face back to meet his gaze, a gaze filled with determination.

"Don't do that. I told you not to hide from me in bed, so I don't want you to do it here either."

Reminding me of the way he'd made me feel in bed had heat creeping through me, taking a breath I answer him with a shrug,

"People usually either think I'm trash because of how I grew up or pity me."

His intense gaze doesn't leave mine.

"Then those people are stupid. Your past is part of who you are, but it doesn't define you Rori. I'll never judge you for it and I'll listen if you want to talk about it. But right now, that looks like the last thing you want, in fact I think you need to be fully distracted from the last few minutes."

He grins down at me and I can't help but grin back, "oh yeah, what did you-"

I don't get to finish my sentence before his mouth descends on me.

Gone are the gentle touches and kisses we've shared during the afternoon, this is hard and demanding. He pulls me towards him until I'm straddling him on his beanbag, my hands balanced on his shoulders, and he dives into my mouth over and over. His hands grip my arse, anchoring me down against him so I can feel his hard length under me. I rub against him, needing the friction and moan into him. He runs his hands up my sides, taking my hoodie with him until he's forced to break our kiss to pull it over my head.

"Fuck Rori, you're so beautiful," he groans as he takes in the blue lace bra underneath.

I reach down to pull his t-shirt up and he leans up so I can get it over his head.

"So are you Jake," I tell him as I run my hands over his toned body, feeling his muscles flex under the skin.

His hand goes up to my hair and he releases it from the messy bun I had it in, before skimming down my back and popping my bra. It falls to his chest, and he pushes it away before raising his head to suck my nipple into his mouth and I let out a satisfied groan. With one hand massaging one of my tits, his other tickles along the waistband of my leggings.

"Are you wet for me Rori? Will I find you dripping when I slide my hand inside your pants?"

His words vibrate against my skin and I grip him harder.

"Yes Jake, touch me."

He slides his hand inside my leggings and down over the

lace fabric of my underwear, while his other hand continues to tug my nipple. I gasp as he strokes his finger along my folds until he finds my clit.

"So fucking wet Rori," he groans as he works my clit with his fingers.

He finds my mouth again and I return the kiss frantically, needing him closer. His finger moves from my clit and before I can catch my breath, he sinks it inside of me.

"Fuck, Jake that's so good."

I know we're alone and no one can see what we're doing, but being outside makes it even more of a turn on and I tell him so. He smirks as he adds another finger.

"Are you a secret exhibitionist Rori? Do you like the idea of someone watching you ride my hand until you can't take anymore, and you scream for me?"

God, his words. It's never been like this. Stuart was my first and I didn't know what I was doing. Then things got so bad it became more of a chore to keep the peace. Even the occasional one night stand I've had since hasn't felt anything like this. Jake continues to slide his fingers in and out of me as his thumb circles my clit. I can feel my orgasm building, but I don't want this to end. Jake's piercing green eyes find mine as he curls his fingers inside of me.

"Give it up Rori, let go and cum for me."

Then he sucks my nipple into his mouth. And that's all it takes to make me fly, crying out his name as the orgasm crashes through me. He continues with softer strokes as I come back down to earth, falling onto his chest.

"You're so fucking beautiful when you cum baby."

I can't speak, my breathing is still uneven as I let him hold me against him.

But this isn't going to be all about me, not this time. I slide down his body and start to undo the buttons of his jeans then reach inside his boxers and free his hard cock. Gripping the base, I lean forward and run my tongue over his length.

"Rori you don't-"

I don't let him finish.

"Shh Jake, it's my turn," I grin back at him, before dipping down and closing my mouth around his head.

He groans as I circle my tongue, slowly taking him further in. He's big and I know I won't be able to take all of him. His hands grip my hair as he moans my name, not hurting me but tight enough that it sends thrills through me. I work my hand and mouth together, sucking him into my mouth as I swirl my tongue over him. I can feel and hear how much he's enjoying it and I want to take him over the edge, the same way he does to me. I quicken my pace and he groans louder, tugging my hair he tries to pull me away.

"Rori, you need to stop I'm close," he grinds out.

But I ignore the pull and instead bring my other hand down to cup his balls and squeeze gently. Seconds later he explodes down my throat, and I swallow every drop as I release his cock.

"Fuck Rori that was amazing, you're amazing."

I don't have time to respond before he stands and then pulls me up as well. Guiding me to the seating area he sits me down before pulling my leggings and underwear down my legs. His jeans are still loose around his hips, so he strips them off and throws them with the rest of our clothes. Kneeling in front of me he hooks his arms under my thighs.

"I'm gonna need a minute to recover after that gorgeous, so before I sink my cock into your pussy, I'm going to spend some time making sure it's nice and ready for me, I want another orgasm from you before I fuck you."

And then his tongue is on me and I'm already squirming. He laps at me as his hands glide over my skin and I push my hips into him, wanting more. His light stubble rubs against me, setting off ripples of pleasure and I moan as he sucks my clit. His hand reaches up to cup my breast and I reach down to grip his hair as he brings me closer. All it takes is his finger sliding into me again to send me shooting off like a rocket.

"I love the sounds you make when you cum for me babe, it makes me so hard."

And with that he's sliding on a condom I didn't even see him get and plunging into me. I've barely recovered from my last orgasm but the way he's thrusting inside me keeps me on the edge of another explosion.

"Yes Jake, it's so good, don't stop."

"Couldn't if I wanted to, you feel so good Ror."

I smile at the shortening of my name and lose myself in how good this all feels. His thrusts get more urgent, and I know he's close. Burying his head in my neck, he reaches down to flick my clit and we both cry out as we give in to our orgasms. He holds himself above me, so he doesn't crush me, and fixes me with those green eyes as he regulates his breathing.

"Best date ever," he grins, and I laugh with him.

He's right, today has been perfect. I can't remember the last time I felt so happy and free, and it scares me a little. I've been through a lot, I don't want to get hurt again, and we might have agreed to take this slow, but I already know he has the power to break me. Jake pulls me from my thoughts with a soft kiss.

"You're in that head of yours again. Come on, let's take a shower."

I let him help me up, picking up our clothes as we make our way back inside. I haven't seen all of the apartment yet but what I have seen is impressive. This time he leads me down a hallway to his bedroom and again I'm blown away. His room is huge, with a massive bed as the focal point. The walls are a dark grey, but one side is again filled with floor to ceiling doors that look like they open onto a balcony. I don't get to see much else as he steers me into the biggest bathroom I've ever been in.

"Wow, Jake this is immense."

The bath is huge, we could both fit and still have room. I watch him turn on the shower and water springs from a multitude of heads in the glass encased walk in. Taking me by the hand he leads me inside. Soaping up his hands he starts to gently wash my body and once again, I give in to the feeling of getting lost in his touch.

CHAPTER 19
Jake

The sun is starting to set as I cuddle Rori into my side as we lie on my bed. I don't know how it's possible to feel as at peace as I do right now, it's only our first date, but I do. She's amazing. I had her again in the shower, I couldn't resist her curves as I washed her body, and after wrapping her in a towel we came to relax on my bed.

My heart broke for her when she told me about her childhood. I didn't want to push further, so soon, for more information, but I'm also so glad she felt she could tell me. We're just touching the surface of getting to know each other and I already know I want to know everything about her.

"This bed is so comfortable," she mumbles into my chest.

"Isn't it, I love this bed, in fact you're the only other person that's ever been in it. Apart from Belle anyway."

She looks up at me surprised and confused.

"Seriously? Did you just get it last week?" she grins.

"Smart arse," I say as I poke her in the ribs, and she wriggles as she laughs.

"I told you, I haven't dated, and the occasional one nighters I had were never here. Other than Jen, you're the only other woman that's even been in my apartment and I've lived here since a month after Belle was born."

She sits up now, crossing her legs as she does, the confusion deepening. She's fucking breathtaking like this. Hair, wet from the shower, falls around her and she still has a pink glow from the warm water and the sex.

"Something on your mind?" I ask, already an idea where this might be going.

"I don't know if it's appropriate to ask on a first date, it might be a bit too personal," she says before biting on her lip.

I reach forward and tug it out of her mouth then lace our hands together.

"I know we're taking this slow Ror, but you can ask me anything, I'll tell you if it's something I'm not ready to talk about."

"Well I was just wondering about Belle's mum."

Yup, that's what I thought.

"Clearly I know you're not together. Jen's never mentioned her at all, but with you saying no other woman has been here…"

She trails off, looking nervous again about where to take the conversation. I knew she'd ask. I know I don't have to tell her, it's probably too soon to share stuff like this, before we know where this is going. But something makes me want to tell her. Not just because of us, but because she's spending time with Belle when she's at Jen's. So, I sit up and rest against the headboard then take a deep breath to clear my head before I start.

"The woman who gave birth to Belle is called Melinda… and we haven't seen her since the day Belle was born."

I ignore the confusion on her face and carry on, I need to get this out in one go or I won't be able to.

"Melinda and I dated at school, young love that ended abruptly after my mother died. We lost touch when we all moved on to different things. I bumped into her again in a bar a few years ago. I'd had a few drinks and we ended up back at the apartment I lived in at the time. I'd always wondered if what we had might have developed further had it not been for mum dying so we started seeing each other again. My company was already doing really well at that point, and it soon became apparent that she enjoyed my lifestyle more than me. I wasn't overly bothered, I'd already realised I shouldn't have started things with her again. We dragged on for a couple of months and then I ended it. She came back three months later and told me she was pregnant…. but she didn't want the baby. She wanted me to pay for her to go private for an abortion."

I pause for a minute to gather my thoughts. It's still a subject that makes me angry beyond words, as well as sick at the thought of my daughter not being here. Rori squeezes my hand but lets me be.

"I didn't want that. I might not have had any thoughts on settling down right then but as soon as I knew she was going to have my baby, I wanted that kid more than anything. So, I asked her to think about it, said I could support both of them. That even though we weren't together we could raise our child together, and that I'd always provide for her as well as the baby, and maybe we could try again to be a family. When she asked to meet up a few days later I thought she'd changed her mind, but then she dropped the next bombshell. She told me that while she wanted my money, she had no interest in having to raise a kid to get it, but if I was that bothered, she'd carry on with the pregnancy in exchange for money. And I agreed. I'm not proud of myself, I didn't think of how she felt about any of it, I just wanted her to have the baby. So, I agreed to it, with conditions. I told her I wanted her to stay with me until the baby was born and that I wouldn't give her any money, other than normal living expenses, until she was too far along to have an abortion. I think I thought I could change her mind. I might not have wanted to be with her, but I wanted to give our baby a family. So, she stayed with me, and it was awkward at first but as time went on it got easier. Yes, I was transferring money to her monthly, a lot of money, like we agreed, but I thought we'd developed a friendship at least. I thought she was realising we could do this together. When Belle was born, she was a little underweight, so she had to spend a couple of days in the NICU. Melinda begged me to stay with her, so she wasn't alone, and I did, thinking the experience of giving birth had bonded her to our daughter and that she'd want to stay. I sat with Belle for hours, every time I text Melinda to see if she needed me, she replied saying she was fine and needed to rest and that I should stay where I was. So, I did. It wasn't until the next morning, when I hadn't had any replies from her, that I went back to her room. It was empty. There was an envelope on the bed addressed to me. She'd signed over all of her parental rights then left. She'd even had it done officially with a solicitor. I haven't seen or heard from her since."

I'm not looking at her when I finish, so many emotions are swirling around my head, and I feel raw and exposed.

"Thank you."

That makes me look at her, and when I do, I see tears running down her cheeks. Before I can question her words, she speaks again.

"Thank you for trusting me with Belle's story. I can't imagine how hard that was for you, and I know we're still getting to know each other, but what I do already know is that you're a great dad. You're raising an amazing little girl, and you're both so lucky to have each other, believe me I know what the alternatives are like."

Her words are like a blanket wrapping around me, and still not wanting to look like an emotional mess in front of her, I pull her back into me and just hold her.

We stay like that for a while before she pulls away.

"I think it's time for me to go home," she smiles.

It's the last thing I want.

"You don't have to, you could stay the night," I suggest.

I can see she's tempted but she shakes her head.

"Not tonight, it's been an amazing day, it really has been the perfect first date, but staying over so soon isn't exactly taking things slowly."

She's right, I might not like it, but she is.

"Ok, you're right, and you're also right about how perfect this has been. Clive will be taking you home though, no arguments."

She nods her head and I text my driver before getting dressed.

I walk her down to the car and bring her in to plant a soft kiss on her lips.

"It's kinda weird to think you're going to see my daughter before I will," I say as I open the door for her.

"It is a little weird, but she's a great kid, so I'll enjoy my morning princess tea party," she smiles.

"I'll text you soon gorgeous, sleep well," I say as I close the door.

Heading back upstairs I pull out my phone and see how many messages I've missed, both from the boys and Jen. I decide to deal with Jen first.

Jen: I'm going to assume she forgave you given how silent you've both been

Jake: She did, I've just put her in my car to come home, don't scare her off when she gets there

Jen: Would I do such a thing dear brother *thinks about what baby photos I have to hand*

Jen: no seriously, I can't believe the coincidence and I may be scarred for life now that I know you're the person from her

stories, but you both deserve some happiness, I hope it works out

Jake: thanks Jen, we're taking it slow but I like her a lot, love you sis

Now to deal with the boys. I ignore the many messages that have rolled through the group chat, they're mostly taking the piss and asking if I got laid yet.

Jake: you're all ridiculous, do you have nothing better to do?

Damien: Oh he's alive! But seriously, you're replying, you fucked up already?

Jake: thanks for the vote of confidence

Sean: I can't believe how that happened this morning! What happened when we left, where is she now?

Matthew: I'll never forget the look of horror on Jen's face when the penny dropped

Damien: that reminds me, where has this girl been if you're the best she's ever had, maybe she should have dinner with me

Jake: I will break your face arsehole

Damien: he bites again, someone's smitten

Sean: stop it, we'll never get the gossip if you keep winding him up

Jake: we walked, we talked, we decided to take it slow, when we stopped for coffee I send some messages and set up a first date picnic on my roof terrace then convinced her to have our first date immediately, she agreed, I've just put her in my car to go home

I can see they've all read it, but I get no replies, so I decide to shock them even further while I'm on a roll.

Jake: oh and I told her the full Melinda story

Yeah, that gets a reaction

Damien: Holy fuck, who the fuck are you right now?

Sean: fucking called it, he's in lurve

Damien: please tell me at some point during all this you actually got laid

Matthew: Damien you have a one track mind

Matthew: I'd put money on he did though

Jake: have I mentioned you're all arseholes

We banter back and forth some more and they eventually let it go. But it's not long before I have Matthew ringing me.

"Surely you're done taking the piss," I don't bother with hello.

He laughs at the other end.

"I am actually, but I am ringing about your girl."

My girl.. is she? It has a nice ring to it. *Slow Jake, you're moving slow, you can't let Belle get hurt.* That sobers my train of thought. When I don't say anything, he continues.

"Remember when Jen asked me that favour."

"Yeah didn't she want you to read something?"

"Yeah she did, and I did, and I was impressed, really impressed, so I invited the author in for a meeting on Wednesday and I'm going to offer her a deal."

I have no clue why this involves me, but I keep listening.

"Jake, do you not remember her talking about her new flatmate at the same time...the author is one Aurora Bales."

I'm silent, letting his words sink in and then I laugh.

"Jesus Christ, how many more ways can our lives be linked?"

"You can say that again. Anyway, I thought you'd want to know the meeting is at eleven on Wednesday, in case she doesn't tell you and you felt like wandering past my building to casually bump into her. Like I say, she's good, I expect to have her signed by the end of the meeting."

I smile to myself, we all know Sean is a hopeless romantic but clearly Matthew has his moments as well.

"Thanks for the heads up mate, I'll check what my day looks like."

"Thought you might", he chuckles, then we say our goodbyes.

I fall asleep thinking about our day, hoping that I'm not getting into something I shouldn't, and planning what I can do on Wednesday.

CHAPTER 20
Rori

I brace myself for the questions when I walk through the door to the apartment. Liv and Jen are sat on the sofa with a bottle of wine, already pouring one for me. Seeing my confusion Jen grins at me.

"I just text Jake to check you were both ok and he said you were on your way, soooo....."

I sit and take the glass, taking a sip before saying anything.

"Sooo... how weird is this gonna be?" I ask cautiously.

I don't want anything to put my current arrangements at risk, I really like being here. Jen smiles at me though.

"I'm not gonna be all, you can't date my brother, Aurora. You're adults, I want you both to be happy, if it's together that's even better. But I meant what I said, save the sex talk for Liv, gross," she shivers.

Liv laughs at that.

"I'm always here for the sex talk my friend, Jake is hot."

Jen groans from beside her and I join in the laughter. My phone buzzes before I can say anything else.

Jake: don't let my sister hassle you, and don't believe a word she says about me, I had an amazing day with you, speak soon beautiful

"Aww you've got it bad," Liv giggles as I look up, "that look on your face says it all, tell us everything." Looking to Jen she adds, "apart from the sex."

Putting my phone away I settle into the sofa.

"Well you've clearly all worked out who everyone is and what a massive misunderstanding last night was. We walked through the park and talked about everything and decided we're going to take things slow. Really slow. You know my history, I'm nervous about dating, but I can't deny we have a connection. We're not going to tell Belle anything, I'll still see her when she's here and I'll only see Jake when it's just the two of us. So, everything stays separate while we get to know each other. Then he convinced me that our first date should be immediately," I shrug.

"Ooo I like it, he couldn't wait to see you. But hang on, as much as I love you, you're not exactly dressed for a date, where did he take you?" Liv asks.

I smile as I tell them about the rooftop picnic to recreate our first meeting on the train. I don't mention the sex but I'm sure they both work it out, especially as my hair still isn't quite dry. Jen's mouth is hanging open when I'm finished.

"Well shit, I didn't think he had it in him, I don't know how I feel about my brother being romantic," she smiles, but I can see she's impressed with the thought he put in.

"So, when are you seeing him again?" Liv asks.

I don't want to feel nervous that we didn't make plans, we are taking it slow after all, but I thought he might have hinted at when he wanted to see me again. But now isn't the time to share that, not while I'm talking to his sister.

"I'm not sure yet, it'll depend on when we're both free and his commitments with Belle obviously."

I'm exhausted from the day; the talking, the sex, the starting it all off with a hangover. It all catches up with me and

I'm yawning before I finish my glass of wine. Leaving them to it I head to bed and fall into a deep sleep thinking about Jake.

I can hear Belle playing in the living room when I get up the next morning. As soon as she sees me, she runs to hug me.

"Aurora I'm so glad you're here, can we bake again? Can we? Please," she pleads with those gorgeous green eyes.

How did I not see the resemblance, her eyes are identical to his.

"Woah Belle, I just woke up! But yes, we can, if you give me time to have some breakfast first."

"Yey!" she shouts, then happily goes back to playing while I head to the kitchen.

Once I've had my coffee fix, I set everything up and call her over and we get started. I liked Belle from our first meeting, but now, knowing she's Jakes daughter, it makes this time even more special. We make brownies this time and she especially enjoys licking the bowl. When I see the chocolate covering her mouth and nose, I can't help but laugh.

"Take our picture again Aurora," she jumps up and down excitedly, so I of course indulge her.

Jen has been watching from the table the whole time and I don't miss the smile on her face as she witnesses the bond we are creating. It's not long after we're finished that Jen tells her it's time to go home and she lights up at the thought of seeing her dad. After putting our baked goods into a container for her to take, she gives me another hug before skipping out the door. I finish cleaning up then decide a long soak in the bath is my plan for the afternoon. I'm relaxing in the bubbles when I get a text that makes me smile.

Jake: so my daughter's new bestie makes a fucking good brownie

Rori: I heard your daughter did all the work, the new bestie is

just along for the ride

Jake: oh she's told me all about how Princess Aurora lets her weigh the 'gredients' and mix it all up and even lick the bowl

Rori: yup, see, it's all her doing, I can take no credit

Jake: we'll agree to disagree on the brownies, but you can take credit for the giant smile on her face when she talks about you, so I'm going to choose to ignore how weird it feels that she's talking about the woman who's pussy I was balls deep in yesterday and just say thank you for making her day

I nearly drop my phone in the bath when I read that last one. How can he be so sweet and filthy at the same time.

Jake: too crude

Rori: nope, just nearly dropped my phone in the bath

Jake: hold up, you're in the bath

Rori: yup

Jake: so you're naked right now is what you're telling me

Rori: certainly am

Jake: you're killing me babe

Jake: but on that note, duty calls, I have important colouring tasks to complete

Rori: have fun

I set my phone back down and sink back into the bubbles, a content smile on my face.

I haven't seen Jake since Saturday, but we've shared a couple of flirty texts and hopefully I'll see him at the weekend. Today all I can think about is my meeting. After Jen told me what she'd done with my writing, I received an email from Woodhouse Publishing, inviting me to a meeting today. Knowing how nervous I'd be, I took the day off work so I wasn't rushing to get here and wouldn't have to go back if this meeting isn't good. I get here early so I sit with a coffee while I try to calm my nerves, before heading into the building. The front desk sends me to the fifteenth floor where I'm greeted by Mr Woodhouses assistant, who takes me to his office. As I walk in my eyes go to the man sitting at the desk, a man I recognise. He stands with a big friendly smile and holds out his hand.

"Aurora, or should I call you Rori?" he laughs as we shake hands.

I'm speechless so he continues.

"Let me guess, Jen didn't think to tell you I'm one of Jake's best friends?"

Finding my voice again I sit as I say, "Actually she did, but that was when he was just her brother and we didn't realise who we were to each other. I'll be honest it, completely slipped my mind with everything that's happened since. Also, Jake didn't exactly give me the work history of his best friends when he mentioned you all. Is this going to be a problem?"

My nerves go into overdrive wondering if this is over before it's even started.

"Let me guess, he just described us as arseholes and left it at that," he grins, before adding, "and no, not a problem at all."

Relief floods me and I smile back at him, "Then please call me Rori, and he absolutely called you all arseholes before he went on to tell me how much you all mean to him, sounds like you're a tight group."

"That we are, we've all been there for each other since we were kids, Jake is pretty much my brother at this point, and I love Belle like she's my own. But we're not here to get all soppy about those arseholes, let's talk about you," he grins.

I like him. He puts me at ease, and he clearly has a strong affection for his friends.

"I really like your work Rori, I was amazed this was your first book, how long have you been writing?" he asks, and my nerves settle some more.

"I started about four years ago."

I wouldn't normally give someone new this much detail, but this is a unique situation.

"I grew up in care from the age of six, escaping into my head got me through a lot of pain and lonely times. Four years ago, I pretty much hit rock bottom and instead of caving into it, I worked on myself and wrote as a way of taking back my life."

I don't go into more detail, while Jake knows about my childhood, he doesn't know anything about Stuart or what happened that night, and I don't want him to find out from his friend. Matthew seems to sense how I'm feeling.

"Rori, let me assure you that client confidentiality always comes first for me, regardless of your relationship with my friend."

I give him a grateful smile, "Thank you. Jake knows I was in care, but obviously not every detail of what I've been through, I'm not sure anyone's ready for that story, despite my therapist encouraging me to write about it."

He looks at me for a minute before saying, "Based on what I've read, I can only imagine a true story about your life would be something really special Rori, and if you ever do try to write it, I would never share it without your consent. But we'll leave that for another time. Like I said, I love what I've read, and Jen said you already had more written that she hasn't read yet. So, I'd like to offer you a deal to work with us to publish your book."

I nearly fall off my seat at his words, "Are you serious?"

My voice is barely more than a whisper, I'm so shocked. This is my dream, I can't believe it's within reach.

"Completely serious, you're good Rori. If you sign with us, we'll lead you through the process step by step. You'll have someone assigned as your editor and they'll guide you in changes etc, it can be a long process, but worth it when you see your first book in print," he smiles.

I'm overwhelmed right now, and I don't know what to say, so I take a minute to breathe deeply before speaking.

"This is amazing, I never thought I'd get this lucky so quickly, and I know I don't have any right to make any kind of demands, but can I possibly ask a favour?"

He looks amused as he says, "Well you can certainly ask."

"I don't for one second doubt the abilities of your staff here, so please don't think that. But when you've lived my life, trust is not easy. Confiding in people isn't easy, and I imagine both of those things are important when working with an editor."

I pause, taking him in, and see a strange look on his face that I can't place. Before I can continue, he sighs and cuts in.

"You want Jen don't you?" he asks.

I nod my head in reply.

"Jen could have had a job here from the start, but she's never wanted my help, maybe you'll entice her to join us. All I can do is make her an offer, which I will, but I need to know you'll work with someone else if she won't do it."

I think over what he's saying, he's offering me an amazing opportunity and I can't force Jen to accept his offer.

"I appreciate you trying, it means a lot, so yes, if she says no, I'll work with someone else."

His smile widens now.

"Fantastic, let me get you some documents that detail what I'm offering you in terms of fees etc. I don't want you to read them now, take some time to look it all over and we'll meet again soon to negotiate anything you're not happy with."

His phone buzzes while he gathers some paperwork and

he stops to reply to a message, shaking his head fondly as he does.

"Welcome aboard Rori," he says as he hands me an envelope.

"Thank you so much for this opportunity," I reply, tears threatening to spill.

"I believe in you Rori and-"

He's cut off by a knock on his door and his assistant pokes her head into the room.

"Mr Woodhouse, sorry to interrupt but your, erm, financial advisor is here, and he says it's urgent."

She looks a little flustered as she delivers the message but Matthew just grins.

"I'm sure it fucking is, send the arsehole in."

I'm startled that'd he'd talk about a business associate like that, until the door swings open and I'm staring at Jake. With a massive grin on his face, and an equally massive bouquet of flowers in his hand.

"Hey beautiful, I hear we have something to celebrate."

CHAPTER 21
Jake

R ori stares at me, mouth wide open, just the reaction I was hoping for, as Matthew shakes his head from across the room. When he'd told me about today, I knew he'd meant for me to just bump into her somehow, but that's just not me. And I know we've only had one date, but this is a massive achievement and I wanted to recognise that for her.

I approach her slowly to give her time to recover from the shock, then bend and give her a gentle kiss on the cheek.

"These are for you," I say as I hand her the flowers.

She takes them and for the first time since I walked in, I see the hint of a smile.

"How did you know?" she asks but then seems to catch on and her gaze goes to Matthew, who doesn't look very impressed with me.

Ignoring me he rounds his desk to stand in front of her.

"Rori, let me start by apologising, but I also want to assure you that you can believe what I told you, I would never discuss your work with anyone outside of you, me and your editor. I told this dickhead I was going to be offering you a deal thinking he might want to take you out to celebrate, not make a grand entrance in my office. Did I mention he's an arsehole?" he smirks.

Shit. Might not have thought this through. She nods her

head and looks to me so I do what I can to back him up.

"It's true Ror, you can trust him. I have no idea what you write, it could be kids books or travel writing, but getting a deal to publish is epic so I wanted to celebrate with you if you want to."

She smiles again, this time a big happy smile.

"I can see how much trouble you're all going to be. Matthew this doesn't change anything but thank you for reassuring me, I'll read everything when I get home. And Jake, thank you for making the effort, it's really sweet of you, I'd love to celebrate."

Relieved that my plan has paid off, I grin as I take her hand and lead her out of the office, aware that Matthew is still shaking his head, but is now also grinning at me.

Once the lift doors close behind us, I cup her face in my hands and press my mouth to hers, her soft lips responding to mine immediately. I deepen the kiss, sucking her bottom lip into my mouth, before pulling away as the lift reaches the ground floor.

"Wow" is the only thing she says as the doors open, and I smile down at her as we walk outside.

"So how are we celebrating exactly?" she asks as we climb into the back of the waiting car.

I link our hands together before replying.

"Well, I'm aware how you feel about fancy dates, but I think something so important is a good reason for something a little bit fancy, don't you think?"

I throw in a wink for good measure.

"I never said I didn't like fancy, just that it wasn't necessary to try to impress me all of the time," she reasons.

"You're right, that is what you said, still, today you deserve fancy."

I don't need to explain further because as I say that the car comes to a stop outside the restaurant I've chosen. It's one of the best in London and has a waiting list months long, but I know the right people to make this happen on short notice. We're greeted at the doors and led through the main restaurant, then towards another corridor, Rori looking confused when she realises we aren't being seated. We finally come to a stop outside of a door and our server opens it then steps aside.

"Everything is set up as you requested Mr Holmes, please let us know when you're ready for your meal."

I thank her and we step inside, where Rori immediately lets out a gasp.

"Oh Jake, what did you do?"

What I'd done, was to book a private dining room, which I'd then asked to be decorated with fresh flowers and candles, with the table in the centre of the room and a bottle of champagne on ice next to it. Pulling her over to it I hold her chair back for her to sit.

"What I did was plan an appropriate celebration," I say as I take my seat, finally resting my gaze on her face, only to be met by teary eyes.

"Shit Ror, what's wrong? Is it too much for technically only our second date? Am I freaking you out?" I ask, concerned I've fucked up. I want to get up and hug her but until she tells me what's wrong, I keep myself seated.

"That hadn't even crossed my mind actually, although it probably should be freaking me out. I'm just blown away by the effort you've gone to yet again, I don't deserve all of this."

Relief washes over me and I reach out for her hand over the table.

"Are you kidding me. Ror you just got yourself a publishing deal, that's fucking huge, and this might not mean much, seen as we've only just started to get to know each other, but I'm proud as fuck of you. I can't wait to see your book in print, although I'm hoping you might tell me about it and not keep me hanging for release day."

Now the tears are running freely down her cheeks, Jesus Christ, I really wish I understood women. Sensing she needs a minute I just carry on stroking her hand with my thumb until she's ready to talk, pouring her some water from the jug already on the table. She takes a drinks and a couple of deep breaths before she squeezes my hand and looks at me.

"Jake you have no idea how much it means, regardless of how long we've known each other. Liv's the only person that's ever told me they were proud of me."

I know she'd told me she grew up in care but fuck me, how can no one, other than her best friend, have ever told her they're proud of her.

"I know you didn't have an ideal childhood but did your foster family not give you that kind of praise? I know it must be different growing up that way, but surely they cared for you."

I see the sadness in her eyes, and I regret my bluntness.

"Sorry Ror, I'm just a little shocked."

"Don't be sorry Jake, you didn't do anything wrong, and no, my childhood wasn't quite like that. It was for Liv, she had a really nice foster family who she was with for most of her childhood and they still have a strong bond. But I wasn't an easy kid, I fought or ran away a lot, so I bumped around from family to family, never really letting anyone in and eventually ended up in a group home until I was old enough to leave."

I take a minute before I speak, I'm so angry for the lost child she clearly was, that no one was there for her when she needed them. But she doesn't need to hear that from me right now. So instead I get up from my chair and move around to kneel beside her, trying to show her I'm here for her.

"I can't even imagine how hard and lonely your childhood

was, sweetheart, but what I do know, is that what you've achieved today is even more impressive when you've done that on your own. You're so strong," I tell her, kissing her gently before continuing.

"Now, I think I brought you here to celebrate, not make you cry, so how about we pop this champagne and eat some amazing food."

And with that, she's smiling again, and I take my seat, pressing the button on the table to signal we're ready for the first course.

"So, tell me about your writing," I say once the servers have left again.

She spends the next fifteen minutes telling me all about her books and how excited she is to have this chance to be published, her face lighting up while she talks. She's so beautiful, I can't help but drink her in as I listen to how passionate she is about writing. When the second course is delivered, we move on to other topics and again the conversation flows, she's so easy to talk to and spend time with, I'm already thinking about when I can see here again.

Before I realise it, we've been here two hours.

"Do you need to leave soon to pick Belle up?" she asks.

"I don't, I have a nanny just for after school, so she never expects me home until just after five anyway. That's why I thought it easier to clear my schedule for the afternoon, so I was still home when I needed to be. I hope it's ok that I couldn't take you on a big night out instead."

I'll never apologise for having to be there for my daughter, but fitting in time around her isn't going to work for everyone, so I feel the need to make that clear up front, so she knows what she's getting into with me.

"Of course not. Jake this has been amazing. The food, the decoration, the effort you've put in for me. It doesn't matter what time of day it is. The way you put Belle first with everything is exactly how it should be, and I'd like you much less if you didn't."

She's so genuine and it gives me hope that we could possibly make this work.

"Actually, talking about Belle, I should show you this. After her telling you about licking the bowl, I'm sure you'll appreciate it," she smiles, as she searches on her phone then passes it over to me.

I'm speechless. In fact, I don't think I'm breathing. Looking down at her phone I'm staring at my daughters beautiful, chocolate covered face, with her head pressed against Rori's, as they smile into the camera. I was too shocked in the park to really process them hugging, obviously I knew they would continue to spend time together. But this picture brings it all home to me. They look so perfect together, but at the same time I also see the pain it would cause if this doesn't work, and it terrifies me. Pulling myself together I hand the phone back to her and try not to let my emotion show.

"That's a great pic, can you send it to me?" I ask.

"Of course," she replies, looking like she wants to say more but doesn't.

We're distracted from potential awkwardness when our dessert and coffee turn up. Thanking the server, I tell her we won't need anything else, and we'll be out when we're done. I don't need any interruptions for what I'm planning next. Standing, I offer her my hand.

"Dessert can wait a little while," I grin as she takes it and stands.

The room has a sofa in the corner, and I take her to it, pushing her down to sit as I kneel on the floor in front of her.

"What are you doing."

"I was in the mood for a different kind of dessert," I reply, as I run my hands up her naked legs, slowly, not taking my eyes from hers.

"Jake, we're in a restaurant, stop!"

I don't stop, I reach the top of her thigh and pull her forward slightly.

"It's a private room Ror, they only come back if I ask them to, relax."

I can see the conflict in her eyes, but I still reach for the elastic of her knickers and start to slowly pull them down. She might want to pretend she's conflicted, but she lifts up so I can drag them all the way down and over her shoes. I press small kisses back up her leg, watching her as I do. She's so beautiful, all I want to do is devour her, so I do.

CHAPTER 22
Rori

Wow, just wow. I'm snuggled into Jakes side in the back of his car as we drive back to my place. This day has been amazing in so many ways. I never expected to be offered a publishing deal today, or have Jake surprise me just because he wanted to celebrate with me. No one has ever done that before.

When he took me over to that sofa in the private room, I was adamant it wouldn't end the way I could see he wanted it to. But then he started touching me, small touches that had me burning up for him, desperate for more. So, I pushed my fear of being caught aside and went with it. And holy shit am I glad I did. He ate me like we hadn't just shared an amazing meal already, laughing as I tried to stay as silent as I could. Then he proceeded to bend me over the sofa and fuck me into next week. Strong, hard strokes pounding me over and over until we both collapsed under our orgasms at the same time. Then he straightened up both of ours clothes and led us back to the table, so we could finish dessert and coffee, and while we did, he went back to telling me how amazing I was and how proud of me he was.

It's confusing, I've never had this. Stuart was never like this, not even in the beginning. I wasn't kidding when I said Liv is the only person that's said that to me before.

"Hey beautiful, where'd you go? I can see that brain of

yours working overtime right now."

Jake interrupts my thoughts with his observation, and I don't want to lie to him, but I'm not ready to tell him everything yet, so I give him part of it.

"Sorry, I didn't mean to space out on you. I guess I'm just a little overwhelmed, like I said, I'm not used to this. I know you probably think I want to take it slow because of my childhood and all my trust issues, and that's certainly a part of the reason."

I pause, deciding how to word the next part.

"Rori, you don't have to tell me anything you're not ready to share, I never want you to feel pressured to do anything."

The concern on his face is what sways me to continue, he's so genuine.

"I'm not ready to tell you all of it, but what I will say is my last, well actually only, long term relationship wasn't a good advertisement for dating to say the least. It ended a few years ago, and I've not been a nun since, but it left me with a lot of baggage to work through, I'm still working through it."

I end on a sigh, because sometimes I wonder if I'll ever fully move on from my past. Turning my head so he can look at me fully he plants a gentle kiss on my cheek.

"I'm happy that you felt you could tell me that. And I'm happy that I got to share this day with you. And I'll be happy to go as slow as we both need because you're special Ror. I want to see where this can go, and I want to show you, you can trust me and I'm not your past. Don't feel sorry or guilty about needing to take it slow and work through things, we both have baggage after all.

We're pulling up at my building as he finishes speaking and I throw myself into a hug with him, emotions threatening to overflow. I think he senses I can't talk right now, and he just holds me silently for a few minutes until I'm ready to pull away.

"Thank you for today Jake, for all of it, I'll never forget it."

"Anytime gorgeous, I'll text you soon to make plans for our next date."

He winks as Clive opens the door for me.

I watch as the car pulls away then head upstairs. I manage to keep it together all the way to the apartment, but as soon as I'm inside, the tears start, and I drop myself down on the sofa as I give in to the emotions I'm feeling, and let the sobs come.

I'm still crying when Liv and Jen get home, running to my side as soon as they see me.

"Aurora what happened?" Liv asks as she puts an arm around my shoulder.

I try to form a sentence but all I get out is, "Jake…Jake.." before Liv is rubbing a hand down my back.

"What the fuck did my dickhead brother do?"

Well at least I know she'd be on my side, but I can't let her think he's upset me, so I pull myself together and say,

"He was so nice to me," and start sobbing again.

Jen looks confused, but not Liv, she looks at me with sympathy and understanding as she whispers,

"It's ok Aurora, he is nice, he's not him. Now tell us what he did that was so nice."

So I do, I tell them all about the meeting and then Jake surprising me and how I barely held it together in the car after. Once I'm done, Jen still looks confused.

"So, it's great that my brother found his way back to the sweet guy he used to be, but am I missing something?"

I look at Liv and she sees the question in my eyes.

"I didn't tell her Aurora, it wasn't my story to tell, I only said you'd had a really bad time a few years ago and she knows about how we grew up. Let me make some tea then we can talk more if you want to."

They both get up and potter around the kitchen leaving me with my thoughts. I trust Jen, I really do. I want to tell her, offer her an explanation, but I'm not ready to tell Jake. As if reading my mind she comes back with a plate of biscuits and as she sit she says,

"You're my friend Aurora, and just like you're keeping this thing with Jake separate to Belle, I can do the same with him and you, I won't tell him something you don't want him to know."

Liv brings the tea over and we're all sat huddled together again. I need to tell her, I need someone else to know what I've been through, so I take a deep breath and dive in.

"His name was Stuart. We met in the group home when I was 15, he was 17. I didn't want anything to do with him at first, I never did, trust isn't easy, so I avoided everyone back then. Well apart from Liv. But the longer we were in there the more he tried to win me over. He was really sweet. He'd buy me little presents and watch TV with me. After a while I gave in and kissed him. We were inseparable after that. Nothing else happened, we just hung out and kissed. A couple of months later he was ready to leave care and he got a builder's apprenticeship and somewhere to live. But he didn't leave me behind. We'd still meet up and he'd take me on dates. I lost my virginity to him on my 16th birthday. I thought he loved me. I suppose he did in his way. But he liked to be in control and tell me what to do. I guess I was so desperate to be loved I just went along with it. We'd been together two years when he decided to move to Glasgow for a job. He said it was better money and cheaper bills, and he asked me to go with him. So, I said yes. For the first six months it was great. I loved playing house, finally feeling like I had my own little family. I got a job as well and tried to make friends. But then he started to change, got more controlling. He didn't want me to go out with my new friends. At first, I argued with him, sometimes just leaving anyway. But then I'd have to come home, and he'd be furious with me. The first time he hit me I was shocked. He didn't even apologise afterwards. He told me it was my fault. It only happened a couple of times, but it was enough to stop me from seeing my friends. He wouldn't let me come back to visit Liv and would get angry when I tried to call her, so that all stopped as well."

Liv grips my hand at this point. She's crying quietly as I speak. We've talked about it a lot and I know she doesn't blame me for losing touch with her, but I still feel guilty.

"Things got worse and worse. He was horrible to me, would say mean things about the way I looked, or tell me how useless I was at housework and stuff. I didn't realise he was already on drugs at that point. But I stayed. I thought he would change. I just wanted to keep him, and at that point I didn't think I had anywhere to go anyway. I barely spoke to him for fear of upsetting him. When I found out about the drugs, I told him I was leaving. He didn't take it well and trashed the flat we were living in, hitting me a few times before locking me in and going out. I didn't know what to do so I waited to see what would happen. When he came back, he had flowers and chocolates and was like the old him. He apologised over and over and said he would stop, that he wanted the life we'd planned, and he'd change. So, I gave him one last chance. For a few weeks it was great again. It was hard to trust him, but he was sweet and helped with things at home and gave me compliments. So much so that when he made a move one night I gave in, and we had sex. It'd been months, it was never that great anyway and after his comments I felt so self-conscious that I never wanted to, something else he complained about. It was only a couple of weeks after that when he started using again and this time, he was worse than ever. Four weeks later I found out I was pregnant. I knew then that I needed to get away. I was on my way home to pack my things, I didn't even want him to know about the baby. I just wanted to protect my child from all of the pain I'd been through, both then and as a child. I was on my way up the stairs when someone flew around the corner and crashed into me, sending me flying. The next thing I remember is being loaded into an ambulance and seeing lots of police. When I got to the hospital, I found out Stuart had been killed, drug deal gone wrong, and the person who crashed into me was the culprit. Then I found out I'd lost my baby."

I let out a long breath when I'm finished. The only people I've told all of that story are Liv and my therapist, but I feel a little lighter telling it to Jen. When I turn to look at her there are tears running freely over her face.

"Aurora, it sounds lame, but I am so sorry for what you've been through. I promise you I won't tell Jake, you tell him if and when you're ready, but I know all he would want to do is help you heal. I'm always here for you if you want to talk, you're so strong," and with that she throws herself at me and hugs me tight.

A bottle of wine and a takeaway later we finally get back to talking about the book deal, which makes Jen flap her arms around again.

"Oh yes missy, that reminds me, I got a call from Matthew this afternoon, what did you do?"

She fixes me with that mam glare she's perfected.

"I told him I wanted you as my editor," I shrug, as if it's no big deal, "so are you gonna be?"

I smile sweetly now, hoping to convince her.

"I've purposefully stayed away from him and his business since I finished uni, wanting to do things my way, but he did make me a really good offer."

I grin, because I'm convinced there's more going on here than just a job.

"soo…", I prod her.

She shakes her head before replying, "so…don't make me

regret this."

CHAPTER 23
Jake

"Daddy, Daddy."

I grin as my little girls come racing through the living room and throws herself up into my outstretched arms.

"Woah there Angel. Where's the fire?"

I laugh as I cuddle her, sitting us down on the sofa.

"Daddy, can we have a party? Please Daddy, please say yes".

Now I'm not gonna lie, my daughter's pleading eyes are hard to resist, but I'm baffled by this request. "What kind of party angel? Do you want to have a tea party with you dolls?"

It wouldn't be the first time I'd cut up tiny sandwiches and cakes and had pretend conversations with Elsa and Ariel. She looks like me as if I'm stupid. When did my baby get so sassy?

"No Daddy don't be silly, a proper party with balloons and pretty dresses and music, for Aunt Jen's birthday"

Ah, now it makes sense. Jen is twenty seven in a few days, and we went shopping for a gift this morning, clearly her mind has been working overtime since.

"How about we invite Aunt Jen over on her birthday and we can order food and get her a balloon to go with her present?"

I offer, knowing I'm about to fold to whatever she says next.

"No Daddy, that's not the same. I want everyone to sit at the big table and have tea, with us wearing pretty clothes and lots of balloons and a cake and then some dancing, please Daddy please."

She throws her arms round my neck and snuggles in, of course, she's bringing out the big guns.

"Who is everyone darling?"

I already know she's going to say the boys, she's only ever known them as her family and a night in with the usual suspects seems doable, they'll even cave to her dress code.

"Me and you and Aunt Jen and Uncle Sean and Uncle Matthew and Uncle Damien and Liv and Aurora."

Well fuck, I wasn't expecting the last two names on her list. I'm taking too long to reply, and she taps me to get my attention.

"Please Daddy, I love Aunt Jen so much and I want her to have a fun birthday."

Oh I'm sure she would have fun, mainly at my discomfort if this happens the way Belle wants it to, and how do I tell a six-year-old that no we can't do something nice for her Aunt's birthday.

"Ok Angel, leave it with me and I'll see what I can do."

Hugging me tighter, she squeals her delight before jumping down to run back to the toys she was playing with earlier. What the fuck do I do now. It's been six weeks since the morning in the park. Six amazing weeks to be honest. I like Rori, a lot. We've been seeing each other two to three times a week. The boys decided to change our Saturday night out to a Friday night in so that I could make the most of my only child free night. On those nights I date the shit out of her. We've been to the theatre, out for food and dancing, we even did an escape room event. Then one or two nights during the week she'll come over to my place once Belle is in bed. We always spend it in my room with the door locked, just in case she wakes up. On those nights we talk about anything and everything or we snuggle up and watch a film.

She's talked more about her childhood both before and after she was removed from her mum, but she never discusses the bad relationship she referred to after the day I surprised her in Matthews office. Her book is going really well. I know from Matthew that he expects it do great things once it's released, which will lead to further releases and hopefully she can ditch her office job. Although she's nervous about all of it and doesn't want to get her hopes up. So yeah, it's going well with us, slowly is working out how we wanted it to, we're getting to know each other. Don't get me wrong there's still plenty of sex mixed into these dates, she's fucking hot, I can't not touch her, and the sex is off the charts good. But we haven't talked again about mixing our worlds, about Belle finding out about us. I don't know if I'm ready for that, if she's ready for that. Hell, I don't know if Belle's ready for that. I need help.

Jake: SOS

Matthew: what's wrong is Belle ok

Sean: where are you

Damien: what's happened

Jake: mm, ok now I feel like a dick, Belle's fine it's not an actual emergency

Damien: you are a fucking dick

Matthew: ffs prick

Sean: what do you actually want then

Jake: Belle wants to have a party at our place for Jen birthday, a meal, cake, balloons, fancy clothes and dancing

Damien: how the fuck does that lead to SOS you idiot, when we

doing this then

Jake: Belle wants to invite Rori

Matthew: and…..

Sean: still not seeing the SOS

Jake: what do you mean..and… Belle doesn't know anything about Rori, we're taking it slow, it's too soon to have a fucking family dinner

Damien: give me strength, can one of you let this fuckwit in on what the rest of us already know

Jake: the fuck does that mean

Sean: you like her dummy, you have heart eyes whenever we see you, haven't seen you this happy in years aside from Belle obviously

Jake: I do not have fucking heart eyes, yes I like her, did you not read the bit about taking it slow, I can't let Belle get hurt

Damien: Jesus Christ this is why I just fuck and don't date, you're literally falling apart right now over having a meal that involves Belle and your girlfriend

Jake: she's not my girlfriend

Sean: well that's the funniest thing I've heard all day, err yes she is

Jake: TAKING IT SLOW

Matthew: right, let me be the voice of reason yet again

Damien: please do

Matthew: Jake you see her 3 times a week, you date, you fuck, neither of you see anyone else, SHE'S YOUR GIRLFRIEND, we all know why you're cautious and we get it, we really do, but if you don't think about the next step then going slow turns to standing still, you don't have to tell Belle you're dating, just invite her as Jen's friend, take the chance to see how she is around Belle and then talk to Rori about what she wants next

Damien: what he said

Sean: ooo Matthew you are good at this

Jake: she's going to be amazing with her, Belle comes home every week telling me all about the things they've done together

Sean: maybe she'll bring dessert, her baking is fucking good

Jake: are you fucking kidding me

Sean: well it is, and you've just said they get on great so I don't know why you're in crisis still, I mean unless Belle is just an excuse of course

Jake: wtf are you taking about

Damien: nice one Sean

Matthew: are we going there, are we sure he's ready for it

Jake: will one of you tell me what the fuck you're all talking about

Sean: we all understand taking it slow for Belle's sake, but we also know that you're scared for you as well

Jake: I have no idea what you're talking about

Damien: it's making my eyeballs bleed reading this, mate, Melinda might have fucked you over but you haven't made a connection with any woman since your mum died, you're scared to fall for her

Jake: bullshit

Matthew: told you he wasn't ready for it

Jake: there's nothing to be ready for, that's not true

Damien: if you say so

Matthew: ok

Sean: mhmm

Jake: you're all arseholes, I'm leaving

Slamming my phone down, I stand up to pace the room. They aren't right, this is all about Belle. But aside from the bullshit at the end the rest made sense, she could come as Jen's friend and we could both control ourselves for the night. It would be nice to see them together, hearing stories from both Belle and Rori always fills me with hope and I want to see that relationship for myself.

CHAPTER 24

Rori

"Will you stop fiddling with your dress, you look amazing." Liv says from beside me in the cab.

"I'm so nervous Liv, what if I fuck up, what if she can tell, it's too soon". I whisper back to her.

I've felt like this for 3 days, ever since Jake told me about this party. Things have been going great with us, I really like him, which terrifies me. Also terrifying, spending the night with his friends and family, his daughter, pretending we're not together. Pretending is fine, totally understand why he doesn't want her to know yet, but I don't want to slip up and act too familiar with him.

"Aurora she's five, she's not going to know, and even if she did, would it be so bad, surely she's got to find out you're his girlfriend sooner or later," she shrugs.

"Don't use that word," I hiss back, only to see her roll her eyes.

We've never had that conversation, never talked about where this is going. I mean I want it to carry on, even if I am a fuck up who still has issues to deal with. But he might not, he might be getting bored with me.

The cab stops and I blow out a breath as we get out. Jen doesn't know about tonight, so we had to leave the apartment before she got home and hang around in a bar before coming here a half hour before she's due to turn up. Jake told me Belle had asked us to wear fancy dresses. I have no such thing. So, Liv took me shopping during our lunch breaks. I wanted something that would look good on me but also impress Belle, I have a feeling she'll expect Princess Aurora tonight. The dress we decided on is deep pink and lace. The top half has spaghetti straps and a sweetheart neckline, giving me modest cleavage. It moulds around my torso before flaring out from the waste with netting underneath to give extra oomph. I'm wearing simple nude stilettos with it. I've curled my hair and pinned it to one side, so it flows down over my shoulder.

We reach the door to Jakes apartment, and I take another nervous breath before knocking. The door swings open and Belle flies through it, me bending just in time to catch her in a hug.

"Hi sweetheart," I say as she steps back, "you look so pretty princess."

And she does, wearing her Belle dress up costume.

"I'm so glad you're here Aurora, will you please do my hair? Daddy couldn't get it right," she giggles.

"Of course," I say, standing back up so I can walk inside.

Just as I realise Jake is standing a few feet behind her she shouts,

"You look so special, Daddy doesn't she look like a princess!"

I finally meet Jakes eyes and the look on his face blows me away. It's a combination of heat and lust, but there's also emotion there and I can't quite decide what it means. He clears his throat before answering,

"Yes Angel, Princess Aurora looks beautiful"

God, he looks good enough to eat. In keeping with the theme he's wearing a dark grey suite with a lemon tie, which I realise matches Belles dress, and that just makes him even hotter. I can barely speak so I whisper a thank you as Belle drags me down the hallway, presumably to do her hair. As we reach the living room, she drags me in there instead, where I'm met with Sean, Matthew and Damien. Who all just stand and stare at me. Well this is awkward. Matthew breaks the silence,

"Rori, it's good to see you again, you're looking lovely tonight"

"Isn't she just" Damien smirks from the side.

Jake must have followed us in here because I hear the grumbling noise coming from behind me before Damien starts to laugh.

"Oh I am going to enjoy this party"

I decide to ignore him and address them all,

"It's nice to see you all again, but I think a little someone needs me to fix the hair her Daddy apparently failed at tonight, shall we go sort you out Belle?"

She pulls me away and I leave the room without making any further eye contact, but I do hear Jake practically growl,

"Damien I will fucking throat punch you if you look at her like that again."

Which makes them all laugh again, including Liv.

After I've fixed Belle's hair, she wanted it plaiting, we head back to the living room, just in time to hear Jen shouting hello from the door. We all follow Belle's warning to shush, only Jake allowed to speak to shout he's in the living room, then shout surprise when she gets there. And she's definitely surprised, especially when her gaze lands on me and Liv. After thanking Belle for organising her party and offering hugs to the boys she heads to us.

"Well this is gonna be interesting," she smirks.

Liv laughs, "Tell me about it, I'm not sure she's took a full breath for the last two hours."

"Would you two stop, we're supposed to be acting like we barely know each other, that's not gonna work if you two keep whispering about us."

Before we can say anymore, Jake gets everyone's attention.

"Ok guys, Belle has planned everything, including the decorations, so it's time for everyone to head up to the roof."

We all move towards the staircase, Belle holding my hand the whole way, and make our way up to the roof terrace. I gasp as we get outside, it looks amazing. A full table and chairs, big enough for all of us, has been set up. There are twinkly lights strung around and multiple sets of weighted down balloons. The fire pit is also lit, and I can't help the blush on my face as I look to the seating area, thinking about what happened there the first time I was here. When I turn back to the table, I meet Jake's eyes and he grins, he knows exactly what I was thinking. We take our seats and Belle insists I sit next to her with Jake on the other side. Sean sits next to me, then Liv, Damien and Matthew, with Jen taking the seat between him and Jake. The distraction of admiring the set up means I only notice when we sit that there are wait staff out here with us, who immediately start serving drinks before bringing food up from downstairs. Well this is a fancy dinner party.

Before we start eating, I excuse myself to use the bathroom. I could have waited but I need a minute to process all of this before dinner conversation starts up. Heading downstairs I lock myself in the main bathroom and lean onto the counter, looking at myself in the mirror. I've barely been in here a minute when there's a knock at the door and Jake calls, "It's me".

I unlock and open the door and he's inside before I realise, locking it again behind me. Then he's on me, gripping my hips and kissing me hard, and I'm opening my mouth to let him slide his tongue over mine. When he pulls away, we're both panting.

"Fuck Ror you look stunning, I had to touch you if I've got

any hope of making it through the night with you so close."

His grin is infectious and I'm soon giggling.

"You look pretty hot yourself"

He gives me another quick kiss before disappearing out of the door as quick as he came.

I spend a few more minutes touching up my lipstick and generally calming myself down, before I go back to the roof. I don't miss the pointed looks from Jen and Liv, or the giggles from Jakes friends, as I sit down, but thankfully they don't comment. The food is served, and we all dig in, the conversation flowing between everyone. I've heard a lot about Jakes friends, and obviously I now have a working relationship with Matthew, but it's the first time I've spent time with them socially and they're a lot of fun. Sean is like a puppy, he seems to get excited about everything and I've heard him teasing Liv a lot. Matthew seems to be the sensible one of the group, whereas Damien is the dark and broody one. But the banter they have back and forth and the way they adore Belle is a wonder to watch. Belle herself has been a joy all night, telling me about school and her friends and asking what we can bake next time she stays at Jen's.

Once we finish the main course, we all sing happy birthday to Jen at Belles insistence, and while that's happening a cake is brought out, complete with candles. Once she's blown them out and thanked Belle for such an amazing party, the cake is cut and served as dessert. I'm just thinking that everything has gone more than smoothly when Belle decides to rip the rug from under me.

"Aurora, do you have a prince?" she asks, full of innocence.

Of course everyone hears her and goes silent, so I try to deflect.

"This cake is so good Belle, did you choose it?"

I'm pretty sure I hear Sean snort a laugh beside me. Belle

doesn't take the bait.

"Like in the film, do you have a prince that gives you a big kiss and will you get married to him?"

Sean is fully giggling now and the other two don't sound far behind him. I just want the ground to open up and swallow me, I can't even glance in Jakes direction for fear of what I'll see on his face. Thankfully Jen comes to my rescue, and I couldn't love her more right now.

"So Belle, Aunt Jen is going to teach you a life lesson right now. Princes are all great in the books and movies, but in real life, us strong girls look after ourselves and don't need rescuing."

I'm not sure if Belle is confused or her young mind has already moved on, but she doesn't ask again, and the conversation starts back up. I on the other hand, still can't speak, or look at the man sitting two seats to my left, who I think I might want to be my prince, but I'm terrified he'll hurt me beyond what I'll recover from.

CHAPTER 25
Jake

From the mouths of fucking babes. My daughter is killing me right now. As is Rori's dress. She looks like perfection and sin all rolled into one, and I've wanted to strip her out of it since she walked through the door. I've watched and listened to the two of them all night and it's completely fucked with my head. Belle adores her and Rori returns all the attention she gets from her. They've chatted about so many trivial things that are life and death for a five-year-old, and not once has Rori ignored her or told her to quieten down, or been anything other than completely enthralled by her.

They didn't see me follow them when they went to fix Belle's hair. I stood in the hall and watched through the partly open door as Rori gently brushed through her hair and then styled it exactly as she wanted it. And why is that fucking with my head. Because with every minute they bond further, I see a future that involves me having a complete family. I see Belle growing up with a mother figure in our home, I see a woman I could love. And that scares the shit out of me. Then the prince conversation, where Rori looked like she might pass out. I wanted to jump in, tell my daughter that I was that prince, that I would take care of Rori. But not only would that have been a wildly inappropriate way to tell my daughter we're dating, but I honestly don't know if I'm capable of giving her that or if she even wants it.

The table has long been cleared and now Rori and Liv are dancing with Belle on the decking. I need to stop staring so I drag my gaze back to the table, to find four sets of eyes trained on me.

"What?"

The boys laugh and shake their heads, Jen groans and face plants the table. I say nothing.

"Brother dearest, you are crazy about that girl, put us all out of our misery and tell her that, then tell Belle."

"What! No, I've already said, we're taking it slow."

The boys now join in with the groans, mumble something about me being a dickhead, and go back inside to find my good whiskey. Jen stays at the table and gives me the look. I cave,

"Say whatever you gotta say Jen."

She leans forward on the table and looks at me.

"I love you Jayjay, I want you to be happy, I want her to be happy, and I think you've got a really good shot at it. I've watched how you look at her all night, watched how she is with Belle every week. She's not Melinda and…"

She pauses, and I can see the pain on her face. I have no clue what's coming but I don't think I'm gonna like it.

"You changed so much after mum died, you shut yourself off from new attachments, she didn't leave by choice Jake, stop avoiding getting close."

I can't look at her and she knows it, so she gets up and goes to dance with the girls. Why does everyone keep bringing up my mother all of a sudden. I mean I probably know why, but I don't want to dive into that right now. This night feels likes a cliff top I don't want to be on, like the decision I make right now will determine my future. I either trust her, and take a leap, asking her to jump with me. Or I set her free to find a future with someone else who doesn't have the complications I do. I'm still thinking about it when Belle appears at my side and crawls onto my lap.

"You tired little angel?" I murmur into her hair, "Have you had a fun night?"

Yawning she cuddles into me more.

"I had the bestest night Daddy, all my favourites are here. I like Aurora visiting me here Daddy, she's my bestest friend now and I missed her."

I can't speak for the lump in my throat. My daughter is already invested, already attached, will already feel the pain of Rori leaving, either by us not working or her moving on from living with Jen. Fuck. Belle is sleeping now, so I stand, keeping her gently tucked in my arms. I meet Rori's gaze as I turn from the table, she's just watching us with the softest of smiles on her lips. Not speaking to anyone in particular I call out that I'm taking Belle to bed and make my way inside. She doesn't stir when I wiggle the dress off her and put her nightie on, giving her a kiss on the forehead, before I silently close her door.

Time to put my big boy pants on and go have an adult conversation. Making my way to the kitchen I find everyone now in here, everyone except Rori.

"Where is she?" I ask, slightly panicked that's she's left. Liv answers,

"She stayed upstairs for some fresh air, said she'd be down soon."

I don't wait for more, I head back the way I came, pretty sure they're all talking about me again, dickheads. I find her curled up on the comfy seats, looking up at the twinkling lights, and my breath catches, absolutely stunning.

"Hey," I call out as I approach, sitting next to her and pulling her legs over mine.

"Hey!" she smiles, "That was quick."

"She didn't even flicker when I got her changed."

"Ah she's had a lot of fun tonight, she'll be worn out."

Running my fingers over her legs I turn so that we're facing each other.

"Can we talk Ror?"

I'm nervous and she can tell, which means she now looks nervous, Christ I hope I don't fuck this up.

"She had the most fun with you tonight, you're so good with her. I know she comes home and tells me about the fun she has with you but seeing you together, fuck Ror, seeing it just hits different. We agreed to take this slow, get to know each other, keep things separate until we decided where it was going. And I'm so glad we did, I've really enjoyed getting to know you, I've especially enjoyed getting to know your exquisite body."

There's that blush again, makes me hard every single time.

"And I'm not saying we have to speed things up ridiculously, but what I am saying is, well, is that I'd like to tell my daughter I have a girlfriend, and then have my girlfriend spend more time with both of us. So I was wondering what my potential girlfriend thought about that….what do you think Ror?"

My heart is thumping in my chest as I wait for her to say something, anything, well maybe not anything. Time seems to stand still while she looks anywhere but at me and her voice is barely audible when she eventually speaks.

"I'm so scared Jake, I'm so scared that I'm too broken to be enough for you, or that you'll wake up one day and realise I'm really not that special and end things, and I'm not strong enough to be hurt again."

I don't even wait to ask permission, I just gather her into my arms and pull her to sit on my knee, kissing the top of her head before I lift her chin to look at me.

"I told you when we first met to get out of your head, that there was only room for two of us in the bed. Now I'm telling you there's only room for two of us in this relationship. You are special and you are enough, you're fucking amazing Ror. But I don't expect you to believe me straight away, whoever treat you so badly you feel this way, needs their head examining. It's not you that's broken, but while you think you are, it's my job to show you you're not, it's my job to show you in all the ways I can how beautiful, talented and special you are, until you trust me enough to believe me, then I'll keep doing it, because that's what you deserve, I'm just asking you to give me a chance, I would never intentionally hurt you."

She looks like she's going to cry, but now I've learned more about her, I know she cries with any emotion she feels, so I'm still hoping they're happy tears. A single tear breaks free at the same time a smile takes over her face.

"Ok Jake, let's tell Belle about your girlfriend."

Grinning like an idiot I pull her in even closer and sink my lips onto her, showing her exactly how happy I am. When we break free, I pull her up from the seat.

"We should probably go back inside with the others."

They're all still sitting around the kitchen island when we get back downstairs. Walking in, hand in hand, they all stop and stare. Owning it, I tug her closer to me and look at everyone watching us.

"What? Can't a man hold his girlfriend's hand when he wants to?"

"Thank fuck," comes from Damien.

Sean is just grinning like a fool and Matthew nods his head. The girls are smiling at Ror, as Jen asks,

"Does this mean-"

I cut her off before she can ask.

"It means you're going home without her tonight and we'll tell Belle in the morning over breakfast."

And there's the blush again, fucking love it. They all quickly make their excuses and leave and I'm definitely not complaining. Once I've seen them all out, I head back to the kitchen where I left her and find her standing at the island with a glass of water. I wrap my arms around her from behind and nuzzle into her neck.

"You have no idea how much I've wanted to have you alone all night, let's go to bed gorgeous."

She turns in my arms but the look on her face has me concerned.

"Jake are you sure about this? About me being here in the morning when she wakes up."

Cupping her face with my hands I smile back at her,

"Completely sure. We'll lock my door like we always do and then in the morning, I'll tell her about us, she already thinks you're amazing Ror, she's gonna be fine. Now can I please get you naked?" I grin.

Taking her hand, I lead her to my bedroom, locking the door behind us as promised. I waste no time in smashing my lips to hers, walking her backwards as I devour her mouth. Reaching behind her I feel for the zip on her dress and slowly lower it down, before tugging the dress and letting it fall to the floor. Taking a step back I run my eyes down her body, from the strapless pink bra cupping her perfect tits, down to her matching knickers and curved hips.

"You're stunning Ror," I say as I start to undress, "how wet am I going to find you when I touch that perfect pussy?"

Her eyes widen as I strip out of my trousers and boxers in one motion, my dick springing free.

"I asked you a question babe, use your words."

I know how much she likes it when I talk to her like this, but she struggles with the confidence to return it. I move in closer again and run my finger down her neck and over her collar bone, feeling the goosebumps spring up under my touch. Leaning down I run my tongue back up the path my finger took until I reach her ear and whisper,

"Are you wet baby?"

I feel her gulp before she nods her head and quietly breathes out, "yes."

My mouth lands on hers again and I sweep my tongue inside, my hands in her hair, loosening the fastening until it cascades around her. I guide us onto the bed, lying side by side, still kissing her, one hand holding her head to mine as the other runs up and down her body. Parting her legs, I slide my fingers inside her knickers and along the length of her pussy, swallowing the moan that escapes her. I dip my finger inside her.

"Fuck, you're more than wet, you're soaked."

I remove my finger and bring it to my mouth, sucking her arousal from it.

"I'm gonna need more of a taste than this babe."

Moving down the bed, I pull her knickers down her legs and throw them to one side then move back up her body before lying flat on my back. I pull her over to me, gripping her arse until she's straddling me, my cock pressing against her stomach.

"Sit on my face Ror."

She looks unsure, so I kiss her again, pushing up off the bed to grind against her. She pulls away from the kiss, panting as she looks down at me.

"Jake I've never done that before."

Stroking her hair, I still the rest of my movements so I can focus on her face.

"If you don't want to that's fine, but if you're just nervous because you've never done it before, trust me, I'll make sure you really enjoy it."

I pause for a second to let her think, before I resume my hands exploration of her body, unclipping her bra as I slide over her back. Slowly she starts to move up my body and I gently encourage her by hooking my arms under her legs. When her tits are in line with my face I reach up and suck a nipple into my mouth and she moans above me. Moving to the other tit I give that nipple the same attention, sucking it before releasing it with a pop.

"Keeping moving gorgeous, I need more of your perfect pussy."

Once her knees are on either side of my face, I reach up to grip her hips and pull her down onto my face, pulling my flat tongue over her folds before focusing on her clit. She gasps above me, but she stays rigidly still. Pulling away from her clit I gaze up at her.

"Does this make you uncomfortable babe?"

I don't want to stop but I will if she really doesn't like it.

"It's not that, I just don't want to squash you!"

Trying not to laugh I grip her arse, "You won't squash me, I promise, don't overthink it."

I pull her back down onto my mouth, sliding my hands under her to part her lips before I dive back in, groaning as I taste her again. I feel the moment she relaxes and starts to let go of her inhibitions. My hands back on her arse I pull her even closer, reaching up to palm her tits as I suck on her clit. I twist and tug on her nipples as I lick and suck on her clit, her wetness coating me, her quiet moans and whimpers shooting straight to my dick. This isn't the first time we've been together with Belle in the house, so I know she won't start screaming, but fuck I wish she could. Her movements get more erratic as she rubs against my face, and I know she's close. I up my speed, sucking her harder until I feel her shatter above, her legs tightening around my head and as she whispers my name over and over. I lick her slowly until the shudders stop, then coax her body back down, until she's lying on top of me again.

"Jake, that was, fuck, that was so good."

Her face is flushed, eyes bright, she's beautiful.

"Well I did try to tell you," I grin, before flipping her over and settling between her legs.

"Your pussy is the best thing I've eaten today, I could do that all day every day and still want more of you"

I dip down to kiss her, letting her taste herself on my tongue, before reaching over to the bedside cabinet to get a condom. Moving back over her I position my cock at her entrance then slowly slide inside her until I'm buried to the hilt.

"Fuck Ror."

I rock slowly, swirling my tongue over her nipples as I do, taking my time to appreciate her pussy hugging my cock.

"Jake, I need more," she whimpers under me.

"Tell me what you need Rori."

I stop moving and drag my mouth from her tits to wait for her answer.

"I need it harder and faster."

Fuck me, she doesn't use her words often but when she does, it's like a switch flicks in my brain. Sliding one hand between her and the mattress, I grip the back of her neck, while my other arm hooks under her knee and lifts it up to her body, and then I let go. I thrust into her hard and don't stop, over and over, harder and faster, pulling her body against me as I do.

"Shit Rori, you feel so good, so fucking good."

She moans her agreement, gripping her arms around me, her fingers digging into my back. I continue my pace, feeling the tension build inside me, I know I won't last much longer. Letting her leg go I reach my hand between us, finding her clit I start to rub over it in time with each thrust into her. I see her slap her hand over her mouth to stop her screaming and I bury my head in her neck to muffle my groans. Seconds later I feel her contract around me and straight after my orgasm rips through me like a freight train. I stay where I am, my cock twitching inside her until I feel the last of the ripples of her orgasm, then slide out and collapse on the bed next to her. I'm never going to be done fucking this woman.

CHAPTER 26
Rori

I wake up confused until I remember I stayed at Jakes last night. Then that confusion is quickly replaced by nerves. He wants to tell Belle, today, with me here. When he told me he was ready to move forward last night, I was terrified. I still am if I'm honest. But the things he said to reassure me were so perfect that I couldn't do anything but agree to give this a shot. I haven't spent the full night with him since the first night in the hotel, and while the sex was earth shattering, as always, falling asleep with him was amazing. After we'd fully exhausted each other with multiple orgasms he pulled me into his body, cuddling me from behind and kissing me softly as he told me to sleep. I don't know that I've felt so safe and..nope, not that other word, not going there at all, just safe, which is a pretty massive thing in itself.

Pulling myself from my thoughts I realise I'm alone in bed and the ensuite also looks empty. Sitting up, I notice a pile of clothes in the space that Jake has vacated, which I assume are for me to wear. Dragging myself out of bed, I go to the bathroom to freshen up before getting dressed. His clothes are baggy on me but not ridiculous once I've pulled in the toggles on the joggers and turned up the bottoms. Opening the bedroom door, I hear voices and follow the noise, finding them in the kitchen. I take a deep breath and slip into the room. Jake spots me first, smiling brightly as he mouths 'good morning' and grabbing Belle's shoulders to turns her around until she sees me.

"Aurora!" she squeals, rushing towards me. "You came back, are you here to play with me?"

She's hugging my legs for dear life as Jake makes his way over to us.

"Hey Angel, why don't you come and sit down for breakfast, Daddy wants to talk to you."

We all move over to the island, and he lifts her onto a seat, motioning for me to sit as well, which is when I realise, he's been busy. On the island is a literal breakfast buffet; croissants, fruit, yoghurt, as well as bacon, sausages and scrambled eggs. He fills a plate for Belle and puts it in front of her.

"Daddy makes the best breakfast Aurora," she says around a mouthful of egg.

I feel like I'm in a daydream as I take a seat and he passes me a plate, telling me to dig in. So I do, because food is a great distraction when I have no idea what he's going to say next. He takes the seat on the opposite side of the island.

"So Belle, Aurora didn't come back she stayed here last night."

"Like a sleepover?" she asks.

"Yeah Angel, like a sleepover. And the reason I asked her to stay over is because I like her too, I like her a lot, so I was hoping it would be ok with you if she spent some time with us, and sometimes with just me."

As he finishes, he reaches across to me and I stretch forward to take his hand. Belle's eyes go wide as she watches us.

"Daddy are you her prince? Yey!" she proclaims and cuddles into me again.

I still can't speak so I look to him to answer. He's smiling fondly at both of us.

"Something like that Angel, is that ok with you?"

"Yes Daddy, can we bake cakes Aurora?"

"Erm, maybe later," I manage to reply and with that the conversation is over and she happily goes back to breakfast.

Once we've eaten, Jake helps her down and she runs off to play in the living room. His arms curl around me from behind and then his lips find mine in a gentle kiss.

"Told you it would be fine."

We take our coffee through to the living area and take a seat on the sofa, near where Belle is playing, Jake pulling me into his side and draping his arm over my shoulders. And that's how we spend the next couple of hours, with Belle every so often bringing toys over to show me or asking me to join in with a game. It's so normal yet it means so much to me to be here with them. When Belle starts to get restless, Jake suggests a walk to the park, much to her delight, and I take that as my cue to leave, only Jake has other ideas.

"That ok with you? I thought we could get lunch while we're out and then we'll drop you at home afterwards, I know you have work tomorrow."

Looking down at myself, I wonder if he's forgotten I'm wearing his oversized clothes.

"I'm not exactly dressed for going out in public Jake, and I don't think last night's outfit is suitable either."

He just grins at me and pulls me up from the sofa, "Come with me."

Leaving Belle where she is, we walk back to his room, where I find several gift bags on the bed.

"This came before you got up and I put it in here while you were playing with Belle, it should all fit."

Looking in the first bag, I pull out a pair of jeans and the softest cream jumper I've ever felt.

"How did you do this?" I ask as I turn back to him.

Looking sheepish he motions to my clothes on the chair in the corner, "I looked at your things for the sizes and then I looked online and sent some pictures to my assistant, she did the rest."

When I don't say anything he rambles on, "They're a gift, I didn't want you to think you had to sneak out in last night's clothes and I knew I wanted to take you both out today so…"

He trails off as I throw myself into his arms, "Thank you, it's so thoughtful of you, again, it's just gonna take some getting used to, like I said, things like this don't happen to me."

He hugs me against him tighter, "Then get used to it gorgeous, because I intend to treat you exactly like the princess my daughter says you are." Pulling away he leans down to kiss my cheek, "I'm going to get Belle sorted out, showers all yours, take your time"

And then he's gone. Looking in the other bags I find underwear that is also the correct size and a pair of gorgeous red flats. I ignore the labels on everything, I don't want to think about what this all cost, and head to the bathroom. Where I find another bag. When I look in this one, I find the same shampoo, conditioner and body wash that I use at home with a little note inside the bag.

Jen helped me out with this info.

Smiling again at the effort he's gone to, I turn on the shower and take my new products with me. When I get back to the bedroom I dress quickly, the clothes fitting me perfectly and turn to leave. Then I notice the chair again and see he's left a brush and hairdryer on it for me, he really did think of everything.

Once I've tamed my hair, I make my way back to the living room and find Belle dressed and ready to go and Jake tidying up her toys. When he stands and sees me, he pauses, then walks over to me and pulls me in for a kiss. Belle's giggles are what force me to pull away.

"Daddy, you kissed her!"

She's still giggling, and I know I'm blushing, but Jake takes it in his stride.

"Yes, I did, that's what grownups do sometimes when they like each other, is that ok?"

Skipping off to find something she shouts back, "Yes Daddy."

Returning his attention to me he strokes his thumb over my bottom lip.

"I couldn't help myself, you look beautiful Ror."

Blushing again I start helping tidy the toys.

"Thank you, but I'm not even wearing make-up so I think you might be overdoing it."

He spins me back to him and pushes me back until he has me caged against the wall, the heat in his eyes keeping me pinned in place.

"You were hot last night in that dress, you were a goddess last night when you were orgasming over my cock, you were stunning this morning when I woke up and saw you sleeping next to me, and right now you're breathtakingly beautiful standing in my living room wearing clothes I picked for you. The amount of make up on your face doesn't change any of that, it's all you gorgeous."

Okay I think I might be swooning right now, how is he even real. I don't get the chance to respond because Belle comes back into the room and immediately tugs at both of us to hurry up so we can leave. And as I'm walking out of the apartment, hand in hand with Jake, all I can think is, I could really fall for this man, and if I do, and he hurts me, I will never recover from it.

CHAPTER 27
Jake

We've been home half an hour and Belle hasn't stopped talking about Rori and how much fun she's had. We walked to the park, them chatting together all the way there, while I was content to just hold Rori's hand and observe them, and when we arrived at the play area Rori didn't hesitate to join in. She pushed her on the swings, rode the roundabout, bounced up and down on the see-saw, all while I watched. It was amazing. After lunch we walked Rori home, where my driver was waiting, and Belle hugged on for dear life, while they said goodbye. It's like she's always been here, been part of our lives. I never thought this would be me and as amazing as it is, it still terrifies me that it might not last. My door opens and the boys come trailing in, making a beeline for Belle, each of them carrying gifts. Raising my eyebrow, I look at them.

"Did I miss something?"

They ignore me, obviously, and Belle starts jumping up and down when she sees the bags.

"Hey princess, give Uncle Sean some love."

Which of course she does, throwing herself at his legs before moving on to the other two.

"Are they for me?"

She points to the bags they're carrying and they all nod, Damien explaining,

"You did such a good job last night we thought you needed a little spoiling."

She dives into the bags, pulling out new colouring books, crayons, pens, yet another dress up outfit and a new doll, not to mention rainbow Dr Martens and pink converse. I love how they are with her, but seriously. Shaking my head, I give them all a pointed look,

"Are you three for real? Stop spoiling her, I'm not raising a brat."

I think Damien actually growls at me.

"She's not a brat, she's our princess and she deserves to be spoiled occasionally by her favourite Uncles."

"You're her only Uncles, and don't you think you've gone a little bit overboard, it's not like it's her birthday, but thank you."

Belle moves to the table to play with her new toys and the boys sprawl out across the sofa.

"So, how's lover boy doing today?"

"Lover boy, really?" I scowl back at Sean.

"You couldn't take your eyes off her mate, and we all know where you went when she left the table to use the loo," he sniggers.

Yeah ok they've got me there.

"How did it go with Belle?" Matthew cuts in.

"Really well, Belle thinks she's fantastic, we haven't long been home actually, we spent the morning here then took her to the park, had lunch and walked Rori home."

They all look a little confused.

"Tell me you took her home to get changed first and didn't drag her to the park in last night's outfit, she wasn't exactly expecting to stay."

Here we go, I could avoid it, I could lie, but what's the point.

"Erm no she didn't need to, I erm, I sent my assistant a few links and she had some stuff delivered for her."

Yup, they're all silent, open mouthed like they're trying to catch flies.

"What?" I shrug as if it's no big deal.

Damien recovers first, "You bought her clothes, like you actually picked them out and had them delivered here so she had something to wear to take your daughter to the park, did you buy her a new bag to put your balls in as well and when's the wedding?" he grins, knowing I'll bite, and I do, with a kick to his shin.

"Shut the fuck up, arsehole, we were both nervous about telling Belle, I just wanted to make sure she was comfortable and didn't have to do the walk of shame in last night's clothes."

"Well I think its romantic, and after the private dining surprise after her meeting with Matthew, I'm so proud of you!" says Sean as he grabs my cheek.

"Get off me, dickhead."

And then Matthew pipes up with, "I mean you should make the most of it because obviously when I turn her into a world-famous author, she's gonna be so grateful she'll fall in love with me."

I resort to throwing cushions at this point. "Did you all come here to wind me the fuck up?"

"Yeah"

"Pretty much"

"Always"

We're all grinning by this point. Damien and Sean get up to do some colouring with Belle and Matthew plants himself next to me on the sofa.

"Seriously though Jake, she's good for you, it's been so long since you've taken a chance."

"Yeah, I know, just hope it doesn't backfire on me...you really think she'll do well with the book?"

"Absolutely, she's good, if she wasn't, I wouldn't have pulled out all the stops to convince your sister to work for me."

I don't miss the grimace and laugh in response, "Oh good luck with that, she's gonna bust your balls daily, I mean I always hoped she'd reach out to you if she needed anything with her career but still....my thoughts are with you mate."

Still laughing, I join the others and they decide they're staying for the duration, so I pull out my phone to order pizzas. There's a text waiting for me.

Rori: Are you kidding me, Jake this bouquet is bigger than the last one and that was huge, you really shouldn't have, but thank you

Jake: I should have, this weekend couldn't have gone any better, I got to wake up with you, Belle thinks you're amazing and did I mention I can't get enough of your body

Rori: you might have, once or twice, I had a great time and I think she's pretty amazing as well, how's the rest of your day been

Jake: the boys are here, they brought presents for Belle, cos she's got them wrapped around her little finger, and we're just about to order pizza

Rori: sounds good, I won't interrupt you any longer, thanks again for the flowers, enjoy your boy's night

Jake: you can interrupt me anytime gorgeous, speak soon

Finishing the food order, I put my phone away and turn back to the table, completely ignoring the smirks, absolute dickheads.

Monday morning is always busy, but today seems even worse than normal and by lunchtime I am ready to throw in the towel and go home. That is until my assistant calls through to tell me my girlfriend is here to see me. And fuck if that doesn't have me grinning like an idiot when she comes through the door looking mortified.

"I'm sorry, I didn't know what to say when she asked how I knew you and I got all tongue tied and then I just blurted out I was your girlfriend, did I mention I'm sorry."

Still grinning I get up from my desk and shut her up with a kiss.

"Why do you need to be sorry, you are my girlfriend."

She looks like a wet dream, a black pencil skirt hugs her hips with a white blouse tucked into it, I can see the trace of a white lace bra underneath. Black stilettos finish the look. She always looks completely fuckable, but work clothes Rori is next level. I move us to the sofa and we sit.

"Yeah I know that's what you said we are, but I didn't know if you wanted anyone to know, like with your business I mean."

"Ror, I'm the boss, so my personal life is really none of their business, but I'm not hiding it from anyone, and when I sit down with my assistant this afternoon I'll make sure your name is added to my 'can always disturb' list."

She finally relaxes.

"So, as much as this is a great surprise on a shitty Monday, is everything ok?"

"Oh yeah, everything's fine, it's just, well I wanted to show you how much I appreciated the clothes and the flowers yesterday, and it's hard to know what to do for the man who has or can buy anything, so I decided to bake you some brownies and drop them in while I'm on my lunch break."

She holds out a tub from her bag and there's that blush again. Now is probably not the time to have a hard on, but here we are.

"Well firstly, you didn't have to do anything, however, I am very happy you did because these brownies are the best. But secondly, just getting an unexpected visit from you is the best bit."

I pull her in and kiss her again, fuck I want her, like now.

"How long can you stay?"

"Maybe 20 mins, I need to be back in an hour and I'm getting the tube."

"You are definitely not getting the tube, Clive will take you back, and don't argue, this way I get longer with you and I can think of a lot of things we can do in that time."

She sucks in a breath and pushes against my chest to look up at me, "Jake we cannot have sex in your office, someone might come in, or hear us," she squeaks.

I ignore her and get up to lock my door, turning back towards her I fix her with a stare.

"You're right, we probably shouldn't have sex in my office, my private bathroom though, that's a way better idea."

"But...but..."

"Get that gorgeous butt up Rori and move it to the bathroom before I give up on that idea and fuck you over my desk."

That gets her moving, and I push her into the bathroom, shutting the door behind us.

"If you're going to come to my office, dressed like this, it's only going to end one way babe," I tell her as I pull the zip on her skirt and push it down. "Now, I'm going to feel how wet this pussy is for me, before I bend you over the sink and fuck you until you scream my name, that good with you?"

"Fuck Jake, when you talk like that..touch me…please."

I don't waste any more time, taking her mouth with mine as I slide my fingers inside her knickers and push two inside her.

"Always so wet for me baby, I need to be inside you."

I remove my fingers and spin her round, her hands landing on either side of the sink as I bend her forwards with one hand, my other freeing my cock from my pants. And then I remember.

"Shit, Rori, I don't have a condom, I've never needed them at work before."

My head rests on her back, defeated.

"It's okay."

"You're right, it is, I don't need a condom to eat your pussy."

I start to turn her back round, but she stops me, and I meet her gaze in the mirror in front of us.

"No, I mean, it's okay, if you didn't want to use one, I'm on the pill and I know I'm clean, I trust you."

Well fuck me. I'm not sure if I'm more overwhelmed by the idea of being skin to skin, or the fact that she trusts me enough to let me.

"Are you sure? I know I'm clean, it's been months before you and I got tested at my last health check."

"I'm sure Jake, as long as you are."

I hold her gaze, a million thoughts in my head.

"I've never not used one, I was using one when Belle was conceived, it broke, but yes, I want this with you."

I suddenly wish we were in a completely different setting for the first time I fuck her bare, but it is what it is, and I'm not stopping now. Lining up behind her, I pull her knickers to the side and thrust inside her. Fuck me. She feels fucking amazing, so amazing I'm not sure I can last, so I tell her that.

"Rori its too good, I'd love to fuck you like this for hours, but being inside you like this for the first time, I'm not gonna last, hold on baby."

That's all the warning I give her before I pull back and ram back into her, over and over again, her gasping and me grunting with every thrust inside her. I loop my arm around her waist to stop her flying forward and my other hand finds her clit.

"Need you to cum baby."

And then we're both crying out as we fall into our orgasms, riding out the waves as they keep coming over and over.

Jesus Christ, this woman is gonna be the death of me.

CHAPTER 28
Rori

I'm sitting in a coffee shop, passing the time until I meet Jen for our meeting with Matthew. I really can't believe my life right now. It's been just over 3 months since my first meeting with Matthew, and I couldn't have foreseen how quickly things would move. Jen agreed to work as my editor and she did an amazing job, making the tweaks needed to smooth out my book, the meeting today is so Matthew can tell us anything else he wants us to work on and the next steps. And it's not just the book that's going so well. Things with Jake and Belle have been an absolute dream. We spend every weekend together, with me going to their apartment straight from work on a Friday, so we can all eat together. We spend time together for the rest of the night and a part of Saturday, before she goes to Jen's for her usual sleepover, giving Jake and I the chance to spend time alone. Although sometimes we hang out with his friends, who have embraced me and our relationship, and I feel like they're all my friends now as well. Then on a Sunday, we usually pick her up early and have a day out, sometimes just a picnic at the park, other times we've gone bowling or further afield to a theme park. I love all of my time with both of them equally, Belle is such a lovely little girl, so caring and affectionate. And Jake, well wow, what can I say. It melts my heart to see him with his daughter, he adores her and she him. And the way he is with me. It amazes me how he can go from sweet and kind to filthy and in charge at the drop of a hat, and I am absolutely here for both versions of him.

As well as weekends, we also try and see each other a couple of nights during the week, and there may have been one or two more incidents in the bathroom attached to his office. What can I say, my boyfriend is hot. I still have my insecurities, and wonder if the other shoe will drop, but they're not as often and Jake is unbelievably patient with me. I know the L word is creeping into my head more often, although neither of us have said it yet.

Jen slumps down in the seat opposite me, suspicion clouds her face.

"Am I going to regret asking what you were so lost in thought about, because if you're pining over sex with my brother, I don't have time to bleach my brain before this meeting."

Giggling, I shake my head at her, "Don't worry Jen, no bleach needed today, in fact since the moment I found out Jake was your brother I have not once discussed my sex life with you. I was just sitting here thinking about this meeting and drifted on to how many amazing things have happened in my life since I moved back here."

Her face softens and she reaches for my hand, "and you deserve every single one of them, I'm so happy things are going so well, and as for Jake, well I've never seen him or Belle happier, you two were made for each other."

I just smile back at her, not wanting to blurt out that I'm pretty sure I'm in love with her brother, I should probably tell him first.

"Now enough of this soppy shit, let's go see how many errors Mr Perfectionist has found in my editing."

She rolls her eyes and gets up from the table. It's fair to say they've clashed a few times, but I still think there's a spark between them. We head across the street and up to Matthew's floor, his assistant waiting to show us straight in.

"Ladies."

He greets us both with a kiss to the cheek and guides us to sit, before returning to his chair. Jen cuts straight to the point.

"What did I get wrong this time?"

He actually looks a little shocked, and maybe hurt by her comment but he recovers quickly.

"You didn't do anything wrong Jen."

She doesn't look convinced. "You've been sending me emails for weeks about things you're not happy with."

"Look Jen, I'm sorry if that's what you think, that wasn't my intention, I just wanted Rori's book to be the best it can, it certainly wasn't a slight on you. Which is why we're here today, it's done!"

We both look at him speechless.

"It's not often I render two women speechless at the same time," he chuckles.

"Are you sure?" I ask.

"Absolutely. Your writing was already really good Rori and Jen has done an amazing job of fine tuning it to make it ready to publish, which as of yesterday is in the process of happening. I already signed off on it."

"Holy shit," I murmur.

Jen still isn't speaking and has a funny look on her face, but I leave her to her thoughts.

"So now what happens?"

"Well, in terms of this book, I've got a launch night booked in for three weeks on Thursday. As for future books, while we can never fully predict how popular a book will be, I have high hopes for this one. Once we see the numbers for this we'll sit down and discuss an offer for the rest of the series. The contract you signed was for one book, with us having first refusal for the rest, providing you're happy with the new terms offered for the remaining books. I'm quietly confident you will be. And obviously we'll also discuss a new contract with Jen separately, so she can continue working alongside you. How does that sound?"

"Like a dream come true," I whisper.

"Jen?"

She finally looks up at him, although I still can't read her face.

"Erm yeah, sounds good"

"Are there any other questions you have at this point?" he asks us both.

Jen shakes her head and I'm about to do the same when I have a thought that makes me smile.

"Just the one, can I expect your financial advisor to come barging through the door at any second with flowers bigger than his head, I didn't tell him about today"

Matthew laughs at my question, "Not today, unless he's stalking you, I learnt my lesson last time and didn't tell him either."

Not that I didn't appreciate the effort last time, but I already have plans to see him and Belle tonight and I want to tell them together. While Belle is too young to read my book, she's still excited that I'm writing one.

"Actually, there was one other thing I wanted to ask you about Rori. You mentioned in our first meeting that you'd considered writing about your life experiences, I was wondering if you'd developed that further?"

Jen looks at me now, she knows I have been writing about it, she also knows Jake still doesn't know everything about my past. She thinks I should tell him, she also thinks I should let Matthew see what I've written. He watches the silent looks we share and speaks again.

"Look, Rori, I didn't ask to put pressure on you."

I share another look with Jen before I give him my attention again.

"No Matthew it's fine, I don't feel pressured. Yes, I have been writing. The thing is, well, the thing is, my story isn't an easy read in parts, it's very personal, I'm not sure I want people to know everything about me, and also, I haven't told Jake all of it yet."

I look down when I finish, not wanting to see any judgement for hiding things from his best friend.

"Rori, I meant what I said in our first meeting, regardless of who my friends are I would never betray your trust when it comes to your writing. If you're not ready to share with readers, that's completely your decision, but there are also ways around that. What do you think Jen, I assume you've read it?"

We both look to her, wanting her opinion.

"I actually haven't read it, but I knew she was writing it and I know the bones of the story. Without knowing which way Rori wants to take the story, it's hard to give you my opinion, however, as her editor, I would tell her the direction I would encourage, is as a story of strength and survival and a self-made future to be proud of."

I can't help myself, I reach out for her and hug her as tight as I can, tears escaping as I grip onto her. Composing myself I sit back in my chair and chance a look back at Matthew. He's smiling softly.

"Not every story needs a face to make an impact Rori, publishing under a pseudonym is always an option to protect your privacy, but that's not a conversation for today, I'd love to read it, you have my word no one else, either in this office or outside of it, will be given access to your words, think about it, the door is always open whenever you decide you want to share it."

I know he means it. Out of all of Jakes friends Matthew is the most mature, more nurturing towards the others. He's still a fool when they're together, but I know I can trust him.

"I'll think about it."

We confirm a few more things then make our way back outside.

"Rori this is amazing news, I'm so happy for you!" She hugs me again.

"Thank you, are you ok though? You went really quiet in there."

"I'm good, really, I was a little surprised and I've got things going on in my head but it's all good."

"You know where I am if you wanna talk about it."

"I know, thank you, but honestly I'm good. What did you think of the other stuff Matthew said, you really can trust him."

I've been thinking about it non-stop since he brought it up, and even before that, if I'm honest. As soon as I started writing I knew I'd have to make this decision as some point.

"Well, I think I want to send you it initially and then once you've read it, I'll let you send it to Matthew. I'm not going to potentially publish a book without telling Jake everything about my past. But the next three weeks are going to be so exciting, and I don't want anything to put a damper on that. So for now, I'll agree to you and Matthew reading it, once the book launch is out of the way I'll tell Jake everything."

She's smiling at me now, "I really think it's the right thing to do Rori, your story will inspire others that are having a hard time in their lives, and I know Jake will go all caveman and want to burn things to the ground for you, but ultimately he'll just want to be there for you for everything, my brother is smitten with you."

So am I, so am I. And I can't wait to see him tonight and tell him about the launch.

CHAPTER 29
Jake

Tonight is Rori's book launch and I plan to make it a day and night to remember. As soon as she told me the book had gone to print, and a big launch event would take place, I started to plan. These last three months with her have been the best of my life, she makes me happier than I thought possible, a happiness I gave up on long ago, and on top of that she makes my daughter happy. To sum it up, I'm completely in love with her, and I think it's time I took the leap and told her so.

She's taken the next two days off work so she stayed here last night, what she doesn't know is that I've also rearranged my schedule to be with her, and I'm keeping Belle off school so I can pamper them both today. Belle will be coming to the launch party, but she won't stay for the full night. Thankfully Liv offered to leave early with her and take her back to Jen's, with Jen following once the event finishes. I've been watching her sleep for the last ten minutes, but I need to get up before she wakes up or I won't be able to pull off the first of today's pampering experiences. Dressing quickly, I go to Belle's room first and find her playing with her dolls.

"Morning Angel, you ready to help Daddy with our first surprise?"

She jumps up and runs over to me for a hug, "Yes Daddy, let's do it."

We make our way to the kitchen and work together to

make breakfast for Rori, putting everything on a tray when we're done.

"Ok Belle, I'm going to carry this because it has hot coffee on it, but you can carry the balloons."

Because of course, with any celebration my daughter is involved in, balloons are a must. We got them yesterday and hid them in one of the spare rooms. We make our way back to my bedroom and I open the door, letting Belle go in first. Rori is just stirring when we approach the bed and Belle wastes no time in jumping up onto the bed, yelling surprise and shoving the balloons in her face. I can hear her laugh, but can't see her face between the balloons and the six-year-old whirlwind covering her in a hug.

"What's all this?"

"We made you breakfast and got you balloons for you big book day!" Belle announces, shifting over so Rori can sit up.

"Wow, this is so lovely Belle, thank you, I'm sure you did most of it yourself, but I should also say thank you to your Daddy for helping you."

She winks at me as I lean over and kiss her, placing the tray on her lap. When she sees the time, she looks at me confused.

"What are you two still doing here at this time?"

"Baby, I rented out a private dining room just for getting the deal in the first place, I've got to top that for the actual launch of the book, now eat up, we have an entire day planned."

She gives me the look that I'm pretty sure Jen has been teaching her.

"What did you do Jake?"

But I'm not caving this time.

"Nothing you don't deserve gorgeous, I'm so proud of you Ror, let me show you. Now eat up and get dressed."

I throw her a wink and run to the bathroom before she can protest any further.

Once we're all dressed, we make our way downstairs, where Clive is waiting for us, already aware of the itinerary for today. It's not long before we're pulling up in front of her building, Jen and Liv already waiting outside for us. They don't wait for Clive to get out, opening the door and piling in before he has time to move. We all exchange greetings before Rori looks at them both with a raised eyebrow.

"Why are you two here, do you know what's going on?"

They both look at me, so I answer for them.

"They do, they're your best friends and Jen is your editor, I wanted to include them in what I have planned for today, trust me, they'll be more help than I am for most of it, I'm just along for the ride."

"And to pay," Jen adds on the end with a giggle.

I shoot her a look because I know Rori hates it when I spend money on her, getting in first I lean down to her ear.

"I told you this morning, I'm so proud of you and I want to show you that by spoiling you. I'm proud of my sister as well, please let me do this."

She threads her fingers through mine and squeezes my hand.

"Thank you".

Our first stop is dress shopping. Jen immediately stops me from following them inside.

"Nope, this is as far as you go big bro," she says, hand out flat in front of her.

"What, why, how is that fair?" I refrain from stomping my foot like my daughter would.

"This is just the way it is, we'll look after them, you don't get to see what they choose until the finished result tonight, now hand it over."

It's only as I'm begrudgingly passing her my credit card that I hear the laughter to the side of me. Swinging round, I see Damien, Matthew and Sean watching the scene, highly amused.

"He's all yours boys, I'll ring when we're done."

And with that, she turns and marches the girls into the shop, not even letting me kiss them goodbye.

"Come on Romeo, let's go for a pint while they shop."

And just like that, I'm being dragged down the street to the nearest pub. We get our drinks, find a table and I start complaining straight away.

"How come the entire plan for today was my idea and I get kicked out!"

"Why would you want to sit and wait for four women to try on a hundred dresses only to buy the first one, you're getting off lightly if you ask me," Matthew states, taking a long drink of his pint.

It's not lost on me that it's not even eleven and we've all got a pint, but given I'd made sure the girls would get champagne, orange juice for Belle, while they tried on dresses, then I think day drinking is fine all round today.

"So, what else do you have planned for today?" Sean asks, and I know it's the romantic in him that wants to know.

I haven't confided in them about how I feel about her, but seen as they've thrown me this morning I might as well.

"We're all going for lunch and then back to my apartment, I've got people coming to give them all a massage and then do their hair and make-up. While that's happening, I need to pop out to pick up a gift for Rori and then we'll all head to the event. Don't forget it starts at seven prompt."

I stare at all of them to hammer that point home.

"Well I'm hardly likely to forget seen as it's my event"

Matthew says with an eye roll, he seems a little off today.

"Yeah, fair enough, anyway Liv is going to take Belle back to Jen's when it gets too late for her and once the event finishes, I'm taking Rori somewhere."

"And where are you taking her?" Damien smirks, he loves winding me up about the soppy shit.

Blowing out a breath I look at them.

"I'm taking her back to the hotel room we stayed in the first day we met, so I can tell her I love her."

Silence, it's become a common occurrence, so I sit back and wait them out.

"You soppy bastard." Damien, obviously, but he's smiling from ear to ear when he says it.

They all are, they know how big a deal this is. In fact, Sean looks like he might cry.

"I'm so glad you found each other, she's great Jake, she really is."

I turn to Matthew, awaiting his assessment, he looks more emotional than Sean which is impressive but very odd.

"You ok Matthew?"

"Yeah sorry, long night, last minute thing to sort out, I'm really happy for you both, you both deserve this, for the love of god don't fuck it up" he grins at me as I flip him off.

We shoot the shit for a couple of hours before Matthew has to leave to get things finished for the launch and as he's leaving Jen rings to say they're done, so I say my goodbyes and head back to my girls.

When I meet up with them the first thing I notice is all the bags, the second is how pale Rori looks. Rushing up to her, I hold her arms.

"What's wrong, what happened, are you ok?"

She doesn't get the chance to answer before Jen steps in.

"Jake, please tell Rori what your answer was when I asked you what the budget was for this shopping trip."

I'm still inspecting Rori, trying to work out if she's ill, but I answer anyway.

"There is no budget, do your worst little sis. Now can someone please tell me why my girlfriend looks like she's about to vomit."

Clive is loading the bags into the boot at this point and Liv and Belle have moved around us to get in the car. As Jen starts to move away, she smiles at Rori then looks back at me.

"She saw the price tags, I tried to tell her but she's having a bit of a meltdown."

Then she follows the others and gets into the car.

Telling Clive I need five minutes, I guide Rori to a bench and sit her down, she still hasn't said a word.

"Talk to me Ror, tell me what you're thinking."

She looks up at me, tears glistening in her eyes.

"It's too much Jake, the dress, the bag, the shoes, I can't let you spend that kind of money on me, I tried to stop her and get them to put everything back, but she wouldn't."

She looks like she's on the verge of a panic attack, this is not how today was supposed to go.

"Okay, Rori, I need you to take some deep breaths for me and I need you to listen, can you do that?"

She nods her head and starts to breath slower and deeper.

"I know you don't care that I'm wealthy, and believe me it's one of your best qualities, because I know you're with me because you want to be and not because of what I can buy you, but that doesn't mean I don't want to. Because I do. What's the point of having all of this money if I can't do things for people when I want to? I've been planning today since you told me about the launch. I spoke to Jen and Liv and told them what I wanted to do, believe me, Liv wasn't happy about it at first, you might have noticed I also bought her dress. But I told her that this would be one of the most important nights of your life and I wanted to make the entire day special for you, which would only happen if your best friend was included, so she caved and agreed to let me buy her outfit as well. Rori I am so proud of you, but I'm also honoured to be the person who gets to go with you tonight, who gets to say, that's my fucking girlfriend when everyone is heaping well deserved praise on you. Now I'm not saying this next bit to brag, but I need to make it clear just in case you didn't fully realise. I am a multimillionaire Ror, please let me use some of that to spoil you on such an important day."

And now she's crying, and even though I've figured out that this is usually a good sign, I still hate to see them.

"Where did you come from? I keep thinking you're too good to be true and the other shoe is gonna drop, but then you just keep saying the most perfect things."

With that she buries her head in my chest and I hug her, staying silent, because if I open my mouth, I might just blurt out right now that I love her, and I want to keep that for later. Once she's calmed down and sitting up again, I decide to take a different approach to the rest of the day, smoothing back the hair from her face I give her the choice.

"Okay, so clearly you're overwhelmed by everything that's happened so far, so no more surprises for the time being, the plan from here was to take you all to a fancy lunch and then go back to the apartment where I've got people coming to pamper you all with massages, hair and make-up, but I feel like that might be a bit much for you, so if you'd prefer we can go straight back now and I'll get food delivered so we can all just chill before you start getting ready tonight, what do you think?"

She's smiling now.

"I think you're perfect, and yes please, I wanna eat pizza for lunch and do some colouring with Belle before I have to go and be all social tonight."

So that's what we do, and she doesn't stop smiling for the rest of the afternoon.

CHAPTER 30
Rori

I'm alone in Jake's bedroom, putting the final touches to my outfit. Today has been insane and I needed a moment to myself. I can't believe how much effort Jake went to today, or how much of a meltdown I had standing in the dress shop and out on the street. But he was as patient as ever with me and I gave in to his request to spoil me. So here I stand, my hair curled to perfection, falling over my shoulders, my make-up is on point, and I'm wearing a stunning strapless black dress. Because Jen went all out in the shop, I'm wearing a lace corset underneath, something I'm sure Jake will appreciate later, the bones pulling me in and creating an impressive cleavage. The satin gown clings to every curve and the thigh high split to the side shows off my leg. The whole outfit is finished off with black stilettos. Black stilettos with a red sole. Yup, she went there.

I hear a knock on the bedroom door and Jake asking if he can come in. Taking a deep breath, I turn towards the door and call him in. His mouth hangs open when he sees me, which gives me the opportunity to take in how edible he looks in his black suit and tie, hair styled to perfection and the hint of stubble on his jaw. Recovering himself, he closes the distance between us.

"Ror you look absolutely breathtaking, you're stunning."

I know I'm blushing, and I know he enjoys it. "Thank you, you don't look too bad yourself, I'll have the hottest date at the party."

"Of course you will, and your date will spend most of the night fighting the urge to drag you into the nearest bathroom and strip you out of this dress."

He runs his hands down my sides as he speaks, sending electric currents shooting through me.

"But for now, I'll be good, and I have one more thing for you to finish off your outfit."

He pulls a flat box out of his pocket and pops the lid, revealing the most beautiful necklace I've ever seen. The chain looks like white gold and holds a diamond infinity sign with a pearl resting in the lower curve. "Jake, this is-"

"Nope, you don't get to finish that sentence," he starts as he removes it from the box and stands behind me. "You gave me permission to spoil you today and you can't take it back now."

"But Jake you've already done so much."

He guides my hand to lift my hair away from my neck so he can fasten the necklace.

"It's on now, can't take it back Ror, might as well enjoy it."

He turns me to the mirror so I can admire it against my skin. "Thank you, so much, this has truly been a day to remember."

"And it's barely started babe, the car is downstairs, it's time to go."

We head out of the bedroom and I find the others in the living room, we all take a few minutes to admire each other's outfits, especially Belle's, she looks so pretty in her soft pink princess gown. However, once Liv and Jen notice my necklace, they both get more emotional and look at Jake like they know something I don't. Then we're out the door and on our way to the venue.

Matthew has organised the event in a function room at a hotel. He explained it's a showcase event for a few chosen authors with books launching this month and is more of a social engagement for me, with him doing all of the work to promote me. I'm still nervous as we enter the venue, but those nerves soon settle. Jake hands us all glasses of champagne and we start to move around the room. Different people stop to ask me about my writing, but they're all friendly and interested in my work, which puts me at ease. We've been here a couple of hours when I finally get to speak to Matthew alone.

"Oh my god this is crazy, thank you so much for everything!" I pull him into a hug to show my appreciation for him.

"It's my pleasure, you deserve this Rori, and that's never been truer than it is right now."

I look back at him confused, he looks like he wants to say something but is worried about my reaction.

"Is everything ok Matthew?"

"Yeah it's fine, sorry, everything's fine, nothing to worry about with the release. But Rori, I was up until the early hours of the morning, Jen sent me your manuscript yesterday and once I started, I couldn't stop."

"Oh," is the only response I can manage.

I wasn't expecting this conversation, I knew she was sending it to him at some point this week, but I didn't think he'd have the time to read it until after this event.

"I debated saying anything because I didn't want to upset you on such an important night, but I couldn't not after reading it, it's a beautiful piece of writing Rori, and we'll talk more about it once this is out of the way, but I just wanted to tell you that you should be so proud of what you've achieved, and Jen was right, your story isn't about what brought you down, it's about the strength you've found in yourself, Jake's a lucky man, you can trust me not to say anything, but I guarantee you it's a story he'll want to read."

And then he pulls me in for another hug and all I can do is grip onto him, emotions flooding through me. Before I pull away, I sense Jake behind me.

"Is everything ok Ror?" he asks as he pulls me out of Matthews hug and I don't miss the clench of his jaw as he does it, which is weird.

"Yeah I'm good, great, I was just thanking Matthew for everything he's done for me."

I smile up at him, hoping to brush away whatever tension I thought I felt. He looks at me for a minute but then seems to pull himself together and he smiles back at me.

"I was just coming to tell you Belle was starting to get tired so I'm going to take her home."

Okay, maybe things aren't fine.

"Oh, I thought Liv was taking her back to Jen's tonight, was that not the plan?".

Matthew clears his throat behind us, joining in the conversation.

"Jake can I talk to you for a minute in private?"

But Jake shakes his head, "She was babe but Belle's being really clingy, I think this has just been a bit much for her, she doesn't want to leave me so I'm going to take her back, I'll make sure Clive comes back to get you and the girls when you're finished here, it's been an amazing night sweetheart, I'm so proud of you."

And with that he kisses me on the cheek and moves back across the room. I turn to Matthew for reassurance, but his face gives him away.

"What was that all about?"

He sighs and shakes his head. "I'm not completely sure, although whatever it was, I know he's wrong, but I also know you're going to be worrying now for the rest of the night. Look, from here on out it's just people getting drunk and dancing, you've done all of the networking you need to do. If you want to go back with Jake and Belle, you can."

I don't hesitate, something tells me we need to talk, so I hurry across the room and out of the hotel, reaching the street just as they're getting in his car. Catching up with them, I don't give him a chance to protest, pushing in the car behind him.

"Ror what are you doing? Go back to the party."

Belle has already snuggled into my side and wrapped her arm around my front, so I gesture to her.

"As if I'd rather be at a party when I could be getting these snuggles, I'm coming with you."

He looks sad but he nods his head anyway, and we travel back to his apartment in silence. When we get inside, Belle asks me to take her to bed, so we go straight to her room. As I tuck her in, she pulls me to sit on the bed next to me.

"Aurora, why don't I have a Mummy like the other girls at school?"

My heart breaks for her, she's never mentioned her mum before, that I know of, and I don't think the first time should be with me.

"Why don't I go get Daddy princess, and he can talk to you about her?"

I go to get up, but she grabs onto my arm.

"I don't want him to be upset with me, do you think she didn't like me Aurora?" her bottom lips quivering as she asks.

I know I should get Jake, but I can't let her keep thinking this, so I scoop her up into my arms.

"Absolutely not darling, everybody who meets you likes you, you're such a special girl. But you know, not everyone is good at being a mum, and they struggle to look after their children the right way. I think your mum knew she couldn't do the job properly and instead of making you unhappy, she decided to leave you with your Dad because she knew how good a Daddy he would be. I think she loved you very much to want to do what was best for you."

She hugs me tighter then moves back into bed.

"I'm glad my Daddy is your prince Aurora, I love you so much, will you promise not to leave me?"

I do my best not to cry, she won't understand I'm so happy to hear her tell me that.

"I love you too princess, and while we never know what the future holds, I can promise you that you will always be in my heart and I hope I'm always in yours."

She seems happy with that, so I kiss her on the forehead then make my way out her room and go in search of Jake. I find him in the kitchen, with a glass in his hand and a bottle of whiskey on the counter and he looks angry.

"Is everything ok?" I ask tentatively.

He looks up at me and I take a step back at the look in his eyes, he's beyond angry.

"Who the hell do you think you are, talking to my daughter about her mother?" he barks out at me.

"Jake I told her I'd get you but she pushed me for an answer."

"You know nothing about her mother, and instead of letting me, her father, talk to her properly about it you decided to give her some romanticised shit about how her mother truly loves her."

"Jake I-"

"No, I don't want to hear your excuses, you're not her mother, you're not a parent, you have no idea what you're talking about and you had no right to tell her what you did. Then to make it worse she literally begged you to tell her you'd never leave her and you couldn't even do that, I thought we were on the same page here Rori but clearly we're not."

"Jake can you–" his words are like knives cutting into me, the pain he's causing is visceral, but I can't find the strength to make him stop his roll.

"And why couldn't you make that promise Rori, why couldn't you tell my five-year-old daughter that worships the ground you walk on that you'll never leave her, is it because you're already planning to?"

"What? No! What are you talking about?"

"Well you looked very appreciative of Matthew tonight, did you decide now that you're gonna be a famous writer you needed a boyfriend that moved in the right circles for you? Were you hoping he wouldn't mind picking up where I left off?"

I can't listen to him anymore, I've worked too hard, I've protected myself too well, I can't go back down this road, so I leave him in the kitchen and lock myself in his bedroom. Moving quickly, I change back into my regular clothes and leave my full outfit on the chair, finally removing the necklace and placing it on his bedside table. I make my way back along the hallways to find he's now sitting in the living room in the dark, staring down into his glass.

"I can't be here when you're acting like this Jake, I'm going to go home."

He laughs at me but it's bitter.

"So you're walking out, leaving me to pick up the pieces in the morning when she wakes up and you're not here, like I said, you have no idea how to be a parent. If you're going to walk out at the first sign of stress maybe we were never meant to be, maybe you shouldn't bother coming back."

I don't answer, we're both too shut down at this point. Instead, I let the tears flow silently as I let myself out and leave his building. I don't text Clive, I get a cab instead, and then I go home, and I climb into my bed, and I cry and cry and cry. Because I always knew he would break my heart in the end.

CHAPTER 31

Jake

It's been four days since our argument. I say argument, clearly it was more like me shouting and screaming like a fucking idiot until she'd had enough and walked out on me. I haven't spoken to her, I don't know what to say. I said some truly awful things to her, and I know I've hurt her. I haven't spoken to Jen or the boys either.

Still angry on Friday morning, I whisked my daughter off for a weekend away, telling her Rori had stuff to do for the book, and sent a quick text to Jen and the boys telling them I wouldn't be around for a few days. I didn't even get a response from Jen.

I took Belle to Cornwall for the weekend and spent the days playing on the beach and collecting shells. And the more time I had to myself the more I regretted everything I'd said. My mood had started when I saw her hugging Matthew, and while I know, deep down, neither of them would ever do that to me, I also know they were hiding something from me when I asked what was wrong. And in that moment, something just snapped, and I needed to get away, only she followed, and then Belle had to go and ask those questions. I should have gone in and stepped in but instead I listened at the door, heard her trying to justify the selfish actions of Melinda and then not be able to promise not to leave her and a switch flicked in my brain.

So now it's Monday, I've sent a couple of texts since we got back last night asking if we can talk but she hasn't responded to them, and I'm getting a little irritated now, because I might need to apologise but she needs to be an adult and let me. She also needs to realise she overstepped and tell me what the fuck is going on with Matthew.

It's just gone two when my door opens and the boys come bounding in, none of them look happy.

"What the fuck did you do?"

"You can't just ditch us for the weekend without any warning and not explain why."

"Has something happened with Rori?"

That last one was from Matthew and I look up at him, trying to see if he knows more than he's letting on, but he just looks concerned.

"We argued, she left, I needed to get away, so I did, nothing else to say."

I know for a fact I won't get away with just that but I'm really not in the mood for a deep and meaningful with them.

"Well you need to fix it, what happened to telling her you're in love with her, did she not say it back?"

"I didn't tell her, probably for the best, maybe we both just got carried away the last few weeks."

I know that's not true when I say it, but I feel too vulnerable right now to admit how much it'll break me if she doesn't come back.

"Bullshit." Damien doesn't mince his words. "Absolute bullshit, listen I know I'm the first one to take the piss and I generally don't do the touchy-feely stuff, but mate, even I can see she's it for you, you need to fix it."

I don't get the chance to respond because Jen comes flying through my door and she looks like she's out for my blood.

"You're a fucking prick," she fumes across the room.

"Hey sis, nice to see you too," I quip back at her, I knew she'd take Rori's side, but I didn't expect such venom from her.

"Seriously Jake, I don't know even know if I can look at you right now. A full day, it took a full day of watching her sob and shatter to pieces before we could even get her to eat never mind talk."

Matthew tries to calm her down.

"Jen I'm sure once they talk about whatever it is-"

"You haven't told them, have you?"

She's staring at me with absolute disgust on her face.

"You haven't told them what you said to her have you?"

Three heads swivel round to look and me.

"Jake, what did you say?"

I'm still looking at Jen, I've never seen her so angry with me and while I know I said some shitty things, it feels like there's more to it than that.

"Jen, do you not think you're being a bit dramatic?"

Wrong thing to say, absolute wrong thing to say, even the boys know it based on the groans they throw my way. She's on a roll now.

"Dramatic, fucking dramatic, let's see how overly dramatic I'm being shall we. Sean, I'll start with you."

He looks terrified but doesn't interrupt her

"My friend was in the middle of the most important night of her life, a night she deserved more than most, and my brother left that party early, making it obvious something was wrong, because he didn't like how she hugged his friend, his friend of twenty fucking years. Does my anger seem dramatic to you?"

He looks like he's going to say something to me, but she doesn't give him the chance.

"You're up Damien. My friend then followed him home, putting his daughter to bed because she asked her to, when said daughter decided to ask questions about her mother, questions my friend didn't want to answer but felt like she had to, so she told that sweet girl that of course her mother liked her and that her mother must love her very much to know she couldn't look after her and instead leave her with a father that adores her. But this fuckwit decided she didn't have the right to talk to his daughter about something like this. What do you think Damien, am I being dramatic, to want to kick his arse right now?"

Damien fixes me with a glare, but she's still not finished.

"And finally, Matthew, tell me how dramatic I'm being, when I've watched my friend, your client, not even be able to drag herself out of bed because the boyfriend who has promised to protect her, instead, told her-"

Her voice catches and I don't even want to listen to the next part, knowing what she's going to say.

"Told her, that she was not Belle's mother, that she's not a parent and has no idea how to be a parent and when she tried to leave to get some space from the shit he was spewing, he told her if she left not to bother coming back."

I close my eyes when she finally stops ranting, I know she's done, I know how bad it sounds, I know the boys are gonna kick my arse, but none of them get the chance because at that moment my assistant bursts into the room.

"Jake, you didn't answer your phone, it's Belle, you need to get to the hospital!"

We all react on instinct, bolting from the room and racing to the ground level where Clive is already waiting for us. The only info my assistant had was that someone had tried to snatch her in the park, and she was being checked over at the hospital. I'd started trying to call my nanny as soon as we left, and she still wasn't answering.

We're all silent in the car, Damien and Sean sit either side of me, each with a hand on my shoulder, Matthew sits opposite, Jen gripping onto his arm. We're all piling out before the cars fully stops and racing into accident and emergency.

"Belle Holmes, she's my daughter, I got a phone call, please, where's my daughter?" I demand as I reach the desk.

The nurse looks up and takes in the group of us, asking some details, she looks over her screen.

"I'll take you through."

We're taken through a maze of corridors and just as we approach a room, I hear my daughters giggle and I stop, my knees give way but Damien and Sean keep me up, and the tears fall, because she's giggling, surely she must be fine if she's giggling. I pull myself together and walk into the room, where I find her sat on a bed, a doctor in the room and what look to be two police officers sitting in the corner.

"Daddy Daddy you're here, I was so scared Daddy, please make the doctor take me to see her."

I catch her as she dives into my arms, the tears coming again to see that she's uninjured.

"Please Daddy, please take me to her."

She's crying now.

"Take you to who Angel. Someone needs to tell me what the hell happened."

I look around the room at the confused faces before me and then the world goes out of focus for the second time today when Belle utters the words….

"To Aurora Daddy, she kept me safe, but I think the bad man got her with the gun."

CHAPTER 32

Rori

Twp hours earlier

I couldn't face work this morning, so I rang and said I had a bug. They probably wouldn't have accepted broken heart as a valid reason to stay off work, so I figured a lie was the way to go. I stayed in bed most of the weekend, Jen and Liv taking turns to sit with me. I know how concerned they are, I also know how angry they are, and I hate to think that this might cause a problem between Jen and Jake. I can't replay that night without crying again so I'm trying to put it out of my head for a while, which is why I decided to come for a walk this afternoon.

Bad idea, terrible idea, because I'm now looking over at the play area and realising I'm close to Belle's school, so of course she's here with her nanny. And I can't look away. I love this girl, I love her dad, I really thought he loved me after everything he said on Thursday before the launch. But the things he said after, that's not love, and while part of me knows he wouldn't have said them if he knew more about my past, the other part wonders how he could think so little of me to say those things. And then to tell me never to come back because I made the choice to walk away from the argument.

I sit on a bench to watch her play, I'm close enough to see how happy she looks but far enough away that I don't look like a creep. Jake started texting last night and I can't bring myself to reply, he says he wants to talk but I don't know if I can take anymore, and I know I'll break if I see him in person. So I left my phone at home when I decided to get some fresh air.

I watch Belle playing for a while longer and they make their way to the gate, presumably to head home, but as they walk out of the gate a man approaches Diana and they appear to be arguing. I stay where I am, it won't help any of us if Belle sees me, but then I see the man grab Belle's hand and start to pull her along the path and I'm off my seat and chasing after them before I can think about it. As I get closer, I hear Diana pleading with the man.

"Paul, please stop, you don't have to do this."

She's crying, clearly upset and Belle looks terrified. As soon as I'm close enough I shout Belle's name. She turns, and the distraction causes Paul to drop her hand and she runs to me.

"Come back here right now."

As soon as she's close enough, I tug her into my body and hold on tight, why didn't I bring my damn phone, I need to call Jake. Belle is trembling and I stroke her arm as I look towards whoever Paul is and Diana.

"I don't know who you are, but Belle is clearly upset, and I think we need to call her father."

"We're not calling anyone just yet bitch, stay the hell out of our business and walk away, the kid is coming with us."

Paul is getting more worked up, so I guide Belle behind my body and straighten my stance.

"No, she's not, I don't know what's going on here but she's going nowhere with you until I speak to her dad. Diana, can I borrow your phone? I don't have mine with me."

She's frozen still, her eyes darting between me and Paul. We're not too far from the play area but this part of the park is practically deserted so I can't even call out to anyone to help me.

As I'm thinking about what to do, Paul drags my attention back to him when his menacing voice calls out,

"I said she's coming with us, you don't want to mess with me."

When my eyes land back on him, I see he's holding a gun and the fear grips me. I can't let anything happen to this little girl, I have to protect her.

"Please put the gun down, just let us leave and I won't tell anyone, she's just a child and she's done nothing wrong, please let her go."

I plead with him, but I know he's barely listening. Time seems to stand still, I keep Belle pinned to my back, gripping onto her arms so she can't move out into his line of sight.

"I won't say it again bitch, hand her over or I will shoot you."

From my peripheral vision I see two men approaching from the side, slowly, they see I've spotted them, and they motion for me to stay silent, they're here to help, thank fuck. But I still have a gun pointed at me, and Belle to protect.

"Why are you doing this, what do you want, maybe I can help you some other way."

I try, hoping to keep him distracted and looking at me. It appears Diana has also noticed the men approaching and she edges closer.

"Paul let them go, please, it's not too late, but the police will be here soon and then it'll get worse."

I cringe as her words sink in, his eyes get wilder, and he looks around, spotting the men approaching. They stop their movements as his eyes shoot back to me.

"You fucking bitch."

It all happens in slow motion, Diana dives for him and I hear the shot as I spin to protect Belle's body with mine. I hear shouting, screaming and crying and then everything goes black.

CHAPTER 33
Jake

I'm aware of my legs giving way again and someone helping me into a chair, but I can't focus on the room or speak. I'm aware of someone approaching me and saying my name but I can't process, then Matthews voice rings clear in the room.

"Her full name is Aurora Bales, she's Jake's girlfriend and my client, can you please tell us what is going on?"

I finally pull myself together enough to concentrate on the room. Jen is now sitting on the bed comforting Belle, Sean is with them, wrapping them both in a hug. Damien is crouched down at my side while Matthew stands next to us, speaking to the police officer. The doctor announces he's going to pass on Rori's details and once the door closes the officer speaks.

"Earlier this afternoon we got a call from an off-duty officer to say a potential kidnapping was in progress. We immediately dispatched officers to the scene. We don't have all of the information yet, but what we do know is that the off-duty officers witnessed a man and woman arguing, then the man started pulling your daughter with him. At first, they thought it might just be a domestic between a couple, but they decided to watch from a distance in case it got more heated. They then witnessed, who we now know as your girlfriend, approach the couple, calling out Belle's name. Belle was able to pull away from the man and run to Miss Bales. The officers couldn't hear everything being said but they called it in and approached from the side with caution. They said it was clear Belle was relieved to see Miss Bales and after a hug, Miss Bales pulled your daughter behind her to keep her further away from the man. Unfortunately, it then became clear he had a gun and was threatening to shoot Miss Bales if she didn't hand Belle over. She refused. The officers were hopeful they could get to them unseen, however when the other woman present noticed them, she alerted the man, and he lost control. The other woman tried to grab the gun and it discharged, Miss Bales was shot as she pushed your daughter to the ground to protect her."

We're all silent with shock, all I can hear is Jen crying into Sean as he holds them, but it's me who speaks first.

"Is she…I mean…what.."

I can't finish my sentence, the words won't come.

"She was shot in the shoulder and brought here as well, we'll see what updates we can get for you, now that we know who she is, she didn't have any ID on her at the scene."

Before anyone else can speak the doctor comes back into the room and looks at the police and then me.

"She's in surgery, she's lost some blood but they're confident she'll make a full recovery, if you all want to stay here with Belle for now, I'll let you know as soon as she's out."

"Liv is on her way," Jen says to no one in particular as the doctor leaves.

The officers are next, telling me they'll leave someone outside and will be back as soon as they have more details. Damien slips out and when he returns, he has coffee for everyone and a hot chocolate for Belle, but I can't drink it. I can't do anything. I can't believe this is happening, not now, not when she's so upset with me, not when she doesn't know how much I love her. I can't contemplate not getting her back.

It's not long before Liv rushes into the room and Matthew explains what's happening. She crumbles into a chair, trying to keep her crying quiet for Belle's sake. She can't even look at me, I don't blame her.

The hot chocolate seems to lift Belle's spirits and she comes to sit on my knee for a cuddle.

"Daddy, Princess Aurora saved me, she has to be okay, I love her so much."

"Me too Angel, I love her so much as well," I tell her, hoping I get the chance to tell Rori.

It feels like hours have passed before the doctor comes back and we all jump to our feet when he enters the room.

"She's out of surgery and everything went as well as it could, the bullet was simple to remove so it was a straightforward procedure, she'll need physio and will be in a lot of pain, but we should only need to keep her here for a couple of days. She's been moved to a private room now, she's still knocked out but you can sit with her, no more than two at a time."

The relief floods through me, but before we can go anywhere, the police officers come back into the room.

"Mr Holmes, we have an update. It would appear the offender is the boyfriend of your nanny. He was in debt, gambling and drugs, and saw your daughter as a way to make quick money, his plan was to take her and then demand money from you for her safe return. From what we can gather, your nanny agreed to the plan but lost her nerve at the last minute. They're both in custody and we don't foresee any further risk to your daughter."

Leaving me his card they exit shortly after. Matthew approaches me once they're gone.

"Hey, we're going to take Jen and Belle to the hospital restaurant, you and Liv should see her first, keep us updated."

I'm torn between wanting to see Rori and not wanting to let Belle out of my sight ever again, Matthew seems to realise my dilemma.

"She'll be fine, she'll have an Aunt and three Uncles as her personal bodyguards."

I know I need to talk to him about what Jen said but now isn't the time, I'm just so grateful that they're all here. Giving Belle another hug, I let them take her and then follow the doctor with Liv. When we're at her room the doctor leaves us. We both enter and Liv immediately starts to cry again. Rori is asleep on the bed, various machines and tubes around her. She looks pale but peaceful as she sleeps. We take a seat either side of her bed and both reach for a hand.

"You've really hurt her Jake."

It's the first thing she's said to me since she arrived at the hospital.

"I know, I wish I could take it all back, but I can't. I just need her to be okay and then I will spend as long as it takes earning her forgiveness, I need her Liv, I love her."

She nods her head and offers a faint smile. We sit in silence, both lost in our own thoughts, both stroking Rori's hand as we wait for her to come round. When she eventually begins to stir, we both shoot forward, watching for her eyes opening, when they do, she looks between us, confusion on her face as she tries to speak but just manages to croak. Liv holds a cup of water up to her and she sucks some using the straw. As soon as it's down she looks back to me and utters her first word.

"Belle?"

She looks terrified.

"She's fine sweetheart, just worried about you, Ror."

My voice breaks and I swallow the lump before continuing.

"You saved her life Ror, I'll never be able to thank you enough for protecting my precious girl, I love you Rori."

I'm not sure how I expected her to react, I probably should have waited to tell her I loved her, but I'm still gutted when she finally speaks.

"I'm so thankful she's okay Jake, please tell her she was so brave and that I'd love to see her when she's feeling up to it, but I need you to leave."

I reach for her hand, "Rori I-."

But she doesn't let me finish, pulling her hand away.

"Please Jake, I can't be around you right now, please respect my decision and leave."

I look over to Liv, she gives me a sympathetic look but doesn't say anything. I stand and look at her one more time.

"I'm sorry Ror, I'm so so sorry, I hope you'll let me come back soon, but as soon as you're up to it I'll get Jen to bring Belle up, I know she can't wait to see you."

She nods her head and then looks away and I do the only thing I can, I walk away from the love of my life.

CHAPTER 34

Rori

As soon as he leaves, Liv speaks.

"Aurora he's been so worried he-"

"Please don't Liv, I can't do this right now, can you please tell me what happened?"

She fills me in on the details of the attempted kidnapping and my injuries. I feel like I've been hit by a truck and I'm exhausted but other than that I'm hopeful she's right about only having to stay a couple of days. The sooner I get out of here the sooner I can leave London. Which is exactly what I plan to do, screw the working things out in my head, it's time to give in to my flight response. Will I regret it later, maybe, will I miss my new life, absolutely, but I can keep in touch with everyone, and I don't need to be in London to sell my books.

Half an hour later I think I might try sleeping again when there's a knock on the door and Jen comes in with Belle. The tears come as soon as I see her perfect face, totally unharmed.

"Aurora" she whispers, as she creeps forward, clearly a little frightened.

"Hey princess, I'm so happy to see you, I know all this stuff looks a little scary, but I promise I'm ok, why don't you sit next to me so I can hold your hand."

Jen helps her up onto the bed and she grips onto my hand.

"Uncle Sean said the doctors had made you better and you were having a nice sleep, then Daddy came back and said you were awake, did he give you a kiss to wake you up like in the stories?"

She's so innocent, as she should be, I hope the events of today don't affect her too much.

"I woke up all by myself Belle, because I wanted to see you so much, you did so well today darling, I'm so proud of how brave you were."

Taking a breath, I gather the strength to say what I need to.

"Listen Belle, I love you so much, and remember when I told you I would always keep you in my heart and you could keep me in yours?"

She nods her head as I hear the intake of breath from Jen, but I can't make eye contact, not yet.

"Well I have to stay in hospital for a little while, so that I can get better, but they're not nice places for little girls. So I want you to go home with Daddy, and I promise I'll make sure to video call you when you're with Aunt Jen on a Saturday."

Her lip trembles a little, but she doesn't cry.

"I'll miss you Aurora, when will I see you again?"

I have to be honest with her. "I'm not sure sweetie, but I promise to keep in touch with you, I love you."

I finally look at Jen and see the range of emotions sweeping over her face.

"I'm really tired. Would you all mind leaving me to sleep for a while, please?"

I know she's got more to say but she just nods and all three of them leave my room. Finally alone I let the tears take over and eventually fall asleep.

When I wake, it's Matthew I find next to my bed.

"Hey, you're awake, how are you feeling?"

"Like I've been shot."

He laughs at my attempt at a joke.

"Glad it didn't affect your sense of humour."

He passes me a drink and I gratefully take it.

"Rori, Jen told me what you said to Belle, she seemed to think you were leaving? Is this because of what happened with Belle or because my best friend is a cockwomble?"

I manage a small smile.

"It's everything Matthew, if either of those things had happened, I would have been triggered, but I think I could've relied on my coping strategies and worked through it. But both events, only a few days apart, I'm in freefall and right or wrong, I need to run, I need to be alone and I need to regroup."

He doesn't speak for a while but eventually he looks at me with genuine care in his eyes.

"Then let me make a suggestion, I own a cottage in the Lake District, I let writers use it when they need space to write or they're getting bogged down in a storyline, it's empty right now, I'd like to send you there. If you don't want Jake to know where you are, I'll respect that. As long as you let one of the girls tell him you're safe. He loves you Rori, I know what he said was terrible, and now that I've read your story, I know why it'll be hard for you to believe that and find your way back from it. But aside from anything else, I'm your friend as well, and if I can give you the option to just get some space somewhere away from here, instead of you running without a plan, in the hopes you can find your way back, I have to at least try."

"I can't make you any promises Matthew" I sigh but he's not put off.

"I know you can't, nor do I expect you to, but you've been

through a lot the last few days, you need to heal physically as well, you don't need to be running without a place to stay, please take the cottage, I guarantee you will find peace and tranquillity to process how you feel."

He has a point, I don't have a plan at all, but I do need to go, and this would give me the distance I need.

"Okay, I'll go, thank you."

He gives my hand a squeeze.

"I'll get everything ready for you, Jen and Liv will be here tomorrow with your things and we'll get you on your way."

He leaves soon after and I take the opportunity to get more sleep.

The next time I wake its morning, both Liv and Jen are sitting next to my bed.

"Hi sleepyhead, we've been sat here talking for ages and you've not stirred once."

Liv smiles at me but I can see her concern.

"Guess I needed the rest. Did they say I could leave today?" I ask hopefully.

"Yeah they did, they'll be in with the paperwork soon and we've brought all your things, but Aurora are you really sure about this?"

I know they're finding it hard, Jen especially given it's her brother I'm running away from, but I have to do this.

"Yes, I'm sure, I need time to process on my own. I'm not going to disappear completely, I'll keep in touch, and I'll keep my promise to Belle, if that's ok?"

I look to Jen when I say that, she might not even let me talk to her.

"Of course it's ok, every Saturday like you said. Look Aurora, I'm not going to make excuses for him, what he said was awful, but do you think there's any way you'll forgive him in time?"

She's teary when she asks and I want to cry with her, but I keep myself focused.

"I don't know Jen, it's not really about forgiving him for what he said, most of it was true, I guess I was just more invested in all of us and thought we could be a family. And yeah, I heard him when he said he loved me, but let's face it, he'd just been through a traumatic experience hearing what happened in that park, I don't want love from obligation. I made a promise to Matthew as well, so whichever one of you he asks, I want you to tell him that I'm safe and I'm doing what I need to do, that I'm sorry this is what we've come to but I have to put my mental health first and that means I have to leave."

They both just nod, they know they can't change my mind. They both help me dress around my wound and once I have my discharge papers, we make our way outside. There's a car waiting outside, and a driver steps out to take my bags while Jen explains.

"Matthew wanted you to travel as comfortably as possible given your injury. It a long drive but you can ask the driver to stop as many times as you need and there are plenty of blankets and cushions if you need them."

Giving them one final hug, I thank them both for everything and promise to let them know when I get there, then I get in the car and we pull away, away from London, away from my friends, away from the family I thought I'd found.

CHAPTER 35
Jake

I've stayed away for two days, spent time with Belle, spoke to therapists to get advice on how to help her come to terms with what happened, but I can't stay away any longer. Belle is back at school, to try and get her back in routine, so armed with flowers and apologies I enter the hospital. When I get to her room, I find it empty, so I make my way to a nurse's station, where I find out she was discharged earlier today. I thought she might have told me, but I go back to the car and ask Clive to take me to Jen's apartment. I have a spare key, but I never use it, so I knock and wait. As soon as Jen opens the door, I know something isn't right. I follow her in.

"Is she in her room? The hospital said she was discharged and I'm hoping she'll see me now."

We reach the living room where Liv is sitting, eyes red, and they share a look.

"What's going on Jen?"

The bad feeling I got when she answered the door grows and she still doesn't speak to me.

"Jen, where is Rori?"

I'm more demanding this time, but I need her to start talking. She finally turns and looks at me, tears swimming in her eyes.

"She's gone Jake, I'm sorry, she left as soon as she was

discharged."

My heart is hammering in my ears, she can't have, she can't just leave.

"What do you mean she's gone? Gone where? When will she be back?"

I'm frantic now, pacing across the floor.

"She wanted you to know that she's safe, but she needs to leave, she needs time to process everything and deal with her own mental health, she doesn't want you to know where she's gone and she couldn't say if or when she'd be back."

Now I'm even more frantic.

"If, what do you mean if? This is her home, I'm her boyfriend, I fucking love her Jen, you must know where she is, just tell me."

My hands grip my hair, this can't be happening.

"I'm sorry Jake, but you told her not to bother coming back if she left, you really hurt her."

I take a seat before I fall.

"I know I fucked up, Christ I do, I know, but I told her I loved her in the hospital and she kicked me out before we could talk, why couldn't she let me explain?"

My whole world is spinning right now, this is worse than seeing her in that bed, at least I knew where she was, but this.

"Jake, you told her you loved her after she saved Belle's life, she probably thought that's why you said it, because of what she'd done for Belle."

"But that's not why I said it."

I'm shouting now, I know I shouldn't, but I can't help myself, Liv finally breaks her silence.

"Jake, she's one of my best friends, I know everything about her, and I know she can't be here right now, shouting at your sister won't change that, you should go home, we can't tell you any more."

She's right, I should probably apologise as well but I don't, I just walk out and when I reach my car I slump inside and tell Clive to take me to the nearest pub. I sit at the bar and order a whiskey, then another, then another, it would be easier if they left the bottle but that probably wouldn't look good when it's barely midday. I've been here an hour when the messages start.

Sean: where are you, I'm at your apartment and you're clearly not

I ignore it.

Matthew: just tell us where you are, Jen's worried about you

Yeah, still not gonna bother.

Damien: Jake stop being a prick and fucking answer us, where the fuck are you

Fuck sake.

Jake: drunk

Damien: that isn't a place fuckwit, drunk where, you only left Jen an hour ago

Jake: drunk somewhere

Damien: are you aware you're 32 years old, answer the fucking question

Jake: no thanks

Matthew: Jake come on, it's us, you know we're here for you, tell us where you are and we'll come drink with you

Sean: day drink on a Thursday, I'm totally down for that

Jake: she left me, she fucking left me, I have no interest in talking about that right now or even drinking in silence with any of you, leave me the fuck alone

And then a text comes in from Jen.

Jen: I know you're hurting, and I'm trying really hard not to slap some sense into you for being such a prick in the first place after what you've been through the last few days, but you need to talk to the boys, I'll pick Belle up today and bring her here for a sleepover, I doubt you'll have sobered up by bedtime

Jake: tell her I love her

And then I try calling Rori, every time it goes to voicemail, I try over and over again and eventually it doesn't even ring, so I text her, and they don't deliver, well this feels like deja vu. So I silence my phone, I can't turn it off in case she calls, or something happens with Belle, but I can't listen to the incessant dings from the boys still trying to find me. Whiskey is the only answer I need right now, so I tell the barman to keep them coming and thankfully, when I drop enough money on the bar, he does.

I'm not sure how many I've had when I feel someone sit next to me, but I know I can't see properly. The barman drops another in front of me but the person to my left, or it could be my right, swipes it before I can get to it and presumably drinks it for me.

"Hey, thas me, gim back," is what I think I say.

"How much did you pay the poor kid behind the bar to keep serving you?"

I think I know that voice, but I can't even remember the question now so I just shrug.

"Jesus Christ Jake, this is the kinda shit I pull not you, come on, I'm taking you home."

It's when he pulls me off the stool I realise it's Damien, how long has he had an identical twin, there's definitely two of them swaying in front of me. I don't have the fight in me to argue so I let him drag me out of the pub and throw me into the car. That's the last thing I remember.

I wake up, face down on my bed, still in my clothes, and I

have no fucking idea how I got here. My mouth is caked shut and I want to vomit. I drag myself up and make it to the bathroom where I down three glasses of water before stripping out of my clothes. Finding some joggers and a t-shirt, I venture out of my room and immediately hear voices coming from the kitchen. When I get there, they all stop and stare. Sean, Matthew and Damien are sat around the kitchen island drinking coffee, they don't look particularly happy with me, I don't really give a fuck.

"What time is it and what the hell are you three doing here?" I grunt as I sink down on a stool.

Sean gets up and when he returns to the counter, he slides a coffee in front of me as he tells me,

"It's just after nine, you've been passed out for fifteen hours, and we're here because we thought you might choke on your own vomit based on how much you drank you dipshit."

"Well as you can see, I'm perfectly fine so you can fuck off now."

Damien slams a hand on the table.

"Seriously Jake, I'm gonna put my fist through your face if you don't knock this shit off, we know you're hurting and probably angry, but this isn't the way to deal with it."

Standing from the table I pick up my coffee and head for the door.

"You don't know shit, leave me the fuck alone."

And I leave them to it, shutting myself back in my room, I lock the door behind me, send a quick text to Jen to tell her I'll get Belle today, then bury myself back under the covers and beg for sleep so I don't have to think about her.

The next time I wake up it's just after 1 and I feel a lot less hungover, so I jump in the shower, ignoring Rori's shampoo and shower gel sitting on the shelf, and scrub the smell of stale alcohol from my skin. I'm hoping to find my kitchen empty this time, no such luck, although at least it's just Matthew here this time.

"You're awake again then."

"Looks like it," I snap out as I go in search of food.

I find leftover pizza in the fridge and sit down with it.

"Are you ready to talk about it?"

"Nope."

"Not even the part where you thought either of us would betray you like that?"

Yeah, we probably do need to talk about that part.

"I didn't, I wasn't…"

I stop, gather my thoughts and start again.

"I said a lot of things I shouldn't have that night, that's probably the one I'm most ashamed of, for the record I didn't accuse either of you of doing anything, and I couldn't give a fuck that she hugged you, I guess I just got the feeling she was hiding something from me and that hug was about more than the book deal, I'm sorry Matthew, you know I'd never think you were capable of that and deep down I know she isn't either."

I dig into the pizza not waiting for a reply, Matthew always thinks before he speaks, he'll mull over my words, probably call me some names that I deserve, then we'll move on.

"I do know you didn't mean it, I know you were spiralling and lashing out instead of thinking about it first, the thing is Jake, she doesn't know that, and maybe she is hiding something from you, maybe she isn't, that's not the point, the point is you need to be honest with yourself about why you went where you did, and until you do you're not going to be able to fix it. But you are wrong about one thing, of everything you said that night, that's not the thing you should be most ashamed of."

He doesn't expand on that, he just gets up and walks out,

and I'm finally alone.

CHAPTER 36
Rori

Opening the front door, I take my coffee and toast to the bench and sit, watching the early morning sun sparkle against the lake. I've been here just over 3 weeks now and I love it. I've never felt so relaxed. My whole life I've always felt like I was rushing from one thing to the next and finally, I can slow down and do things at my pace.

I'm staying near Windermere, in a cottage with a view of the lake. It's not a huge place, but it's exactly what I need. It has two large bedrooms, both ensuite, a living room and kitchen. I chose the bedroom that also faces the lake so it's the first thing I see when I open the curtains on a morning.

For the first week after I arrived, I basically spent all my time either in the cottage or sitting on this bench. Matthew had made sure everything was in working order and made sure the fridge and cupboards were well stocked. He also organised for a private Doctor to check on me a couple of times to see that my wound was healing well, which it was. It still aches but it's not stopping me from doing anything. That first week I cried daily, I slept a lot and I ate a lot of carbs.

The day I arrived, I text the girls to let them know I was safe, and Jen replied telling me she had Belle for a sleepover and did I want to videocall. So I did. I didn't ask why she had Belle on a weeknight, but given it was the day I left, it wasn't hard to assume. It broke my heart talking to her from so far away, but

I smiled through it, and she was as bubbly as ever. We've spoke on Saturdays as planned since then and she's been the same hyper little girl each time, giving me hope she hasn't been too traumatised by that day.

The last two weeks, I've started to explore more. I went into the village and wandered around the shops, picking up little things I thought Belle would like to send to her later, and then sat and had a coffee while I watched people pass by. I've also been on a couple of lengthy hikes, taking in different parts of the lake. But I also started writing again. I spoke to Matthew at the end of my first week, he wanted to give an update on my book. The early sales were impressive enough for him to be ready to send me the follow up offer for the rest of the series. I may have screamed when I read it, it's a lot of money, in fact I rang him back to ask if he'd made a mistake. He laughed at me. Then told me that no he hadn't made a mistake. Then I asked the burning question; did I need to come back to London to make this happen or could I do it from anywhere. He told me email is a wonderful thing and not to worry about location at this stage. We didn't talk about Jake, but we did discuss the manuscript that dealt with my past experiences. The thing about that book is, Jen was right, it did turn into a story of strength, but it also turned into a story of love.

When I wrote it, I debated long and hard on how I wanted to end the book, and I decided I wanted to send a message of hope. So, I included a chapter about finally moving on, giving myself permission to be happy with someone else, because I deserve to be, and not letting my past overshadow or derail the possibility of a future. I ended the book excited to know where my future would take me. Then the bottom fell out of my world.

Matthew wants to publish it, but he won't until I decide if I'm sticking with that ending or I want to rewrite it. I know what he's really asking, I just don't have an answer for him. Because I'm still so angry with Jake. And I'm still so hurt by the things he said. It doesn't matter which way you look at it, he doesn't trust me with his daughter, he doesn't trust me to always put her needs first, if he did, he would have heard my love for her when I answered her questions that night.

My phone pings and I pray it's not him. He hounded me for the first few days, I didn't answer or reply to any of his texts, but I couldn't bring myself to block his number, so I just kept it on silent. After a couple of days, he stopped calling but I'd still get texts a couple of times a day asking if we could talk. I haven't had any calls or texts for the last 3 days and while it makes me less anxious every time my phone goes off, it also makes me wonder if he's over it, if he's moved on from us, and I don't want to deal with the reaction that causes.

Jen: I hear you signed the new deal, suppose that means I have to as well

Rori: well I am your favourite author and you are my favourite editor, no brainer really

Jen: if I sign it will you come home

Rori: nice try

Jen: gotta take my shots where I can

Rori: video call with Belle later?

Jen: of course, speak soon

I go back inside once my coffee is finished and set up my laptop. All three of my follow up books are with Jen and we discuss those as and when. But I've found myself inspired while I've been here so I'm working on some new stuff. This is what I can do right now. I might not be able to think about Jake, or process what happened in the park, or contemplate how fucked up I still am from my past. But I can write, and right now, that's enough for me.

CHAPTER 37
Jake

It's been over four weeks since she left, over five weeks since I last held her. Considering we'd only been together four months, you'd think it wouldn't hurt this much. But it does. All day, every day. I swing from wanting to hunt her down and hug her, to wanting to shout and scream at her for leaving me, but regardless of which way I swing, the underlying pain of not having her here doesn't change.

I know she speaks to Belle when she sleeps at Jen's because she comes home and tells me all about it. Then she tells me how much she misses her and hopes her book work will be finished soon so she can come home. At this point I don't know much longer it'll be before Belle starts to question if she will come back. And the most frustrating thing is, is that she just won't speak to me, and I just don't understand why. I recognise I was a dick that night, I know I need to apologise, but I feel like she's really overreacted, that if she actually did love me, which she's never said if she did, surely love would be enough to at least stay and hear me out. To at least accept that I had every right to be upset with her, even if I expressed that the wrong way.

On top of everything else, work is a shit show. I threw myself back into it, needing the distraction, but after what happened I have no desire to hire a new nanny any time ever. So, I'm constantly having to rearrange meetings so that I can pick Belle up or asking Jen to do it. Which she does, she'll always be there for Belle, but I know she blames me for Rori leaving so we're not exactly siblings of the year right now. All in all, I'm a miserable fucker, as my friends like to point out, often.

I hear the door open and the giggles of Belle arriving home after her regular sleepover last night. When she spots me, she runs over for a hug.

"Hi Daddy, did ya miss me?"

"Of course Angel, don't I always. Have you had fun?"

She's digging around in her pocket as she answers.

"I had so much fun Daddy, look at my new purse."

She pulls out a small pink purse covered in sequins, its perfect for her.

"That's pretty, I hope you said thank you to Aunt Jen."

"Oh it's not from Aunt Jen silly, it's from Aurora."

I nearly drop my daughter as I shoot my head up to Jen, the question in my eyes, but she shakes her head.

"She sent it to Aunt Jen and then I opened it yesterday when she called me, I'm going to go and put it safe in my room Daddy, love you."

Jumping off my knee she sprints to her bedroom. Jen looks about ready to leave but I can't let her go without asking.

"Jen please, has she said anything? Is there any point in me hoping she'll listen to me? Is she ever coming back?"

"I don't know Jake."

"Bullshit, I don't believe you, if this was just her needing time away after what happened at the park she would have spoken to me by now, and I know I overreacted after the launch event but come on, is leaving for over four weeks now not a little bit dramatic? Just because I said a few things that I should have worded differently, if it's over for good Jen, then she at least owes me the decency to tell me, so we can both move on, the longer this goes on, with Belle thinking she's coming home to us, the harder it's going to be on her as well."

And that's when my sister loses her shit.

"How you managed to build the business you have when you are so fucking stupid is beyond me. You didn't need to word it differently Jake, you needed to not even think it, never mind say it. We've all tried to steer you in the right direction, but you're a pig-headed idiot who wouldn't listen. How many times do I have to say this Jake; Mum had cancer, she didn't choose to leave us."

What the fuck.

"Why are you bringing up mum again, this has nothing to do with that."

"Yes Jake, it really does."

She's not quite as crazy looking now and she comes to sit next to me.

"Jake you changed when Mum died, you stopped letting anyone in. And I don't mean me or the boys, I mean anyone new. You finished school, went to Uni, started a business, and you never once mentioned a new friend, or a girlfriend or anything. You couldn't shut us out because we wouldn't let you, but you've never built a relationship with anyone new since. It's like Mum dying made you unable to trust anyone else entering your life in case the same thing happened to them. When Melinda came back, I think you tried with her because you knew her before Mum died, so it wasn't someone new. And I know what she did was horrific Jake, but you already had issues way before that. When Rori came along, I was so happy for you, but then you just kept talking about taking it slow because of Belle and how much Melinda leaving hurt her, I knw you didn't get it, Jake, you didn't get that people leaving you was making you just as closed off. Rori has been looking out for Belle from the start, and Belle trusts Rori, do you not think that's maybe why she felt comfortable enough to talk to her about her mum in the first place, you might love her Jake, and that is a massive step, but you don't trust her enough because you can't let go of the notion that she might not last forever, so she can't possibly be a mother figure to Belle. So no Jake, you didn't need to reword that she wasn't her mother, you needed to see that if your daughter trusts her enough to confide in her like you would a parent, then your girlfriend had absolutely earned the right to answer her questions without running to you first. And as a side note, it was a fucking good answer. You didn't just hurt her feelings Jake, you shut down any possibility of you ever being a complete family when you made it clear to her that you didn't trust her to be Belle's parent. I love you Jake, I want you to be happy, you have to make peace with the past."

And with that she hugs me then leaves. I don't know how long I sit there, thinking about everything she's said, before I finally do what I should have done weeks ago and talk to the people who've always been there for me.

Jake: So Jen just tore me a new one

Damien: I've always liked that girl

Sean: go Jen

Matthew: about anything in particular

Jake: she thinks my trust issues have fuck all to do with Melinda and actually started when Mum died and that even though I said I was protecting Belle, I really just can't admit how closed off I've been so I was always going to fuck up with Rori

Damien: I'm buying that girl a car

Damien: and a boat

Damien: maybe even a puppy

Sean: at least we helped one Holmes mature into a well-rounded adult

Matthew: anyone else think we've had this conversation already and he told us all to fuck off

Jake: I'm sure you weren't quite as blunt….so you all agree with her then

Damien: I'm buying her gifts mate, I think the answer to that is obvious

Jake: what do I do

Matthew: take a good long look at yourself, maybe punch yourself in the face, then work out how to get your fucking girl back

CHAPTER 38
Rori

I miss Jake, it doesn't matter what I do, I miss him every day. And Belle, six weeks of video calls just aren't enough, I want to hug her and spend time with her, and I know she's started to realise that I've been gone for too long. In fact, I miss everyone, but Jake and Belle, the emptiness I feel at not being with them is intense.

I've done a lot of soul searching while I've been here. I've had to admit to myself that as much as I thought I'd dealt with my past and moved forward, the first real test of that, was to be part of a loving healthy relationship, without letting my past interfere with it. And I failed. I see that now. We spent so much time taking it slow, getting to know each other, building a firm foundation. But I held back the biggest parts of me, the hardest experiences I'd faced, and then blamed him for saying the wrong things when he had no idea what I'd been through.

I've spent hours walking and thinking, analysing our time together, revisiting my past. I've finally grieved for the childhood I didn't get, for the family I never had and for the baby I couldn't protect. But I've also finally accepted that I couldn't control any of those things, that I was not to blame. I've found a peace within myself these last few weeks that I didn't think was possible, didn't really know I needed until I came here.

It's the first time I've been on any kind of break. Never had a holiday in my life. While I saw a therapist after my miscarriage,

I did that while still having to work to support myself and find somewhere to live. Then I moved back to London, straight to a new job, new friends and Jake. But for the first time in my life, I've taken a breath, walked, taken in my surroundings, made time for myself. I know Jake was scared that night, the night he said those hurtful things. And while I never had any intention of leaving, I was still holding things back from him, and maybe deep down he knew that, and it fuelled his fear.

I want to reach out to him, to talk to him and explain everything. But I don't know if he'll want to speak to me after this long. He might have moved on. He might have realised that he can have a relationship and be a father at the same time and found someone else. I'd like to think Jen or Matthew would have told me, but then I made it clear to them I didn't want to talk about him whenever we've spoken. He's probably still angry with me, I ran, not only from us but from the trauma of the attempted kidnapping. He must have been going out of his mind and I left him when he needed me the most.

I've decided I want to go back to London. I may not know how things will be with Jake, but I do know I have friends who I love and miss, and a little girl whose life I want to be part of, even if it's just as her Aunt's friend. Jake told me that wouldn't change if things went wrong with us, so all I can do is hope he meant it. Regardless of if it's too late for us, I want to explain everything to him, and I think I know how to do that. So I do what I've been debating for the last week and make the call.

"Hey Rori, it's good to hear from you, everything ok?"

"Hi Matthew, yeah I'm ok, been doing a lot of thinking and I was hoping you might help me with something."

"Of course, what do you need?"

"I still haven't made a decision about publishing my story, I know you both want me to, but a lot has happened these last few weeks and I always said I wouldn't publish if without telling Jake the truth about my past."

"I understand Rori, there's no rush."

"How is he Matthew?"

There's a pause on the other end of the line and I hold my breath, hoping he's not about to break the news that Jake has moved on to someone else.

"Look Rori, I've always said what you tell me is confidential, and I think I owe that same courtesy to Jake, but what I will say is, he's beating himself up pretty badly for the things he said to you, he's not in a great place right now."

It's my turn to pause now, while I hoped he wouldn't tell me Jake was over me, I also didn't want to hear he's in a bad way.

"I'm sorry if this puts you in a bad position, but I was wondering if I sent you a cover note for the manuscript, if you'd pass the whole thing on to him. I owe him an explanation and this is the only way I know how to give it, he might not want to hear it, or ever speak to me again, but I want to come back to London and I need to reach out before I do."

"Of course I will, send it to me recorded delivery and I'll get it to him without opening it, and Rori, we all want you back."

I pass on my thanks then end the call before settling in to write the letter.

CHAPTER 39
Jake

The last two weeks have been intense. I sat with everything Jen said to me for the rest of the day and realised she was right. My mother's death changed me, it not only hardened my heart, but it made me fear ever being that close to anyone again, for fear of losing more.

The next day I rang a therapist and paid over the odds to be seen the same day. She made me see that I'd built up the day of the book launch so much in my head, had planned it so much, that I hadn't stopped to realise how much I feared being rejected and her leaving me, not Belle, me. So, the first chance I got, I attacked her and pushed her away so that I wouldn't have to hear her say it. I was a fucking idiot. I'd been seeing the therapist every other day since, and it was hard, emotionally exhausting work, but I was coming out of the other side of it now and more focused than ever on trying to make things right with Rori. I'd finally grieved, not just my mother's death, but all of the things we'd missed out on without her,

I'd barely spoken to anyone in the last two weeks, replying to the occasional message so they knew I was alive at least, and they'd all backed off and given me the space I needed. But now I was done hiding, I needed to find Rori and I was done being fobbed off.

Striding down the corridor, I don't give his assistant time to call ahead before I barge into Matthew's office. Not waiting for a greeting, I jump straight in.

"I know you know more than you're letting on, I need to find her Matthew and if you have a way to do that, you need to tell me right the fuck now."

He doesn't flinch at my tone or respond to what I've said. Instead he reaches into his drawer and pulls out two envelopes. One much thicker than the other.

"I was going to come over tonight, I know you've been avoiding us, and I hope it's because you've been dealing with your shit. But you're right, I do know more than I've told you."

I was about to yell at him when he cut me off.

"It's the hardest thing I've had to do Jake but once you know everything, I hope you understand. This was always her story to tell, and while I could sit here and say it's my job to keep my authors work confidential etc, that's not the reason I didn't tell you everything. You needed to deal with your own shit, and believe me, if you'd known all of this and still had the meltdown with her that you had, it would have been so much worse. Again, when you read it all, I think you'll realise that the damage I would have caused by breaking her trust would have been horrific. But she's ready to tell it now, well, to you at least. The smaller envelope is from her, I haven't opened it, the larger one is her manuscript. I read it the night before the book launch and that was what we were discussing before she hugged me. I'll get Belle from school and stay with her as long as you need me to, take it, read it, process it, then come home and we'll talk more."

I stood in stunned silence, this wasn't what I was expecting, but I took the envelopes from his desk and with a nod to acknowledge what he'd said, I turned and left.

Not knowing where to go I had Clive drive me around while I contemplated what to do next. Eventually I asked him to take me to a hotel and I checked into a room so I could be alone with whatever I was about to uncover. Opening the smaller envelope first I pulled out a handwritten letter and started to read....

Jake,

I want to start by saying I'm sorry for leaving the way I did, it wasn't fair, and you deserved better. Having said that, these last few weeks have given me the space I needed to truly let myself grieve and make peace with my past, so I can't regret them. You should have been given a manuscript along with this letter. It's not just my manuscript it's my story. It's not pretty. But you deserve to know everything. Please don't be mad with Matthew and Jen. They urged me to be open with you, but I wasn't ready. I didn't want your pity, I didn't want you to look at me differently. I realise now that it wasn't fair to you to withhold so much of me from you. While I was hurt by the things you said that night, I know part of my reaction was based on my past trauma and had I stayed, and talked things over, things may be very different now. All I can say is, the time we've spent together has been the happiest of my life, and I will forever cherish those memories. But I am broken, I do have a past, and I understand that once you read about it, it will probably just add to your reasons to not trust me enough to see a future for us all. I hope you meant it when you said you'd still let me be a part of Belle's life when she's with Jen. I'm ready to come back to London and if that's changed, I will of course respect your decision and find somewhere else to live. I've left the ending of the book the same as it was when I first wrote it, I doubt I'll ever have the confidence to publish it, but I can always change the ending if I do.

Rori

Deciding I should probably read the manuscript before dealing with my feelings on what she's said, I put the letter aside and settle in to read.

It's dark by the time I get to the second to last page. I got up to put a light on an hour ago, but other than that I haven't moved from the bed, where I've been sat while I read. I've also cried more in the last few hours than I have since my mother died. I cried for the scared child who was let down by the people she should have been able to trust the most. I cried for the young girl who never felt safe or loved. I nearly lost my mind and cried tears of rage for the abuse she suffered from that arsehole, and the heart-breaking way it ended. And then I cried tears of disgust when I thought about the things I said to her, none of which were true even before I read this.

I turn to the last page, wondering what she meant about changing the ending and find the epilogue....

When I started to tell my story, I didn't know how I would end it. Because every story needs an ending, doesn't it? Well, now that I'm at the end, I don't think it does. The reason for that, well there's two actually. They're the two most precious things in my life. Actually, that's not strictly true, while they are undoubtedly precious to me, there's also a third thing that is as well, and that's me. Because with them, I'm the me I want to be, the me I thought was lost, with dreams I thought were stolen. So, some might say this story it about strength or resilience. Maybe about overcoming trauma. But for me, my story is about hope. Despite every inch of me screaming in protest, I let myself fall in love with the best man I've ever known, I let myself fall in love with the most amazing little girl I'm so grateful to call my bestie, I let friends become family. So, I don't choose to be the victim of my circumstance, I choose hope, I choose them, I choose to not have an ending to my story because this is only the beginning.

I didn't think I could cry any more, but now I'm fully sobbing at her words. What the fuck have I done? I need to make this right. Jumping up, I shove everything back in the envelopes and call Clive to pick me up.

Storming back into my apartment, I'm not surprised to hear voices coming from the kitchen, but when I get there, I am surprised that Jen is here as well.

"Jesus Christ, did you send out the bat signal?" I ask Matthew.

He just rolls his eyes and pours me a drink. I ignore the glass and instead walk over to him and pull him into a hug, everyone stops talking and I can feel them staring, but I don't give a fuck. I pull away and seek out Jen next, crushing her against me in another hug. Clearing my throat, I look at them both.

"Thank you, both of you, you protected her when I didn't, you held her confidence and showed her she could trust you. But it's time for me to take over, so as much as I love you both, I am going to go nuclear if one of you doesn't tell me where the fuck she is."

Speech over, I finally pick up the drink and down it. Jen speaks first.

"Jake, I don't know…"

I don't let her finish.

"Jen, I listened, I really did, this isn't a reaction to what I've read, I've been seeing a therapist for the last two weeks and you were right, all of you were, and now that I know what I was doing, I need to fix it, the only change from reading the manuscript is the need to tell her how fucking proud of her I am."

Sean is now grinning like an idiot and the others seem to have a lot to say, but before they can start, Belle comes thundering into the room sobbing, and I gather her up in my arms.

"Hey Angel, it's ok, Daddy's here, what's wrong sweetie?"

"I had a bad dream Daddy" she manages to get out between sobs.

Holding her tight I stroke her hair, helping her calm down.

"It's ok Angel, it was just a dream, you're ok now."

"No I'm not Daddy, I miss Aurora, in my dream she never came back, I want her to come home Daddy, I want her to play with me again and bake cakes and tuck me in at bedtime, that's what mummy's do."

I hear the intake of breath around me and I can't speak. Learning my lesson from last time I gently pull her away from me so I can look at her.

"What do you mean Angel?"

She looks at me, full of innocence and tears.

"Aurora told me my mummy left because she knew she wouldn't be very good at it, but Aurora is really good at, I love her so much Daddy, and you're her prince, so I want to choose her to be my new mummy."

Looking around, I see even Damien is on the verge of tears at this point, and Matthew has his arm around my sister as she quietly cries. Focusing on Belle again, I take a deep breath.

"I love her so much as well Angel, and I'm going to do everything I can to bring her home."

She settles when I say this, hope taking over her face. Sean steps in and sweeps her up into a hug as he tickles her, and giggles ring out.

"Come on princess, I'll take you back to bed and read you a story."

I give him a grateful smile as they leave the kitchen and sink back down onto a stool. Damien is the first to break the silence.

"I hope you've got a fucking plan mate because you're going to need it."

I look up at Matthew, willing to beg if needs be. He shares a look with Jen, and she nods her head. Letting out a breath he turns back to me.

"She's at my cottage in the lakes, she wanted to know if she needed to look for somewhere else to live before she came back."

Grinning, I stand and pull my phone out.

"She has somewhere to live, but I have plans to make and you're all gonna help"

CHAPTER 40
Rori

It's been five days since I sent the letter to Matthew, and I haven't heard anything. On top of that, Jen text me earlier to say Jake had taken Belle away, so we wouldn't be able to FaceTime today. I'm gutted. I miss her so much, and if he's taken her away, it sounds like he's moving forward with their lives.

Deciding I can't spend the day moping, I head out to do some shopping. I'm going to start packing up tomorrow and I want some last-minute gifts to take back for Belle, even if I don't get to give her them in person. I spend a couple of hours choosing things for her, as well as Liv and Jen, then make my way back to the cottage. As I approach the cottage, I'm confused by what looks like a sheet of paper taped to the door. Once I'm close enough I see it's a note.

3rd times the charm, head down to the lake if you still have hope

Nerves fill my stomach, Jake doesn't know where I am and even if he did, he's away with Belle. I haven't blocked his number, but it's been weeks since he tried to contact me. It's possible this is a case of wrong address, or even an elaborate ploy to murder me. But the mystery gets the better of me, so I dump my bags and make my way down the path towards the lake.

As I approach, I notice an area to one side, near the lake edge, that looks set up for a picnic maybe, but I can't see any other people around, so I head that way anyway. When I get there, I see that it is indeed a picnic. Several blankets are laid out on the grass with masses of throw cushions along one edge. A picnic basket is set down on one corner, and next to it stands an ice bucket with champagne inside. It's a clear day, and the view of the lake is breath-taking, it's the perfect spot for an intimate lunch. I'm about to turn and continue searching for any sign of life, when a voice stops me.

"I've had two picnic dates in my life, both of which turned into the best decisions I've ever made, so I'm really hoping my luck continues and you agree to join me for this one"

He's here, Jake is standing behind me asking me to join him for a date, he did all of this. Slowly I turn to face him. He's so handsome. He's wearing the jeans and t shirt combo that I love so much, and his hair is slightly ruffled from the breeze. But it's his face that keeps me locked on him. He looks fragile, vulnerable in fact, unsure of what I might say.

"It's so good to see you Rori, you're fucking breath-taking, please don't leave straight away, there is so much I want to say to you, please stay and let me talk, even if you tell me to leave as soon as I'm done, please hear me out."

I offer a small nod and relief takes over his features. Letting him guide me to the blankets, I take a seat and he joins me, opening the hamper. We remain silent as he starts to set out the dishes, leaving them covered for now.

"Are you warm enough? I have extra blankets if you'd like one to wrap around yourself."

Finding my voice, I say, "No, I'm ok for now, thanks."

"Ok, would you like a drink? There's champagne, or water if you'd prefer."

I can't hold it in any longer, so I ignore his questions and instead blurt out, "Why are you here Jake?"

He sighs and stops fiddling with the food, then takes a seat next to me, leaving space between us. Looking me in the eye he nods to himself, then starts to talk.

"I have so much I want to say to you. I've had weeks to think about everything that happened. Weeks to think about what I should have done differently or not done at all. It's hard to know where to start but I guess the first thing I want to say is thank you."

I'm sure the confusion is evident on my face, so he continues.

"Thank you for sharing your story with me, thank you for still having some level of trust in me to share your past with me. I'm not embarrassed to say I cried as I read it. But not because I pity or judge you. That couldn't be further from the truth. You're amazing Rori. You've been through so much, and to still be such a kind, caring, giving person after all of that. It's me that shouldn't feel worthy, never you. And it may not mean much to you right now, but fuck, I'm so fucking proud of you."

The tears are falling now, regardless of what he says next, just hearing how he feels about my life heals me that little bit more.

"Thank you."

He gives me a small smile.

"I hate seeing you cry, especially when I don't think I've earned being able to touch you yet."

I'd love to be able to throw myself into his arms and let him hold me, but I can't, there's still so much unsaid, and I don't know where we'll stand after this.

"I've been seeing a therapist."

Well that shocks me.

"You have? Is everything ok?"

"Everything's great, well at least it will be if everything goes to plan."

He reaches for a blanket at this point, and wraps it around me, I'm not cold but I don't stop him, it's like he wants to wrap me up in something because he can't touch me himself.

"Jen kinda laid some home truths on me. All this time I thought I was protecting Belle by not dating, and I was to a degree, but she made me realise I was also protecting myself, that I'd closed myself off to new relationships after my mum died because I was scared of losing someone again. Jen, the boys, even Melinda…they were all relationships I formed before she died. You're the first person I've let into my life since she died, and it terrified me. Only I didn't realise that's what it was at the time, so when that fear reared its head, I lashed out instead. I'm so ashamed of the things I said and the way I treated you Ror, I'm so fucking sorry"

He looks pained, and it kills me not to comfort him, instead I move a little closer to him and rest my shoulder against his.

"I'm really glad you've listened to the people around you and gotten some help to understand your emotions. Thank you for the apology, I'm sorry I walked out the way I did, I was triggered by your words and instead of telling you why, I ran. However, it doesn't change the fact that you still said those things, that we were clearly having very different thoughts about where our relationship might end up, that deep down you don't trust me enough."

I let my words trail off, I don't know what else to say. He moves now, kneeling in front of me so he can look into my eyes.

"Fuck it, I have to touch you Rori."

Reaching out, he grabs both of my hands and hold them on his thighs.

"We don't have different thoughts Rori, or at least we didn't then, and I'm hoping we don't now. The day of the book launch I had it all planned out. The shopping, the pampering, the necklace…it was all supposed to lead up to the end of the night, when I would take you back to our hotel room, the room where we spent our first night together. I was gonna explain the reason I chose the necklace I did, the infinity symbol, was because I'm in love with you, and wanted something to show you I wanted more. I was going to tell you I loved you, then make love to you for hours. Then, when we'd worn each other out, I was going to hold you in my arms and tell you I wanted every night to end like this, I wanted every morning to start like this, I wanted you to move in with me."

Wow, just wow. I'm speechless. He's saying everything I wanted to hear, everything I dreamed about. But I'm still not sure if I believe him.

"I can see the doubt on your face, and I'm so angry with myself that it's me who put that there, that I'm the reason you can't trust I'm telling the truth. It is the truth though. When you were dress shopping and I went for a drink with the boys, I told them everything. I'm sure you can imagine the shit I got for being such a soppy bastard."

I smile at that, he's not wrong, god, I even miss those lumps.

"I never once thought you'd cheat on me Ror, especially not with my best friend, but when I saw your exchange I knew something was off, I knew you were hiding something, but instead of talking to you properly, I let all of my fears and insecurities take a hold of me, and said the worst things. I didn't even believe it when I was saying it, but I was so far gone in my own head, I couldn't stop myself. Knowing what I know now makes what I said that night even worse."

I want to believe everything he's saying, I want it so much, but there's still the other things he said that night to discuss, so I steal myself to ask what I need to ask.

"And what about Belle, what about the things you said about my relationship with her, I don't want what happened at the park to guilt you into saying things you don't mean."

I see the anger on his face, and for a minute he's lost to the memories of what she went through that day, and how close he came to losing her.

"I was so wrong Rori, so so wrong, and if I hadn't realised that myself, my daughter certainly dug the knife in earlier this week."

I grin, despite the seriousness of the conversation, wondering what sass she'd thrown at him.

"Before I tell you what she said, I want to tell you how I feel about it. From the very beginning, before you even found out who I was, you have loved my daughter in a way that is beautiful to witness. You play with her, you comfort her, you listen to her and put her needs first, even with us, you always made sure she was ok with everything, and worried about her. That night, I should have been filled with love and comfort that she trusted you enough to talk about how she was feeling and ask you those questions, and I should have been thankful that, instead of taking the opportunity to bash Melinda, you instead made Belle feel loved and special. And instead, I shit all over such a special bonding moment between the two of you and made it all about my insecurities and my feelings. The day I got the call that she'd been taken to hospital, the bottom of my world fell out, and we all rushed to be with her. It was Belle that told us you were hurt, and when she did, I collapsed, and the boys had to hold me up. I might not have fully realised the damage I'd done at that point, but I did feel what it was like to potentially lose you and it crushed me. I shouldn't have told you I loved you when you first woke up, it was selfish, and I know how it must have looked. But fuck Ror, I was just so relieved you were ok. Then you were gone, and I had to sit with everything and replay everything in my mind. We weren't talking the day that happened, you were in that park by chance and as soon as you saw her in danger, you reacted, even though you were justifiably furious with me. You were there when I couldn't be. You protected her from the danger. You took a fucking bullet for her Rori. You didn't act like her fathers pissed off girlfriend, you acted like her mother. You are not only everything I could ever want in a partner, you are also everything I could ever wish for and more, as the mother of our daughter."

Yeah that's it, I'm done, an absolute blubbering mess as sobs rattle through me and I throw myself into his arms.

CHAPTER 41
Jake

I hold her tight as she breaks down in my arms. And yes, I am a piece of shit, because I'm also having to tell my cock this is really not the time to get excited. But fuck, it's good to hold her. I don't speak while she cries, letting her get it all out. I've poured everything into the words I've said to her, all of it from the heart, all of it how I honestly feel. I can only hope I've done enough to convince her to give me another chance. Eventually she sits back in her original position and I instantly miss her.

"I've missed you both so much Jake, it's hurt to be away, but I didn't know how to talk to you, and I was so lost in the memories that the park triggered for me."

I take her hands again.

"Shh, baby, we have plenty of time to talk about all of this as much as you want, I just want the chance to earn your forgiveness, I can't lose you Rori, we can't lose you."

She reaches up and cups my cheek and it's the best feeling I've had in weeks.

"You already earned it Jake, everything you've said has pieced me back together, I can't lose either of you either, I love you Jake."

The smile splits my face and I don't waste any more time. I pull her all the way to me and crash my lips to hers in an earth-shattering kiss.

"I love you too Rori, so fucking much."

Then I'm kissing her again, softer this time, savouring every part of her lips on mine as my hands run up and down her body. Eventually I pull away, I'm not sure that we have enough privacy where we are for what I really want to do right now, so I have to stop before I strip her down.

"Let's eat baby, picnics are our thing remember, and I need to feed you so I can get my hands all over that body once I get you back to the cottage."

She laughs, but helps me uncover the food, before I pour the champagne, thank fuck we have something to celebrate. We eat in silence, just happy to be together. I keep my hand on her at all times, not wanting to give up the feel of her for a second now that I've got her back. Once we're done, I dig out the box I had hidden at the bottom of the hamper and hand it to her.

"You left this after that night and I wanted to bring it back to you, I still want what that symbol represents, so while I absolutely love the ending to your book, I have to tell that you actually can't go back to Jen's, and do in fact need to find somewhere else to live."

She looks shocked for a second, before the penny drops, and she opens the box to find the necklace I gave her before the launch.

"Oh really, well that's annoying, where am I going to find somewhere as nice as Jen's on such short notice."

I kneel behind her and take the necklace from her so I can fasten it where it belongs, then drop my head to kiss her neck.

"Well it's funny you should mention it, because I actually know of a place that's arguably better than Jen's, and just happens to have space for an extra person."

Kissing her again, I turn her head to look her in the eyes.

"Come home baby, come home to me and Belle and make a family with us."

The smile that takes over her face fills my heart with love for this amazing woman.

"There's nowhere I'd rather be."

We spend some time watching the lake, me lying against the pillows with her nestled between my legs, resting her back on my chest.

"You never told me what Belle said to twist the knife."

I smile as I answer.

"Well, she said you did everything a mummy does so well, that she wants to choose you to be her mummy."

I know she's crying before I hear the sniffle, so I move us around so I can wipe the tears away.

"Babe, seriously, the tears kill me, even when they're happy ones."

"I just miss her so much Jake, I was gutted when Jen said I couldn't talk to her today because you'd taken her away, hang on, you're here, is she away with the boys?"

I've been saving this bit until the end, not wanting it to sway her decision.

"Actually, Jen didn't say you couldn't talk to her today, she said you couldn't FaceTime her."

Seeing the confusion, I carry on.

"I did take her away Ror, she's here, you can see her when we get back."

I've barely finished speaking when she jumps up and starts gathering things together. Laughing, I also get up.

"Where's the fire babe?"

She stops and looks at me like I'm speaking a foreign

language.

"Are you kidding me, Jake, she's here, I haven't seen her for weeks other than through a screen, get a move on and take me to her."

Still laughing, I send a quick text then help her gather up our things. Once we're done, I pull her in for another kiss before taking her hand to start walking back up towards the cottage. What she doesn't realise is, it's not just Rori she's going to see, I brought the whole gang with me. I rented a house not far from the cottage and the others have been keeping Belle occupied, while I convinced Rori to forgive me.

As we near the cottage, their cars start to roll onto the drive, and Rori lets out a gasp when she realises everyone is here.

"What did you do?"

"They all miss you and they all wanted to come, probably to make sure I didn't fuck up."

She doesn't get the chance to reply, because Belle come hurtling out of the car and rushing over to us. Rori drops to her knees and opens her arms for her, and Belle doesn't hesitate in diving into the embrace. They hug for a long time, as everyone else wanders over and smiles at the reunion. Eventually, Belle pulls back and looks at Rori.

"I've missed you so much Aurora, are you finished your book stuff now cos I really want you to come back"

"Yes sweet girl, I'm finished what I needed to do, I missed you so much too and I'm coming home."

At that point, Jen and Liv pile into them and they all hug it out. The boys make their way to my side.

"Glad you got your shit together, you soppy bastard." Damien of course.

"Called it from the beginning, our boy is in looove."

Matthew just smirks at me.

"You're all arseholes, you know that, but fuck I love that woman, and as soon as I can, I'm putting a fucking ring on her finger"

They all stare at me for a long minute before breaking out into laughter. Like I said, arseholes.

We spend a couple of hours letting everyone catch up but thankfully the boys catch on to the fact that I need to be alone with Rori and convince Belle to go back to the house for a tea party, while we stay at the cottage. As soon as the cars pull away, I've got her pinned to the door with a searing kiss. She opens for me and I plunge my tongue into her mouth, one hand in her hair and the other grabbing at her ass. When I pull away, we're both panting, but I waste no time in picking her up and heading towards the bedroom. She laughs as I rush through the cottage,

"Are we in a hurry?"

"It's been over six weeks since I've had my hands on you Ror, yes we're in a fucking hurry, but make no mistake, I intend to fully reacquaint myself with all of your glorious body, for several hours."

The heat in her eyes tells me she's completely fine with that. Setting her down on the bed I start to slowly undress her, my eyes roaming over her skin as it appears before me.

"You're stunning Ror, I've missed you so much, are you wet for me babe?"

She moans as I run my fingers down from her face to her tits and tug on one nipple.

"Yes Jake, so wet, go slow later, please just fuck me now."

I love how assertive she's being, and who am I to argue. Standing up, I start to undress.

"Play with your pussy while I get naked baby."

I watch as her hand makes its way down and then she slowly pushes a finger inside herself. I'm so turned on watching her, that I forget what I'm doing and just stare at the sight before me. I snap out of my haze and pull the rest of my clothes off, kneeling between her legs and giving my cock a hard tug. Reaching out for her I pull her hand to me and suck the finger that was just inside her pussy.

"Fuck Ror, you taste so good, but my favourite meal will have to wait, I need to be inside you."

"Yes Jake, now, please."

I take both her hands in mine and pin them above her head. Hovering over her I rest my cock at her entrance and stare down at her, she's so beautiful. I kiss her softly before thrusting fully inside her.

"Fuck me Rori, that's so good, I hope you're expecting this first time to be quick."

I pull back and then thrust into her again and again, my hands leaving hers to roam over her body as I fuck her. I play with her tits the way I know she likes, still not slowing my pace, and keep my eyes locked on hers the whole time. This might be quick and raw, but it still feels different, still feels like we're sharing something on an emotional level that we haven't had before. I can feel myself getting closer, but I won't cum without her, so I reach between us to rub her clit.

"Oh yes, Jake that's so good, I'm so close."

"That's it baby, give it up and cum for me, you feel so good Ror, fuck I love you."

And then she detonates. Her pussy grips me hard as she shakes through her orgasm, and it sends me over the edge a second later. Panting hard, I continue to pump in and out of her slowly, letting both of our orgasms wash over us. I fall to her side, pulling her over with me so I can stay lodged inside her, and kiss her head.

"I love you Rori."

"I love you too Jake, I'm so happy you came for me."

"I'll always come for you Ror, always. Now, I think we need a shower, I want to clean you up so I can get you all dirty again."

And I do, all fucking night long.

CHAPTER 42
Rori

The last 2 months have been amazing. The day after Jake came to the cottage, the rest of the gang headed back to London. Jake however, had decided we needed some time to ourselves, so him and Belle moved into the cottage and we stayed behind for a few days. It was so nice to spend that time with them both. We explored during the day, with me showing them all of the walks and shops I'd found while I'd been there. Belle had great fun on the lake, especially when we hired a boat for the afternoon. Once she was in bed, Jake and I spent the evenings talking and laughing, sometimes about serious stuff and sometimes just about what we wanted for the future. And obviously there was a lot of sex, very quiet sex, but a lot nonetheless. When we eventually travelled home, Jake didn't even ask before instructing Clive to take us straight to his apartment. Our apartment. Which still feels odd to say. Belle was beyond excited by this new development. And it's been a fairy-tale ever since.

Sales of my book are going really well, and I'm currently working on the next ones with Jen and Matthew. Because of how well it's going, I haven't bothered to look for another job, which means we also haven't needed to find a new nanny, as I can pick up Belle from school every day, something we're both relieved by after what happened. Belle still goes to Jen's every Saturday for a girls night, which gives Jake and I time to spend together, usually going out somewhere before coming home for lots of noisy sex.

I've also insisted he goes back to having boys night. The boys still pop in whenever they like for their Belle time, but I told him it was important that I had time with just Belle, so Friday nights are now our girls time while Jake meets the others.

Today is a little different. It's Saturday, so Belle will be sleeping at Jen's tonight, but we're all going out together first. Belle decided she wanted a pampering day with us all, and clearly, we can't deny her anything. So, we're about to head out to meet Jen and Liv for a pre pamper breakfast.

"Jake we're leaving."

"Not without my goodbye kisses you're not," he shouts as he comes down the hall to meet us.

Belle runs back to jump up for a hug, before whispering something in his ear. He smiles at her and nods before setting her down and coming over to me. Pulling me into him, he sweeps his hands down my back and kisses me deeply as he grabs my ass.

"I love you, have a great day with the girls and I'll see you later for date night."

He winks at me as he sends me toward the lift. Clive drives us to the restaurant that is a lot fancier than I expected. Liv and Jen are already seated at the table when we arrive, and have champagne poured with juice for Belle.

"What's going on, are we celebrating something?" I ask as I give them each a hug before taking my seat.

"Nope, just starting off pamper day the best way we know," Jen answers.

They both look suspicious, but I'm distracted by the waiter taking me through the specials, so I let it go. We all enjoy a delicious breakfast, but when I ask for the bill the waiter tells me it's already been paid. Confused, I look at the others and they both deny paying, but don't look particularly surprised either. I turn back to the waiter hoping to get some answers.

"What do you mean it's been paid, who paid it?"

"Mr Holmes called earlier and instructed us to put whatever was ordered on his card, and, well, he also gave us an extra tip for having to tell you what he did."

I can't help but laugh as I turn back to the table.

"Ok what is going on?"

It's Belle who pipes up with an answer.

"It was my idea, I wanted us to have a special day, so I asked Daddy for some extra help."

I'm still suspicious but I give her a hug and let it go.

Our next spot is a spa. I assumed we were just going to a nail bar or something similar, but apparently not. When we walk in there are four ladies already waiting for us.

"Good morning Holmes party, we have your room all set up for you if you'd like to follow us."

We're led into a room where four beds are set up. While the ladies explain we'll be having a full body massage while Belle gets to play with toys already set up for her. I pull Liv aside as we go to change.

"Ok spill it, what is this all about and why do I think Jake is responsible?"

She tries to dodge the question, but I pin her with a stare.

"Ok ok, yes Jake set this up, he called yesterday and said he wanted you to have a relaxing day with all of us before he takes you out tonight, and when I asked why, he just said, because he can."

Jake spending money on me is still something I struggle with. He doesn't go over the top but I'm still very aware of his wealth and I'm not always comfortable with it, especially as he won't let me contribute towards the household bills. However, I can see how much Belle is enjoying the day, so I let it go, opting to send him a quick text.

Me: I know you're expecting this text but instead of telling you off I'm just gonna say thank you. Belle is happy and that's what matters. I love you

Jake: I love you too gorgeous, keep reminding yourself that you're not going to tell me off as the day unfolds, and also, you're so fucking worth it

Me: what did you do

Jake: thank you Jake

Me: Jake….

Jake: gotta run baby, the boys are here to harass me, have fun

I don't reply, I know he won't cave and tell me. So, I get undressed and take my place on the bed.

By early afternoon we've all been thoroughly pampered. After our massage we all got our nails done, including Belle, and then more staff turned up to do our hair and make-up. We were then served afternoon tea with more champagne. Once we're finished with that, we're taken back to the room we were in earlier, but the beds have now been cleared and comfy sofas are in their place. There are also two boxes on the table. Belle rushes over with a squeal and picks up the smaller box, then comes back over to me. She looks to Jen and gets a nod of the head in return.

"What's that you've got Belle?"

"Daddy took me shopping to buy you a present."

"You don't need to buy me gifts sweetheart, you're the best present."

"I wanted to get you something special, so you know I love you forever and ever."

I start to choke up at that and feel both Jen and Liv stroke my back on either side of me.

"Thank you darling, I love you forever and ever as well."

I take the box she hands me and open it carefully. I was not expecting what's inside. Nestled on a velvet bed are a stunning pair of earrings, but more than that, they're an exact match to the necklace Jake gave me before the launch, an infinity symbol of diamonds with a pearl in the lower drop.

"They're beautiful Belle, thank you so much."

I give her a hug and hold on tight, she really is so precious to me. Jen retrieves the other box and pulls an envelope from her bag.

"He asked me to give you this before you open the box."

Taking the envelope from her, I pull out the paper inside

Rori,

I know you're probably crying by now, you're killing me babe and I can't even see them! I told you two months ago that she chose you, we both choose you, you've made our family whole, we both just wanted to remind you of that and of how much we love you. I hope you've had a good day so far and you can shout at me later, but there's still more to come, see you soon gorgeous,

Love you forever

Jake

Laying the note down I take the box and open it. Inside is a bracelet that again matches the necklace and earrings. Only this time, as well as the infinity symbol, there are three charms dangling from the chain around it, each one with a different letter…A, J and B. While Jake still calls me Rori most of the time, he agreed with Liv that my actual name is special and uses it occasionally.

"I don't know what to say, this is like a fairy-tale, how did I get this lucky?"

Jen wraps an arm around my shoulders.

"You all got lucky when you found each other, happiness looks good on you and my brother, I've never seen him like this and if he wants to spoil you occasionally, to show you how much he loves you, let him, just don't tell me how you thank him."

And with that, she giggles as she squeezes me again. Assuming we're done I expect us to make our way back to reception, but I'm shocked again when a team of people stream in with clothes rails.

"Good afternoon ladies, Mr Holmes arranged for us to join you this afternoon. He specifically told me to inform you, Rori, that it is date night, so don't argue, just pick a fancy dress so he can wine and dine you tonight. He also told me to dress Miss Belle for a special date with her favourite Uncles, and that Liv and Jen were to join in the fun because they would be having their own night out tonight, because they deserve some fun as well."

At this point I have no words, so I let them carry me along in the excitement of picking and trying on dresses. In the end I choose a long, red, one-shoulder gown with a thigh high split to one leg. At the advice of the team, I forgo underwear of any kind so as not to show any lines and the bodice style of the dress gives my boobs enough support to not need a bra. I finish it off with nude, open toe stilettos. I wonder where he's taking me to need such a fancy dress. Belle of course, chooses a pink princess dress and the girls look stunning in the dresses they choose. Once we've all had another glass of champagne, we're led back to reception. And that's when the next surprise comes. Standing in reception are Damien, Sean and Matthew, all wearing a full tux and holding flowers. It's Damien who speaks first.

"Ladies, you all look ravishing, Rori, please do tell Jake I said so."

He winks at me before approaching Belle and getting down on his knees.

"Belle, princess, you look wonderful, these are for you from your Dad because he loves you so much."

She takes the small posy from him and gives him a hug.

"Thanks Uncle Damien, they're so pretty."

Sean steps forward next.

"What Damien said, but Rori, please do tell Jake Damien said so."

We all laugh at that as he gives us a grin.

"Liv, these are from Jake, as a thank you for being a constant in Rori's life, and always being there for her, you're an amazing friend."

Liv wipes away a tear as she takes the bouquet, and I am seriously starting to wonder what the fuck is going on. I don't get the chance to ask as Matthew steps forward.

"Ladies you are all a delight and as gorgeous as ever, Belle I'm really looking forward to our night, but first, Jen, these are for you from Jake, for being the best sister he could have ever hoped for, for putting your life on hold to help him raise his princess, for being such a good role model to her, and for giving him the kick up the arse he needed to deal with his crap and go get his girl back, you're amazing and he loves you dearly"

Jen doesn't hold back and throws her arms around Matthew, and he doesn't hesitate to hold her close. There's definitely more to them that they're letting on. Sean cuts in to address the group.

"Ok ladies, this is where you leave Rori. Liv, Jen, if you'd like to come with us we'll drop you where you need to be and then go have our own fun with princess Belle. Rori, Clive is waiting outside to drive you to your next destination."

And with that, they give me quick hugs before we make our way outside, where Clive is indeed waiting for me. I'm still too dumbfounded to speak as we pull away from the curb. This is over the top even for Jake, I have no idea what he's up to, but I hope I'm about to find out.

CHAPTER 43
Jake

I look around the rooftop, checking yet again that everything is set up. My nerves are really kicking in now. Everything so far has gone to plan. Rori has spent the day being pampered and hasn't rang to shout at me for spending money on her, so that's a bonus. I spent the day with the boys, getting the roof ready and accepting their ridicule for being such a soppy bastard. We've strung lights all around the roof top and they're all twinkling brightly now the sun has gone down. We also covered an area of the decking with boards to create a dance floor and each corner has a tall podium housing a thick church candle. There are more candles dotted around the floor area, all inside glass vases so they don't go out. The fire pit is also going, and the seating area has been set up with a picnic and champagne.

When the text comes from Clive to say they're on route, I start the playlist I've been working on, then head down to wait for her. I hear the lift open and her voice floats through the apartment.

"Jake, where are you? What's going on I'm so confused!"

Rounding the corner, she comes into view and I stop in my tracks, my mouth falling open. She's fucking stunning. Recovering myself I go to greet her.

"Ror, you look amazing, you always look amazing, but you are truly breathtaking tonight."

She blushes, she always does, then notices what I'm wearing.

"You're in a tux, I thought this was just date night, do we have an event to go to or something?"

"Or something," I reply with a smirk. "There's nothing 'just' about our date nights baby, and if I occasionally want to get dressed up to celebrate our life together then that's what I'll do, come with me"

I take her hand and she lets me lead her through the apartment and up to the roof. As it come into view, she gasps beside me.

"Oh, Jake it looks amazing, you must have been doing this all day."

"You're worth it."

I pull her in and plant a soft kiss on her lips. I'll not stop if I kiss her harder and I have a timeline to keep to. We make our way over to the picnic and sit down.

"I thought we were due another picnic, after all we do make our best decisions this way."

"Oh really, is there something we need to be deciding on tonight?"

"Maybe."

I open the champagne and hand her a glass then encourage her to eat something. While we eat, she tells me about her day and how much fun she's had.

"The flowers were so thoughtful Jake, what made you do that?"

"The girls have been there for you, Liv for longer, but they're both important to you so they're important to me. I just wanted to show them they're appreciated."

Glancing at the time I realised I need to move things

along, so I stand, pulling her up with me.

"Let's dance sweetheart."

I lead her over to the boarded area and we start to move around the floor to the music. After a few minutes, she pulls back and looks up at me.

"This has been the perfect day Jake, thank you for everything, I love you."

This is it.

"I love you too baby, but maybe we can make it more perfect."

"Don't worry, you're definitely getting laid tonight," she laughs.

Keeping my arms around her, I keep us still, gently swaying to the music.

"I would hope so, but that's not quite what I meant. Since the moment I met you, you've taken over my thoughts. I can't believe I tried to convince myself we were ever only about sex, because you have always been so much more. You complete me Ror, I feel content and happy in a way I never thought I could. I can't believe I nearly fucked it all up."

"Jake we…"

I cut her off.

"I know, I know, but I'm bringing it up because I'm not saying any of this lightly, I know what it's like to lose you, to not be able to hold you, talk to you, laugh with you. I will never take you for granted because I lived the alternative and it's not something I ever want to experience again. You are beautiful, inside and out."

I can see her tearing up, and also maybe starting to wonder where I'm going with all of this, so I take a step back.

"You know the tears kill me baby, but I'll accept them

tonight as long as they're happy ones."

Then I lower myself to one knee as she gasps, her hand covers her mouth as I pull out the ring box.

"I want to picnic with you on rooftops forever, I want to see you raise our little girl with me, I want everything, forever. Aurora, will you marry me?"

She practically falls into my arms, crying and saying yes over and over again. Holding on to her, I reach for her chin and raise her face to look at me.

"I love you."

"Oh my god Jake, I love you so much, I'm so happy, you're everything I've ever wanted."

I slip the ring on her finger and hug her back to me so I can reach for my phone and send a one-word text….now. Thirty seconds later, the door opens, and everyone piles onto the rooftop, Belle leading the way as she barrels into both of us.

"Did you do it Daddy? Did she say yes?"

Composing herself, Rori wraps an arm around her and smiles down at her.

"I did sweetheart, I said yes!"

This has Belle jumping up and down and the others cheering from the sidelines. Rori notices them for the first time and hits them all with the look.

"You were all in on this all day, weren't you?"

They're all grinning at her, and the girls swoop in for hugs as the boys find me and offer handshakes and congratulations. Once we've both been congratulated by everyone, I see Belle tug on Damien's arm, and he bends down so she can whisper to him. Before I can ask, he stands and claps his hands to get everyone's attention.

"Ok so I know we're all very excited right now by this

sickening display of soppiness."

Belle give him a dig at that, and he grins.

"Sorry princess, I'll get to the point. Anyway, as everyone knows, well apart from Rori, Jake has been planning this for a couple of weeks and obviously let Belle know what was going on. Well, last week Belle spent the afternoon with her favourite Uncle"

Matthew coughs at that and Sean pipes up with, "I didn't have an afternoon with Belle last week."

I smile at the love these men have for my daughter, but I'm still confused by where he's going with this.

Damien continues "As I was saying...while Belle was with me, she wanted to talk to me about something serious, something she wasn't sure how to talk to Jake and Rori about."

I have to interrupt at this point.

"What's going on? Belle are you ok?"

I kneel down in front of her and Rori joins me.

"She's fine Jake, she just wanted to share something with me so she could understand it better and we had a good talk about it, didn't we princess?"

Belle looks to us and nods her head.

"We did Daddy, I think you forgot what I asked you, so Uncle Damien helped me lots."

As she's speaking, Damien produces an envelope from behind his back.

"Anyway, as a result of that chat, I did some research and got everything ready so that Belle could tell you all about it."

He hands her the envelope with a reassuring smile. Everyone is staring with bated breath at this point. Belle takes a deep breath and looks at Rori.

"When you were gone, I was sad because I missed you so

much. I told Daddy you're so good at doing mummy things with me so I wanted you to come back so you could keep doing those things, but I think Daddy forgot I said that."

I put an arm around Rori to steady her as her emotions start to get the better of her. I'm still confused, I haven't forgotten what she said, I told Rori about it, I'm not sure what I'm missing.

"When Daddy said he wanted to marry you I was so happy, cos that means you can stay forever. I asked Uncle Damien if that meant you could be my Mummy now."

I look up to Damien and he just gives me a nod.

"He told me how it all works and then said he could talk to an important man for me if I wanted him to, and I did. He said you would need this Daddy."

She pushes the envelope towards me.

"So, can you please be my Mummy now?"

Rori lets out a loud sob and pulls Belle to her in a crushing hug.

"I love you so much Belle, I'd be honoured to be your Mummy"

I'm not even hiding the tears at this point, but before I join in the hug, I open the envelope and pull out the papers. Well fuck me. They're adoption papers. I look back to Damien.

"They're all drawn up and just need signatures to get the ball rolling, it was what she wanted, and you know I can't say no to her."

I turn the papers to Rori so she can see them and she's gobsmacked.

"Jake is this…"

"You're already her mother Ror, but yes, I want nothing more than to make it official."

And then I'm grabbing them both and holding on for dear life. I can hear the crying and murmurs from the others, but it all fades away and all I see is my future wife, our daughter, my family, forever.

EPILOGUE
Rori

I can't believe this day is finally here, or that it's going to be more of a celebration than Jake is expecting. I'm getting married!

Jake's proposal on the rooftop had been perfect. I'd felt the love radiating from him and didn't have to think twice about my answer. Belle's speech was the icing on the cake for both of us. She'd immediately started calling me Mummy and I absolutely cried every time she said it for the first few days. We'd talked after and decided we wanted a small wedding. Neither of us really has family, other than the chosen family we surround ourselves with. So, a destination wedding seemed like the best option.

Which is how I find myself sitting on a balcony, looking out over the ocean in a Mexican paradise. We flew in yesterday and in approximately one hour, we'll be standing on the beach, saying our vows in front of our people. Although it's quite a casual affair, I've still stuck to some traditions. We booked two suites for our arrival; one for the girls and one for the boys. Which means I haven't seen Jake since last night at dinner. Probably a good thing or I might have ruined everything.

There's a knock on my door and I shout to come in. Damien appears a second later.

"Hey Rori, nervous? It's not too late to run away with me instead!"

He says with a wink.

I roll my eyes at him, I'm used to it by now.

"I think I'm good Damien, thanks for coming"

"I was intrigued when I got your message. What's up?"

"Actually, I was hoping you could help me with a gift I have for Jake."

"Sure, what do you need?"

Picking up the envelope from the table, I hand it over to him.

"I just need you to hold onto this until I need it again, I'll tell you when it's time."

He looks confused but doesn't say anything and leaves soon after.

We may be getting married on a beach, but I still wanted a somewhat traditional dress. I went with a long white dress, made with soft flowing material and a lace overlay, so it would be easy to pick up for the walk to the beach. It has capped sleeves with a low sweeping back. The train isn't too long but still makes me feel like I'm wearing a traditional gown.

Once I'm dressed, I give the girls a shout. They've been in the next room getting dressed themselves and helping Belle into her outfit.

When they walk in they all gasp.

"You look so pretty Mummy!"

I nearly tear up again, but I manage to hold it together.

"So do you sweetheart."

Liv and Jen are equally complimentary as we gather our things then head down to reception, where the staff are waiting to escort us to the beach.

When we get there, I stay behind a shelter while Liv and

Jen make their way to the beach to meet the others. Given there's only the eight of us here, I didn't bother with formal bridesmaid duties, but I did want Belle to walk me down the aisle.

When the music starts, we make our approach. I see Jake before he sees me. He looks amazing in his tan trousers and white shirt, the top button left undone. I see the moment his eyes find me and see the emotion covering his face.

As we reach the others, he mouths 'I love you' as he kneels down to hug Belle and tell her how beautiful she is. Then he's standing again and taking my hands.

"Rori, you look incredible."

We're both emotional as the officiant takes us through the short service before asking Jake to recite his vows. He takes a deep breath and looks at me.

"Rori, this last year with you have been the happiest of my life. You and Belle are my heart and soul, you are everything I will ever want or need. I will be forever thankful that my plane was grounded that day. I promise to always love you, to always respect you, to always cherish you. I promise to build a life with you that fulfils us all. I promise to fall in love with you again every day and never be too busy for a picnic date. I promise you forever Rori."

The tears are silently rolling down my cheeks as I listen to his words. Then it's my turn and I hope I can get through this as planned.

"Jake, I love you more than I ever thought I was capable or worthy of. I will always put our lives and family first, I will always be here for you when you need me, I will always say yes to picnics. The love I have for you is limitless, and I can't wait to watch it grow."

I nod towards Damien and he takes the envelope from his pocket, passing it to Jake. He takes it and looks back at me confused.

"What's this?"

"Well, I decided you always get the jump on surprises, so it was my turn for a change. I also thought it was quite appropriate for Damien to hand you the envelope, seeing as the last one he handed over gave me a daughter."

I nod for him to open the envelope and he does. He slides out the picture inside, it's all that's in there. One picture, a little blurred and grainy, with 'Baby Holmes' written above it. He gasps and looks up, tears filling his eyes and before I can speak, he sweeps me into his arms and kisses me like it's the last time we'll ever touch.

The officiant coughs and we pull away, both with stupid happy grins on our faces. Seconds later he pronounces us husband and wife.

"Does someone wanna tell us what's going on?" Damien asks.

We turn to face everyone, and I take Belle's hand.

"Belle is going to be a big sister!"

Everyone is on us then, hugging and congratulating us as well as Belle. She's ecstatic at the idea of a baby.

Later in the evening, I'm sitting on the sand, curled up in Jake's arms, Belle dancing with Sean as we watch the sun go down. I think back to everything that's happened in my life, all of the heartbreak I've been through. All of it that led me to this moment here, this moment of pure happiness, of a life with friends who became family, of a husband and daughter who complete me, and of a new life growing inside me. Hope really did win.

VICKI'S BOOKS

Her Hopeful Heart is the first book in the, From the Heart, series. Matthew and Jen's story will be next!

ACKNOWLEDGEMENTS

I want to start by saying.... Never did I ever think I'd be writing an acknowledgement for my own book!

Firstly, I want to thank my amazing husband, David. Not once, from start to finish, did he doubt that I could do this. He read everything I wrote to help with editing, gave me feedback and suffered through a long and painful conversation about one chapter in particular that made both of our brains hurt!

Secondly, I'd like to thank my sister, Amy, for being way better at cover designs than me.

And lastly, but by no means and less important, thank you to everyone who read the book in the early stages and gave me the encouragement to continue.

If you've enjoyed Her Hopeful Heart, please leave a review on Amazon and share it with your friends.

Vicki

Printed in Dunstable, United Kingdom

67700542R00160